THE POINT OF NO RETURN

DEVYN SINCLAIR

To my ninjas—you know who you are.

AUTHOR'S NOTE

Dear Readers,

This book is meant to be fun and fantasy. However, within that, there are some themes and situations that could be disturbing to some readers. No book is worth your mental health. So if you feel you might need to know a bit more, the full content warnings for this book are available on my website.

www.devynsinclair.com

PROLOGUE

MARIUS

The crowd on the steps of the opera house was loud. Clamoring. We'd seen crowds like this in our days, but never here. Never right below our feet.

Even in the wake of the fire that nearly destroyed this building, there hadn't been a group of people so large and so rowdy. The people carried cameras and music floated above the crowd in quick snippets. Opera. Beautiful.

Across the plaza, a sleek black limousine appeared. The crowd all came to attention, focus on the car. This must be the girl they'd all been waiting for. The singer who was supposed to be a prodigy. An undiscovered talent.

She would come and go like the other talent I imagined.

People surged forward as soon as the car came to a stop. Two large men forced themselves through the crowd to create a bubble. The car door opened, and then, nothing. I got a glimpse of a lean body and a baseball hat. No hint of who she was or what she looked like.

The crowd leaned so far forward, pressing into the bubble around her that it looked sticky. Viscous, as they tugged her up the stairs and into the newly busy cacophony that vibrated beneath us.

Yet another voice, Alexandre said, annoyed.

Erik laughed once. *At least this one will be pretty.*

After two hundred years of silence, adjusting to the constant noise in the building below was a struggle. It felt like a constant hum, waiting for us to focus and follow the vibrations until we could hear clearly.

Below us, the girl and her guards were nearing the top of the stairs. She was about to disappear from my view. A breeze off the river spun through the air, delivering the scents of the summer city. River water and wine, croissants and sweet perfume. Lilacs and lotus and a hundred different flowers.

The last scent slammed into me with the force of lightning.

MINE.

The roar echoed through my mind and was reflected back by the others. My long existence was forever cleaved into two. Before I'd experienced that scent, and after.

My mate.

Our Mate.

I'd thought it was a myth.

That was Erik. We knew it wasn't a myth, but rare enough that it felt that way. A mate. One singular being that matched you in every way. Was meant to you. Whose soul belonged to you.

Or us, bound as we were.

Mine.

Any more forceful and my growl would echo through my bound stone form. I felt the building beneath my feet crack, my power trying to rip itself loose in defiance of the fucking sun and the magic that was binding me here. That was my *mate* and I needed to get to her. *Now.*

Don't break yourself, Marius. Erik said. *You can't get to her broken on the street below.*

That was the only thing stopping me from tearing myself apart to reach her. I couldn't reach her if I was dead. That need eclipsed everything.

Even my own life. The pebbles from the cracks vibrated with the energy that I was shoving down.

She disappeared out of sight, the last tendrils of fragrance blown away from her. I didn't know what she looked like. Hadn't gotten a chance to see her because she'd been hiding.

I felt the singular shift in purpose between the three of us. No longer merely attempting to escape our connection to this place and retaking our power. But having her. Protecting her. Making her *ours*.

We'd heard her name enough over the past weeks, spoken through the stone. It was the same name that now floated up from hundreds of mouths in the crowd spread out in front of the opera house.

Christine.

CHAPTER ONE

CHRISTINE

*M*y own face stared back at me, twenty feet tall. I was decked out in full costume; the image divided in two. On one side I was in full armor, holding a sword directly vertical, staring into the camera. The other side I was feminine. Dressed in flowing white and looking delicate.

Joan D'Arc.

I was never going to get used to that.

This was the *airport.*

Quickly, I looked around to see if anyone had noticed that it was me that was staring out at them in the transportation section of Charles de Gaul.

Of course they hadn't. It was the morning, and I

looked like I'd just crawled out of Paris's famous catacomb system after an eight-hour flight.

I would be lying if I said this was the first time I realized exactly how big this was going to be, but every time I saw something like that billboard, it hit me all over again. It was hard to wrap my head around.

Checking the notes on my phone again, I made my way towards the arrival doors, lugging my too-large suitcases with me. People who traveled light when they were going somewhere for a month amazed me. It felt like I'd packed up my entire life to come here.

But then again, if this went well, it would change everything.

There. A line of drivers stood with signs for their passengers. My stomach flipped at the thought that I was one of those people. It was like being in a movie. A man in a suit and a driver had a sign that said 'Daniels,' but he was already looking at me.

If he was in any way connected with the opera, he would know what I looked like. He smiled and gave me a little half-bow. His English was flawless, with that accent that I loved. "Miss Daniels, welcome to Paris. My name is Raphael. I'm here to take you to the opera house."

He motioned, and another man standing behind

him came to take one of my suitcases while he took the other.

"Thank you."

"Did you have a good flight?"

I smiled. "Could have been worse. I slept most of the time."

"I imagine that will help you adjust to the time change."

"I hope so."

We passed out of the doors, and I froze. Raphael was heading straight towards a limousine. The long kind with dark windows that looked like they'd never been touched by a speck of dirt in their life. The other driver was already loading my suitcases into the trunk.

"Miss Daniels?"

I swallowed. "When they said they were sending a car, this wasn't what I expected."

"Ah. Yes. Originally, they were merely sending a car. But this car, and my services, are being provided for my Monsieur Chagny, and are at your disposal for the rest of your stay."

My mouth dropped open. "That's...nice of him."

Raoul Chagny was the major benefactor of this entire production. The fact that he knew who I was stunned me enough. But a limo and a driver? That was over the top.

Raphael shrugged and opened the back door of the car. "He wanted to put you up at the Ritz as well, and would have, had it not been for the opera's unique accommodations for this show."

If I'd known I would be getting into a limo, I might have dressed better. My leggings and cropped t-shirt didn't exactly scream rich and famous. The whole Ritz thing was a thought that I couldn't even touch yet.

I scratched my previous thoughts off the notepad in my brain. Yeah, there was no way that I'd anticipated it would be like this, billboards aside. I'd tried to shelter myself from the firestorm of media attention that brought me here, and pretended that it didn't exist as best I could. But time was up on that front, and the reality was going to be a lot to take.

He closed the door as I slid into the car. This was wild. The only other time I'd been in a limousine was for prom, and that was almost…wow like eight years ago? And we'd been packed into a limo smaller than this like a sardine can. Tulle and tuxedos everywhere.

There was nothing but room in this. It almost felt wasteful.

Raphael slid into the driver's seat, and the other man retreated. He must be with the airport. Or maybe this company. "Relax, Miss Daniels. We will arrive at the opera house in no time at all."

"Thank you."

I checked my email as we drove. It killed me, the amount that I was paying for international service. But with this contract I could afford it. And it wasn't like I could just live off the grid for a month.

The notifications on all my social media apps were in the thousands. Every time someone re-tagged me in the original video, or saw me on the streets of New York, I was tagged.

Now I knew how celebrities felt when they were hounded by paparazzi. It was relentless. Easier to let go of that presence completely than to deal with it. But that being said, I wasn't quite ready to let go yet. I clicked open one just in case and found a picture of myself from minutes before climbing into the limo. Leggings, t-shirt, and all.

The translation read: *Christine Daniels just landed in Paris! Joan D'Arc here we come!*

Oh boy. I'd hoped that no one would notice me yet. I should have done the baseball hat and glasses thing. They were in my bag, but I'd been naively hopeful about not needing them. Because I knew one thing: while the people in New York were excited, the people in Paris were frantic.

"Raphael?"

"Yes, Miss Daniels."

I sighed. "Someone took my picture getting into the car. We may be dealing with some press when we arrive at the opera house."

He nodded and met my eyes in the mirror. "Do not worry, Mademoiselle. Monsieur Chagny has arranged security for the opera house. I will inform them of your arrival."

Security.

That made sense. Everyone was a little nervous about this, even though it was exciting. We didn't want any accidents or copycats destroying this production or putting anyone in danger.

Raphael made a call, quiet French floating back to me through the open divider.

I closed the app, ignoring the fact that replies and tags were already pinging, and checked the schedule. The whole cast had been rehearsing virtually for weeks, but separately. I'd learned all the music and had been coaching with the director and the conductor. Not with any of the other cast. Even with the internet, timing music over a video call wasn't worth it.

Plus, there were cast members from all over the world, so hosting a full-length rehearsal session on location wasn't feasible. Especially with the restoration of the opera house still under way. But we were ready.

Rehearsals started tomorrow morning. One week of putting everything on its feet. One week of tweaking everything with all the elements put together, and two weeks of performances. That was the plan.

There had been hints by everyone from the producers to the director that if the show was doing well there could be extensions. But I wasn't counting on that. I'd done enough performing that I knew verbal hints and promises were not the same as a guarantee.

So in my mind, it was a month. If it ended up being longer than that, so be it.

Glancing out the window, I watched as we pulled into the outskirts of Paris. Graffiti and the *métro*. Motorcyclists who rode in-between the cars like there was a great deal more space than there was. People living their lives, blissfully unaware of the chaos that surrounded mine.

Not that I wasn't grateful. I was. It was just...

Meeting the cast all together wasn't going to be easy. It wasn't a secret that many of them didn't believe that I deserved to be here.

I shut those thoughts down. They wouldn't help

anything. All I could do was my job, be friendly, and hope that everyone didn't completely hate me.

But secretly, I was afraid that they were right. It was basically an accident that I was here, and nothing more. I couldn't even disagree with that.

The movement of the car and the time change—despite the sleep that I'd gotten on the plane—lulled me, and I drifted off, caught up in dreams of me showing up and everyone laughing and telling me that it was a joke.

Incredibly different to the dreams that I'd had on the plane. Those I was intimately familiar with. Recurring dreams of me in the dark, running from someone chasing me. But the dreams weren't scary. The person or thing chasing me wasn't doing it to kill me or hurt me. No, there was a breathless anticipation in those dreams that *when* I was caught, the adrenaline would make what happened after that much better.

I'd never been caught in the dream. Not since I started having it years ago. But I also had flashes when I woke up, inevitably reaching for my vibrator. The smell of grass and the press of bodies together. Of pleasure that was raw and unfiltered and left me gasping. It was the only recurring dream that I had, and Meg never let me forget it.

Of course, waking up from *that* dream on a plane

full of people wasn't ideal when what it made me want to do was have privacy. I understood the old 'think about baseball' thing now. Only for me, it was singing one of the arias from the show in my head until I could breathe again and my skin didn't feel like every touch was from that phantom chasing me and making me want more.

It was the sound of people that woke me. Tinted windows were my favorite thing in the world right now. We were pulling up in front of the opera house, and just like I'd predicted, there was a crowd. Cameras were already flashing and there was at least one news camera. Regular people too, with phones waiting for me to get out of the car.

I dug in a bag and found my sunglasses and hat. They were *definitely* needed now.

"Please do not exit the car until security arrives, Mademoiselle," Raphael said. "We will take care of your bags. Do not worry."

"Thank you."

"I will also text you," he said. "If at any time you need my services, simply call or text me. And that includes anything from driving to picking up coffee."

I laughed nervously. "You don't have to do things like that."

"On the contrary, Miss Daniels, it is my pleasure." He looked over his shoulder and smiled. "I am being paid an absurd amount of money to be at your beck and call. It will not bother me in the slightest."

Another laugh burst out of me. Real this time. "All right. Thank you. For that, and for being honest."

"Of course."

Through the crowd, two men in suits were pushing to the car. They were security if I'd ever seen it. They were so big that they practically formed a human wall. Thankfully, they created a bubble around the door where they could pull it open.

The world was nothing but sound. "This way, Miss Daniels."

But I could barely hear them. One man pushed through the crowd in front of me. The other one was at my back, hand on my shoulder, holding me in the small opening that they were keeping clear. Questions hurtled into my ears and the flashes of the cameras blinded me.

I looked down at the ground and let the hand on my shoulder guide me. The only thing that I could do right now was to make sure that I didn't trip and have a new video of my clumsiness going viral. I understood celebrities now because I was one. I didn't love it.

A warm breeze hit my back, and I put a hand on

my head to make sure that I didn't lose my hat. I didn't need photos of bad plane hair on top of everything else. But that breeze felt good. Calming and settling. Almost as if the city were greeting me and welcoming me with a touch on the shoulder. That was a weird thought, but it was still how it felt.

Managing to break free of the crowd, there was a third man that rushed us through the doors and made sure that they were locked behind us. They were filming through the doors, of course, but at least that was something that we could control.

"Our star has arrived, I see." Another French-accented voice sounded from behind me. This one I knew, at least a little.

Anne Giry was what every person's mind imagined when they thought of a French woman. Tall, aided by spike heels and a severe bob that was nearly as sharp as her jawline. Clothes that looked effortlessly chic on a frame that was thinner than a rail.

But she was unfailingly kind and had already helped me more than I could say. I wasn't exactly sure what her title was, but she did everything. Helped with the conservation effort of the opera house and the re-building. I was pretty sure that she had a producer credit on the show, and she was one of the principal people in charge of the marketing of the entire project.

Simply speaking, without her, this project wouldn't be nearly as big as it was now.

I was just relieved to see a friendly face. "I'm here. Barely."

She laughed, light and tinkling. "Yes, I saw you had a welcoming party."

"In a way, it's good that we're all staying here at the opera house," I said. "Will give them fewer opportunities to try to find me, and we'll all have to deal with less press."

"Less press isn't exactly what we want, but I understand what you mean. If you're all right with it, I'll schedule some interviews so that there's a little less hunger around you."

I shrugged. "As long as it doesn't interfere with any rehearsals and I have an interpreter, that's fine with me."

"I'll make sure. Now let's get you up to your room. That way you have a chance to settle in before tonight's meeting." She gestured towards the stairs that led up towards the theatre itself, and I followed.

"You're showing people to their rooms?"

"Not people," Anne said with a smile. "Just you."

"Oh."

The place was *gorgeous*. The restoration was something you barely noticed. So seamless that it didn't seem possible that this building had been a burned shell until a year ago. Anne mentioned that the restoration wasn't totally complete. The statues on the roof would undergo restoration after the run of the show ended, along with the rest of the exterior.

I would have plenty of time to look at it all later. We wove through the public hallways, and then through a small, nearly invisible door that let us into the secret areas of the opera house. Sets, costumes, props, housing, food, all under one roof. Just like it used to be.

People were everywhere back here, and thankfully I wasn't getting stares as we passed. Everyone was doing their jobs. The residential rooms were upstairs near the roof. There was chatter, and I saw a long hallway filled with semi-private bunk beds. Better than nothing. I turned into the door and she caught me by the arm. "No."

I looked at her in surprise. "Really?"

"Our star staying with the chorus? People would talk."

They probably wouldn't. This wasn't the eighteen-hundreds now. But I followed her down the catwalk, which overlooked a large portion of the deep and complicated backstage.

A different hallway was lined with doors at certain intervals, and ended with one large wooden door that looked like mahogany. As we passed the other doors, I noticed the small nameplates on the doors, with names in curving script.

This was the named cast. Which one was mine?

My stomach twisted and jumped with nerves as we kept walking. I already knew which room it would be, but it still made me nervous all the same. Anne didn't stop until we reached the end of the hallway, and on that door, was my name.

Christine Daniels.

"Here are your keys to your apartment and the artist's entrance to the opera house. I'll leave you to get settled," she said, glancing down at her phone. "Your bags are already inside, and the general meeting starts at six. With the party, of course, after that. Welcome to Paris."

"Thank you," I said. I owed her a lot more than that, but I honestly didn't know what else I could say.

"I'll see you soon."

She didn't bother to stay and see my reaction to the room or anything, already lifting her phone to her ear and the click of her high heels echoing back down the hallway after her retreat.

I took a breath. I was here. I made it. "Welcome to Paris," I said under my breath.

CHAPTER TWO

CHRISTINE

*M*y room was almost as big as my New York apartment.

I froze when I pushed the door open, because I was convinced that this was a mistake. It wasn't, but I still couldn't believe it.

This was the one part of the opera house that hadn't stuck with the original decor and layout. Instead, this room—if you could really call it that—was a sleek and modern apartment. I had a kitchen with a breakfast bar, a bathroom, a living room and dining table, and a fucking amazing bed in one corner. If this was where I got to live, then sign me up for the show to get extended.

My bags were sitting on the bed, just like Anne said. There would be time to unpack later. Right now, I just wanted to shower and change into something that didn't make me look like a drowned gym rat before the full cast meeting.

That was a lie. I wanted to explore every facet of this beautiful room in a way that would make a perfect movie montage for a rom com. Including jumping on the bed. But I didn't.

I only allowed myself to take a brief look out one of the two large windows that overlooked the Paris street below. This was the original window shape at least, and the original stone of the walls.

It was rough under my fingers, and if I looked closely, I thought I could still see the shapes of smoke from the famous fire. The stone was cool against my palm.

Christine.

I jumped back, whirling. There was no one there. Of course there wasn't—I locked the door behind me. *You're just exhausted.* After the flight and the excitement, I was dragging. All I needed was a shower and some coffee. That was it. I would be fine, and definitely not hearing things. Definitely not voices in my head. I wasn't going to be that kind of method actor. No voices like Joan of Arc.

Heaving one of my too-large suitcases down

onto the floor, I grabbed some clothes and my bathroom bag, and showered. I was too nervous to enjoy it. Now my mind was spinning forward to meeting everyone.

Should I take a nap? Or would that mess up my already fragile sleep schedule?

A loud knock made me jump. "Christine, you lovable bitch, are you in there?"

Rolling my eyes, I stood and made my way to the door. Meg nearly tackled me when I opened. "Oh my *god you're here!*"

I laughed, trying to catch my balance while my best friend hung onto me like a monkey. "I am officially here."

"And you've got the best room in the house," she said. "Holy shit."

The flush rose up to my cheeks. "Yeah. Sorry about that."

Meg snorted. "I'm not if I can come hang out here sometimes."

"Of course."

I noticed there was another person standing in the door. "Meg, do you want to introduce me to the person who now thinks that we're both freaks?"

"Right." She spun back to the door and took the girl's hand. "This is Tori. She's awesome. Also corps de ballet. We bonded on the flight over."

"Nice to meet you." I held out a hand, and she shook it with a grin. "I promise you don't have to be scared of me. If it weren't for that video, we'd all be in the corps."

"I think it's awesome." There wasn't anything to make me think that her words weren't genuine.

Meg practically danced her way over to the kitchen and ran her hand along the countertop. "This is fancy."

"It's honestly way more than I expected. Everything has been." I looked at her. "Raoul Chagny sent a limo to the airport for me."

"Fuuuuck." She elongated the word dramatically. "You don't happen to know a surgeon who could transplant your vocal chords, do you? Because I'm going to kill you in your sleep and take over your life."

Glancing at Tori, I smiled. "She's kidding."

"It's true," Meg confirmed. "But it's also true that my love is violent. So don't cross me."

I laughed. "I don't know what to do with myself now. I could easily sleep more, but I don't want to fuck up that schedule so early in the trip."

"That," Meg said, "is actually why we're here. We thought we might explore a bit? Get some coffee and croissants. Act like idiot Americans?"

"That sounds amazing." But there was one factor that Meg hadn't considered.

She'd been my best friend for a long time, since before we both ended up at American Ballet Theatre. To her, I was just Christine and not *Christine Daniels, opera sensation.*

"There's just one problem."

"Oh?"

I pressed my lips together. "There was a swarm of people outside the opera house waiting for me because someone saw me get into the limo. Security had to get me through the crowd and escort me into the building."

"Crap," she said under her breath. "Yeah, I forgot about that."

"Believe me," I said. "I wish I could explore Paris like that wasn't a thing that was going to happen. But it probably is. So why don't you guys go, and you can bring me something back?"

"That seems unfair," Tori said. "Not like any of this is your fault."

"No." A thought struck me.

Raphael said that he could take me anywhere that I needed to go. Did that include this? Would he know a place that we could go that might be free of that kind of crowd?

"Hold on a second."

I found my phone where I'd tossed it on the bed. Just like he'd promised, there was a text from him and his number. Inputting it in as a contact, I dialed.

"Miss Daniels?"

"Raphael," I said. "If me and two of my friends wanted to have coffee some place discreet without the kind of crowd that we ran into today, would you know a place?"

"Of course," he said. "It will not be a problem. Should I come pick you up now?"

I smiled. "That would be great. The artist's entrance, please. Oh, and Raphael?"

"Yes."

"You can tell Monsieur Chagny that I'm thankful for the limo, but at least for now, I think something a little less conspicuous would be helpful."

He laughed. "Of course. I will be ready to pick you up in fifteen minutes."

Meg and Tori were staring at me. "What the fuck was that?"

"So the limo guy, the driver. Apparently he's just...*my* driver while I'm here. I didn't ask for it, but if he's getting paid either way, might as well use him, right? The guy seemed ecstatic to have such an easy gig. Plus, he said he knows a place where we can go and be inconspicuous."

I still grabbed my hat and sunglasses along with

my purse, just in case. And like the absolute mess that I was, I knocked over my airport bag, spilling everything onto the floor.

"Of course."

My friend laughed, bending down to help me clean up the mess. "Got a new one, I see?" She held up a book with a muscled man on the cover. I flushed, even though Meg was *well* aware of my reading habits.

"I like that one," I said, clearing my throat. "Wanted the real copy for this trip instead of just digital."

Tori looked at the cover and grinned. "What is it?"

"Let me see." Meg examined the image. "Moon, wolf, rippling abs. I'm going to guess werewolves?"

"Yes."

Meg laughed. "Christine is a big fan of romances. And if a hot werewolf swept into her life, she'd bang him at the first opportunity."

"Like you wouldn't?" I muttered, shoving the rest of the stuff back into the bag.

"No," she said. "You're right, I totally would. And besides, Europe is a better place for that to happen, right? All those legends and abandoned places." Her smile was teasing. "If I find you in the catacombs, I'll know what you were looking for."

"You're the worst."

"No I'm not. Because once you're done with all the naughty books, I fully expect you to pass them on to me."

I looked over at Tori. "With all the press, there wasn't much I could do. So I basically stayed home. Learned my lines and music, and read books."

"You don't have to justify it," Meg said. "Everyone is a bit of a monster fucker at heart. Get your freak on and all that. Christine would sell her soul to fuck a monster. She even has dreams about them."

I blinked and glared at her. Tori didn't need to know that about me on the first day. "I don't know about the soul thing. But you benefit from my romance books," I said, sidestepping the talk about the dream. "Don't even pretend that you don't."

"It's true," she twirled a pirouette. "I have learned some moves. I'll have to come and borrow that book," she said with a smirk. "And to do other things in this glorious apartment." Meg looped her arm through mine as we walked out and I locked the apartment behind me. "You know, I think being your best friend is going to have some advantages."

"Thanks," I said with a snort. "Tell me how you really feel."

She pushed my arm. "You know what I mean, bitch."

"I do." Neither Tori nor I could hold back our laughter. "Now, any news that I should know?"

"Only *everything*," Meg said, glancing at our new friend. "Tori is almost as good at finding out about drama as we are."

"Tell me."

"Let's wait until we're in the car," she said. "Because this is something we don't want anyone to overhear. It's about Désirée."

My eyebrows rose into my hairline. That was bound to be interesting. Meg pulled me faster towards the stairs, so we could start our very first adventure in Paris.

CHAPTER THREE

ALEXANDRE

*T*he sun shone in my eyes. It always did this time of day. Why I didn't simply change my position in the morning so that it didn't, I wasn't sure.

That wasn't true.

By looking west, I got the most spectacular view of Paris. Every day in the morning and evening, the city sparkled. Even after two hundred years, that view was worth the sun in my eyes.

Laughter rang up from the streets below. It often did, so why did I notice this laugh? The voice that came with it seemed to dance across the stones of the streets and the opera house before it landed before me.

I moved my limited gaze, trying to see the owner of the voice. Three women were running up the steps from a black car and into the opera house. Racing with smiles on their faces, wild and free. The one in the center—that's who the voice belonged to.

The whole world narrowed to that sound. That laugh. Like everything changed and the sun in my eyes became a golden glow that hovered in the world now that I was hearing *her*.

They'd finally rebuilt enough to perform. I knew that. I wasn't happy about it, but we knew. They were going to recreate the show that killed us—that killed hundreds. Getting free of this place would be ten times as hard with a crowd traipsing in and out. But now we had a mate. One who was in the opera below us. Was that her voice?

You heard it? Marius asked.

Yes.

Is it her?

There had been whispers through the opera house for months. The young singer with a voice like magic that was coming to revive the opera. Was she the one who laughed? Was she the one who'd called to us through the very stone? The scent had come from the crowd, and we hadn't seen her. But that voice…

I hoped it was her. Because the sound of her made my body sing even within the restraints of this punishment. Our mate.

I don't know. I answered.

What if it is her? Erik asked. *What do we do?*

I understood the question. How could we find the answer to the question that our souls had answered for years in the place we hated the most? How could we find her and make her ours when the eyes of the world were on her?

It was the time of the day where I began to be restless, longing for the freedom of night when I could release myself from stone and finally live again. Today more than ever, when I wanted to see her. Hear her voice near to me and see if what moved deep within was real or an echo of a dream we'd buried.

What we always do, I said. *We watch, and wait, and when the time is right, we'll figure it out.*

Marius's dry laughter echoed in my head. *Lot of good figuring things out has done us until now.*

That was true, but even now, I knew this was different. This wasn't something we could put off and pretend didn't exist. It couldn't wait for the years to pass and for an opportunity to slip into the center of our aim. This, we needed. I needed.

There was no room for doubts in this. We couldn't allow that.

If it was her? The woman they all spoke about and the one whose laugh woke me within stone? Then we would have to do something about it.

I was now counting the minutes until the sun fell away.

CHAPTER FOUR

CHRISTINE

a few hours later, I was back in my apartment, caffeinated and nervous. The production meeting started in less than half an hour, and after that, a casual party for the cast and crew to mingle and get to know each other the way that we hadn't been able to over the internet.

What did you wear to something like this? I already knew that outside of Meg, Tori, and Anne, meeting everyone was going to be a crap-shoot at best. So I needed to ride that line of professional and fun. God, this was already impossible.

Tori and Meg told me what I already knew: Désirée was pissed that I'd taken her place as the lead, and she'd told multiple people if there was a way for her to get rid of me that she would take it. I already figured that I'd have to watch my back. This just solidified it.

I ended up in black skinny jeans and casual sneakers, with a black sheer top over a conservative bra. The sleeves were solid. I'd worn this exact thing to a different cast party in New York. Granted, that was a very different feel. But after scooping my hair off my neck and putting it up? I felt very Parisian, and at the moment that was enough for me.

Clothes? Check. Make-up? Check. Keys? Check. Everything was ready, and I still had time. But I would much rather leave now and work on learning the best paths through the opera house than leave later, get lost, and be late. I left my hat and glasses behind. I couldn't hide from the people in the production, even though nerves and habit made me want to.

The nearest stairs were a metal spiral staircase that spun down three levels to the stage floor. We'd taken them earlier to meet Raphael, but had gone to the back of the theatre instead of the front.

Even getting later in the evening, there was still a fair amount of commotion back here, with trades-people working on the set. I sidestepped two men carrying a large panel of painted wood that looked like a forest, and stopped looking where I was going for one second.

I bumped into something—someone—and was about to fall straight on my ass before he caught me by the arms. "Whoa," he said, French accenting lilting his words. "Are you all right?"

"I'm fine." I looked up, and anything else I was going to say got completely lost in the pale blue eyes locked on mine. That was entirely aside from the stark jawline and softly curling hair that reached his shoulders. Not to mention that he was tall. Well over six feet and leanly built with muscles that showed through his clothes.

Holy. Fuck.

Meg had told me that I was going to fall for a beautiful French man. When she said that, I rolled my eyes and declared that I wasn't coming to Paris to fall in love. Just to do my job.

Looking at this man's face, I could go back on my word as easily as he just caught me. "I'm sorry. Was trying to avoid one thing and bumped into you instead."

One side of his mouth tipped upward. It was a smile, but there was something deeper to it that didn't quite make sense. And then it was gone, and I was left wondering if I'd seen it at all. "Luckily I don't mind catching beautiful women."

Suddenly I felt dizzy. Like the two of us were caught in a frozen moment, time and space pulling me and this man together for a suspended second. Like there was more to me tripping into his arms than my own clumsiness, but some element of fate. Obviously, I needed more sleep.

I shook my head to clear it. This wasn't a movie. I was just an idiot, and way too clumsy for someone who was a ballerina.

"If he hadn't caught you, then one of us would have." Another voice spoke, and I turned to find two others watching our exchange. Equally gorgeous. Equally tall and built. Blond and dark. My body started to tingle, like it couldn't quite get a hold of the fact that I was close to this much delicious, masculine energy. If this was the kind of stage crew that they hired in Paris, I needed to come here more often.

And again, I felt that pull. That breathless tension that sought me like an arrow. Towards the two of them. All three of them. A hook low in my gut that told me these were men that I needed to know.

What the fuck was that? Then one smiled and knocked me back into myself with the way my body reacted to that smile.

I was already blushing, but their words just enhanced it. "Well, thank you for the rescue."

"Our pleasure," blue-eyes said.

Our. Even though it was just him that caught me. They were all staring at me with interest. Of course they knew who I was already. Everyone did. That's all it was. They just saved the star from falling on her ass. They'd probably use it against me later. All the breathless hope went out of me and left me feeling like a limp balloon.

I stifled a sigh. "Just point me in the direction of the house?"

Blue-eyes glanced over my head, and then released me, pointing. I'd been so comfortable with his hands on me that I hadn't even realized he was still touching me until the places where his hands had been were cold. "Over there," he said. "That door will take you to the side of the seats."

"Thank you."

"You're welcome." He looked at me a moment longer, and there was no way that I could move while he had me pinned with that stare. It was only him finally looking away that had my feet moving.

I needed to get a serious grip. Tired or not, I couldn't be falling over stage hands and losing my head over beautiful men. But like hell was I going to forget that face. Any of their faces. Part of me wished that this was a romance we were staging. I wouldn't mind practicing a few *lines* with those lips.

Okay, Christine. Calm the hell down. If Meg were here, she would tease me about wanting one of my romance novels to come to life. But was that a bad thing? I could think of worse things than being romanced.

There were a few people milling around the auditorium already. I went to the front and center section of the audience and took a seat near the back of it. I wanted to observe as long as humanly possible. Hopefully, it would all go smoothly.

Suddenly, I heard my voice. Singing. A sound that I would never forget as long as I lived. Not only did I know the aria like the back of my hand, I knew exactly what video was playing, though I didn't know where.

"Wow," I heard a low voice. "I mean, you made it seem like she can't sing. That's nuts—her voice is awesome."

"I don't particularly care if her voice is 'awesome,'" another voice said. "I care that she hasn't earned it. Just because you have a voice doesn't mean you go from being a fucking ballet dancer to the lead in an international show. It's ridiculous."

Clearly, being introduced to the cast was going to go well then.

Two girls walked down the aisle past me, and I fought the urge to shrink down in my seat. It would be so easy to do it and lean into that story about me. That I didn't deserve this and I was lucky to be here. Hell, those were things that I thought about myself.

But she was right. I did come from the ballet world. Which meant that I knew more than most how to deal with catty colleagues. It would be a month in hell if I didn't show strength now.

So I didn't duck down in my seat. I just scrolled through the emails on my phone until they passed me, and when they turned to move into the seats, I smiled. They both froze. One of them turned pink and looked horrified. I guessed that she was the one that said she liked my singing.

The other one just stared at me. Assessing. There was a flash of brief terror there, because she knew that if I went to Anne and told her what she'd just said about me, she'd be on the first plane back to wherever she came from.

"Hello," I said.

"Hi," the blushing one said.

The other said nothing, though she nudged the first girl with her elbow and they moved to the middle to sit down. I caught the flash of different emotions on my new enemy's face. Anger at what she still felt for me, and gratefulness for me not taking revenge. At the very least she'd be hesitant to talk about me like that again in public.

In private, I was sure she wouldn't care.

Enemy might be a stretch, but right now, enemy until proven friend was the only way to survive.

As soon as they sat down, their heads were together, whispering. I didn't try to listen to what they were saying.

Slowly, people filtered in from all directions. The backstage areas, the lobby, the side doors like I'd come through. The division between cast and crew was clear enough. All the crew sat together to the left, in the next section over. I assumed all the people sitting around me were in the cast.

Meg and Tori sat a few rows away, my best friend waving with a wink. She knew that I didn't want to draw attention to myself, and the moment I started talking with anyone, I would. A few I recognized from my days auditioning and dancing, and some I didn't recognize at all.

"Don't worry, everyone," a voice called out. "I'm here."

All heads turned towards the smiling blond man who was clearly joking. Him, I knew from a distance. Everyone knew him. Taylor Peak was one of those people that made opera *cool*. He was playing the King. He, at least, I wasn't worried about.

I should have brought my hat. I knew I shouldn't hide, but after my one bout of bravery with the girls,

I wanted to again. Instead, I settled for looking down at my phone as the rest of the cast, crew, and creative team came in.

People vastly underestimated the amount of people that it took to put on an opera. Even more since we were all living in the opera house.

There were probably three hundred people in this auditorium, the pleasant hum of chatter making feel me more comfortable being ever so slightly anonymous.

Out of the corner of my eye, I saw another commotion as Desirée Michaels came in and sat near the front. She'd been the assumed person for this part until my virality stole it from underneath her. I needed to make sure I didn't eat or drink anything around her. Would she poison me? I didn't think so, but stranger things had happened.

That was the other part of Meg's gossip. Désirée was so enraged that I'd been chosen over her that she threatened to quit the entire production and was apparently now being paid more than any other cast member just to get her to stay. Having her name attached to the show alone was enough to make it worth it.

My viral fame was going to bring in new people to the opera. The younger generation. But Désirée had credit with the traditional opera crowd. She would bring in those people.

Anne stepped up in front of the orchestra pit, clipboard in hand, and it was like the lights had dimmed for a performance. We all dropped into hushed silence and waited.

"Hello, everyone. Welcome to Paris, and the banner production of *Joan D'Arc* at the new Paris Opera House."

Applause.

"You all have your schedules and room assignments. Rehearsals begin tomorrow at nine. After this meeting is adjourned, you may see Emily for your key to the cast and crew entrance."

A small woman waved from the front row. She'd already given me mine, I realized, so I wouldn't have to wade into the crowd of people that would be aiming for the person with the keys.

"I must emphasize how important it is that the cast and crew entrance be kept locked at all times. There will be an attendant there around the clock, in case you forget your keys and to prevent any incidents. But please help us avoid that in the first place by simply keeping it locked."

She went over a few more housekeeping things. The kitchen schedules and bathrooms for the members of the cast with more communal housing. But I wasn't listening. My brain was distracted.

All the way to the right, under the shadow of one of the boxes, was the man who'd saved me from falling on my ass a few minutes ago.

He leaned against the wall, arms crossed, the look on his face bored as he watched Anne. Mildly amused, if anything. Even that expression was enough to make me inhale like I was gulping water.

I wasn't this person. There was a reason that Meg teased me and that I loved reading romances. I was awkward when I wasn't on stage. If I ran into the three of them again, I wouldn't know how to act.

Another man came out of the door behind him, quietly standing next to him. His friend. One of the ones that had been there when I almost fell. They spoke, but the way they melted into the shadows made my heart pound. Clearly, no one else had noticed them. Weren't they part of the crew? They had to be.

Now that I could, I looked. The second man was just as gorgeous as the first. Much darker hair and a more solid build. I needed to get myself in check if I was already drooling over two different crew members. Internal show relationships were tricky at best.

"And of course, we want to welcome our star," I heard Anne say. "Christine Daniels."

I startled. Anne was looking directly back at me, and now everyone in the cast and crew was too. I waved, wishing desperately that I didn't feel like a target had just been painted on me.

Anne, seeing that I wasn't getting the response that she expected, moved on to the next point, and the attention shifted away from me again.

Reflexively, I looked back towards the men in the corner, and froze. The looks on their faces were far from bored. The heat in those shadows could set the room on fire. All three of them were there now. All dark and gorgeous, and all staring straight at me.

CHAPTER FIVE

CHRISTINE

*T*hey'd certainly gone all out on the catering.

In the lobby of the opera house, there were tables with *piles* of amazing food. And this was Paris, so amazing meant that there were chefs on site to make the food that couldn't sit out on platters. Pastries that were lighter than air and wine that was likely going straight to my head after a long flight and jet lag.

And at the same time, there was no way that I wasn't drinking it.

Outside the glass doors, there was a crowd. Cameras trying to get a glimpse of us from the bottom of the stairs and fans that had somehow tracked down the fact that there was a party tonight.

Thank fuck for Raphael. He'd taken us to a neighborhood far away from here, where it didn't seem to matter who I was. No one had noticed, and it was perfect. Since no one knew that we left, there wasn't a crowd to greet us at the opera house when we came back.

More than just the cast and crew were at this party, though, the producers and financiers were here too. As they would be at the gala before we opened.

Meg came over to me with a glass of wine, drinking most of it in one go. "Well, this is lame."

"*Meg*," I whispered, trying to hold in a laugh. "It's the first day. You can't say that."

She rolled her eyes. "Of course I can. No one cares what I say. I'm in the chorus. Besides, you know that it's true."

"I won't say that."

"Out loud," she muttered, draining the rest of her wine.

She wasn't wrong. This wasn't much of a party. But then again, I hadn't really expected it to be. If we were in New York we'd call it a 'mixer.' So that everyone mixed and got to know each other. Not that anyone other than Meg—and maybe Tori—was going to talk to me.

Where I was standing there was a ten-foot bubble, and no one seemed willing to step inside it. "Do you think they hate me?" I asked quietly.

"Are you serious?"

I looked over at her. "Does it seem like I'm kidding?"

She sighed. "I think they're scared of you. Brand new talent coming in from nowhere? That's got to be intimidating."

"What's intimidating?" Tori asked. She was in the middle of eating fruit off a stick that she'd covered in chocolate from the fountain.

"Discussing whether everyone won't talk to me because they hate me or because they're scared of me."

"Oh, they definitely hate you," Tori said, mouth full. "One-hundred percent."

I glared at my best friend. "You were saying?"

She glared right back. "You really wanted me to tell you the truth about that?"

"Well, if I know they hate me, it makes it easier. I don't have to be in limbo about it. If they hate me… I'll just have to deal with it, I guess. Do my job."

"They won't hate you at the end," Tori said. "I've known you for like ten seconds and I love you.

They're all just more afraid of Désirée and getting on her bad side. And liking you? That puts them on her bad side."

That wasn't surprising.

Across the lobby, Désirée Michaels was speaking with Anne and another one of the investors. And she was pure glamour. Heels as high as heaven with a tasteful pencil skirt and dark top that made her look like she'd been born in Paris even though she was as New York as they came.

She looked over at me like she knew that I was watching. No smile, merely a sip of wine before she looked away.

In comparison to her, I looked like a teenager in this outfit. It wasn't hard to make the leap to why she hated me. I was singing a role that everyone thought was rightfully hers, and not only that, but right now she looked like the epitome of class and I look like a kid that worked at Hot Topic in the Secaucus mall.

Not that I'd ever be caught dead in New Jersey.

"If looks could kill," Meg said.

"I need to make sure she never touches anything I drink," I said.

Tori laughed, snorting and covering her mouth with a napkin to hold in chocolate. "I'm sorry. You dying isn't funny, but the idea of Miss High and Mighty over there trying to be sneaky? Hilarious."

I grinned, sipping a little more of the golden wine.

"Miss Daniels?"

Meg and Tori's faces went blank and polite. I turned to find Anne behind me, smiling, Raoul Chagny by her side.

"Christine Daniels," Anne said. "You're familiar with our angel investor Monsieur Chagny?"

"Of course I am." I stretched out a hand. "It's nice to meet you."

He smiled brighter. Much younger than I'd originally thought, he was handsome. Brown hair and green eyes, he was the kind of guy that could sweep you off your feet without a second thought. "It's an honor to meet you in person," he said, his English lightly accented. "Though I'm not sure if you should be calling me the angel. Not when Mademoiselle Daniels has the voice of one."

I blushed, and he took my outstretched hand, lifting it to his lips briefly. The room went silent, and it wasn't just my imagination. Everyone within sight hushed, watching us with interest.

"Thank you very much," I said. "It's an honor to be here."

"I'm very much looking forward to hearing you sing in person. Madame Giry has promised that I might attend some of your rehearsals."

Anne nodded and glanced at me. "Of course. After all, without you, this production wouldn't be happening."

"I hope we all live up to your expectations."

Raoul leaned in. "I doubt you could do anything but exceed them."

There was a breathless moment where I wasn't sure what to say. How did you respond to that? Was he flirting? I'd never been good at flirting, and though Meg and the other girls in the company had always turned being a ballerina into a dating selling point, I felt like I'd missed that class.

Even if I wanted to flirt, I didn't think I could. Not after I'd encountered those guys earlier. Because the feeling in my gut was so *visceral* in reaction them that this paled in comparison.

But I had to say something. "I wanted to thank you for Raphael. He's already been amazing."

Raoul's smile only grew wider. "It was my pleasure, of course. I simply couldn't bear the idea of our star having to take the *métro*. And of course, if you need anything else during your stay, feel free to let me know."

I could practically hear Meg bursting behind me. "Thank you."

Anne put her hand on his arm. "I'm sure you and Miss Daniels will get to know each other well."

He inclined his head and smiled at me. "Duty calls."

They moved on to speak to more of the producers, and I was free to down what was left of my glass of wine.

"What the hell was that?" Meg asked.

"What?"

Tori laughed. "He looked at you like he wanted to eat you. But like, in a good way."

"I doubt it."

Meg looked at Tori. "Christine wouldn't know if someone was into her if they did it in sky writing."

"Hey."

"You're going to pretend that's not true?"

I sighed. "No."

"Exactly. And I don't think that having the biggest financier of the whole production wrapped around your finger is a bad thing, babe."

"Not exactly going to make me more popular with the rest of the production, though."

She made a face. "Fair point."

From one of the entrances to the theatre, I saw my knight in shining armor enter the lobby, along with his friends. They were a trio in my head, already inseparable. His eyes found mine like a heat-seeking missile. My stomach dropped through the floor, and it felt like the temperature rose.

"Who the *fuck* is that?" Meg asked quietly.

"Someone who wouldn't need to use skywriting," I said.

And I was incredibly aware that all three of them were hot enough to light me on fire without having to rent a plane. They could be a billboard walking straight towards us the way they were.

They didn't seem to mind the ten-foot bubble that everyone was keeping. I glanced around, and no one was watching me anymore now that Anne and Raoul had moved on. They weren't even in the room anymore. Maybe that meant that I could breathe.

"You haven't fallen down again yet, I see."

"No," I managed with a smile and raised my empty glass. "I've managed to keep myself upright. Barely."

He laughed, and his friends laughed too. They looked at me the way that *he* was looking at me. With keen interest and a heat that I wasn't sure I was perceiving correctly. The same way they'd looked at me in the theatre that made my heart pound.

That kind of heat was reserved for darkness and silk sheets. Moaning and shared breaths. Not the middle of a mass of people.

"I never got your name."

"Alexandre," he said. "This is Erik, and Marius."

"I'm Meg," my friend said, pushing in front of me. "And this is Tori. We're the friends and bodyguards."

Alex raised an eyebrow, and I wasn't sure that there should be anything about that one single gesture that was so hot. Maybe because he was French? I had no idea. But it was.

Erik was smirking.

"I hope that Paris has been treating you well so far?" Marius asked.

"So far, though, I haven't gotten to see much of it. Just got off the plane this morning."

"Then we'll have to make sure that you see more of it," Alex said. He looked around. "I'm sure that we could find a better party than this one."

"Now," Meg said. "You're speaking my language."

"Meg, I can't just leave."

She turned to me, a look on her face. "Of course you can. You're the star. You could take a shit on the stage and they'd find some way to justify it and turn it into good press."

I groaned. "Why am I friends with you?"

"You love me."

"Unfortunately."

Meg punched me in the arm and then pulled me away from Tori and the guys. "You're telling me that you would rather stay here, with everyone staring at you, then sneak out for some drinks with guys that look like *that?* Chris, there's one for each of us."

I glanced around. She wasn't wrong. The bubble around me was still solidly in place. I'd spoken to Monsieur Chagny and some of the investors. There wasn't really a reason that I needed to stay.

"Okay," I said, relenting. "But we cannot stay out all night. Rehearsal."

She smirked. "When have I ever stayed out all night before a rehearsal?"

"You want a list?"

"No." She dragged me back to them. "We're in."

I held out a hand. "But we need to be careful," I said. "If the paparazzi find out where I am…"

Alexandre winked. "Don't worry. I'm sure we know a place where we can lose them."

They started walking back towards the theatre, and I lowered my voice. "You know that going with people that they don't know, *in Paris*, is the start of that movie where the girl gets kidnapped, right?"

Tori laughed. "They're part of the crew, right? Even if we don't know them now, I'll wager we'll know them perfectly well by the end of the run."

"If we're lucky we'll know them better by the end of the night," Meg whispered.

"You two are going to be the death of me," I said.

"I need to go to my room and get a hat. Glasses just in case."

"No need," Erik said, turning. There was a hat stuck in his back pocket and he offered it to me.

"Are you sure?"

"I am very sure." The look in his eyes told me that he wasn't talking about the hat, and my stomach did a little flip. Now that they weren't hiding in the shadows, I could actually, properly look at Alex's friends. More than I had backstage. In those moments, I was pretty sure that I'd blacked out.

Erik was tall, black hair shining like raven feathers under the lights of the hallway. The rolled-up sleeves of his shirt showed corded forearms that led to what looked like an incredibly toned body. Not exactly shocking. The crew of these shows had to move things well above their weight all the time, and regularly. I doubt they even needed to use the gym with the kind of workout they got backstage, both building and operating.

Marius was blonde and had an easy smile that I could see charming himself out of any trouble that he could get into. If I didn't know that he was French, I could have pegged him as a cowboy.

All three of them were tall and built and everything you wanted when you were going out on the town in an unfamiliar city. Melt-in-your-mouth delicious. Meg's way of saying exactly what she'd do to the guys we found attractive back in New York. Though she was a lot bolder about it than I was.

They led us through the now quiet and dark backstage door and to the artist's entrance. It was all quiet, and as soon as we stepped out into the warm night air, I felt better. Even the risk of being caught by cameras felt easier than being surrounded by people who won't talk to me.

Now we were just a group of people walking across the cobblestones and getting lost in the twilight.

"So, where are we going, exactly?"

Marius smiled. "We're going to show you the real Paris."

CHAPTER SIX

ERIK

I might need the others to hold me back.

She was there, and she was real. The beast inside me was roaring with the need to take and claim. That perfume that was somehow only her. Now that I'd experienced it, I never wanted anything else.

Lilacs. Hints of other flowers, but she smelled like that perfect first bloom of lilacs in summer. The way the sweetness hit you and then pulled you in deeper.

That Alex had already touched her skin drove me crazy. I wanted to touch her. Feel her. It was the only fucking thing I could think about, and all I could do was stop myself from visibly shaking with need.

Christine Daniels.

We'd heard the stories. Gargoyles that bonded. Mated. And the women who disguised themselves in order to be with them.

Nuns, mostly. A convenient way to make sure no one asked questions about who—or what—you were fucking. And churches were an easy way for us to hide.

But those stories were still rare. Rare enough that in the time we'd been trapped in the opera, I'd only heard of one other mate. I'd never heard of one for multiple Gargoyles at once.

What did it mean?

Other than the fact that I wanted to pull her into an alley and bury myself in her until we were both blind with pleasure.

When we heard her voice, something woke inside me. Then I'd seen her face. We all had, and that connection we'd all made in those moments backstage. She was *the one*. I hadn't expected that pull.

"Fuck," I said under my breath, and Marius nudged me with his elbow. In French, he said, "Get your shit together, Erik."

"You don't think I'm trying? How are you so calm?"

He laughed once. "I'm not. I'm just hoping that she doesn't see the front of my pants."

I looked back at the three girls trailing us now. Her friends were pretty, but it was like they existed in a fog. I could barely see them when she was standing there.

Christine was stunning, and completely unaware of how compelling her presence was. Graceful, because of her history of dance, and that made your eye stray to her whenever she moved.

Long hair that I wanted to run my fingers through. It wasn't just brown. It was brown that had never been touched, the highlights and shadows being picked up by the street lamps.

And her eyes?

I'd never seen eyes like that. So blue they were nearly violet. When she looked at me, I managed to cover my shock and the instant connection there. The pull in my gut towards her. Deeper than what we knew or felt.

When we sang to her through the stone, it was just a test. Seeing the new singer we'd heard about. Maybe there was something else that pulled us to do that. We hadn't been sure that it was *her* we had scented.

But it was.

Shaking my head, I glanced back again. They were laughing. Walking arm in arm. Even hidden under my hat, I could see a glimpse of glossy lips tipped up into a smile and a part of me that had long since died *wanted*.

Marius was right. I needed to get myself together. He jumped in front of us and started walking backwards. "The usual place?"

"Where else?" Alex asked.

Over the years we'd been trapped here, we'd learned our section of Paris intimately. We could only go so far before our binding pulled us back, and none of us were going to risk being forced into our stone forms where we could be broken or damaged.

But we'd made the best of it. We certainly weren't the only monsters in Paris. And where we were going, there would be plenty. Not that Christine or her friends would know. But it was one of the safest places in the city for humans. None of the monsters wants to risk the club shutting down over a human incident.

"If they're there," I said to Alex. "Please tell me I won't have to get between you."

He seethed beside me. "If they so much as look at her—"

"Alexandre," I said. "They would be fools to try anything in the club. You know that."

"It's not the club that I'm worried about."

Marius gave him a look. "She's staying in our house. If they want to try that, they're welcome."

I cleared my throat and switched to English. "We're just going to have fun. Show the new girls a good time."

"Maybe we should have taken the car," Christine said behind me. There were nerves in her voice.

"It's not far," I said. "Promise."

She smiled, but I felt her anxiety. She had a right to be nervous. Strange city, strange men. But we weren't going to hurt her. Christine Daniels had no idea how important she was to us. Had no idea that she was now the only thing that mattered.

We led them down the steps to the walkway next to the river, and I pointed to the neon sign under the bridge. "See?"

"That's where we're going?" Her blonde friend looked curious and eager even as she looked me up and down. That wasn't going to happen.

"It is," Alex confirmed. "Best party in the city."

Christine smiled and shared a look with her friend. "That's what we signed up for."

I gestured, and they walked first into the club.

"What are we doing here?" Marius asked. "Not physically. What are we doing with her here?"

"We have to start somewhere," I said. "There are worse things than drinks and dancing."

"Fair enough."

But as we followed them into the club, I couldn't help but echo his thoughts. What *were* we doing here?

CHAPTER SEVEN

CHRISTINE

*B*eing in the art scene in New York, I'd been in my fair share of underground clubs. This one blew them all away, by far. Neon lights lined the walls and integrated with machinery and clockwork gears. Steampunk that was also a rave.

The club kept stepping downward, like a giant staircase. Each lower level held something different. Dance floors. A bar. Lower down, I saw tables and couches and curtained alcoves.

And the place was absolutely packed.

We showed our IDs to the bouncer, and he waved us through. I turned around fast enough to notice that none of the three guys were carded. They were regulars here then.

Marius caught my eye and smiled before coming to my side. "Welcome to Club Spectre."

"You come here often?"

He grinned, even as he waved to someone passing. "Enough."

"Good to know. I thought I would be the celebrity. I guess you three are."

Reaching down, he took my hand and pulled me deeper into the club. "We're not celebrities," he said. "This place is just home."

Where he had my hand, there were tingles and heat. Ever since all of this happened and I was vaulted into the spotlight, I hadn't been able to go out or even try. Nobody tells you that when you become famous, suddenly you have to second-guess everyone's motives.

I tried to go out on one date in New York and ended up walking into a swarm of reporters that the guy had tipped off in order to try for his fifteen minutes of fame.

That paranoia lived in my gut, and I hated it. "Why are you guys doing this?" I had to raise my voice over the pounding rhythm.

"What do you mean?" Marius helped me dodge dancers and took me down further. He guided me, steering me away from a group of people gathered near a bar, and I felt him tense. Then it was gone.

He pulled me all the way down to the lowest level with the couches and alcoves. One glance at one of the club attendants and they found us a private booth that was covered with gauzy curtains. Even if there were people in here looking for me, that would make it one step harder.

The others were right behind us, passing through the curtains and sitting on the plush benches.

"I mean," I said, looking at Marius, who still had my hand in his. "That so far in my recent celebrity experience, people who don't know me and are nice to me usually want something from me. So if that's what's happening, please just tell me so we can get it over with."

Meg looked at me, concern in her eyes. I hadn't told her about some of the things that had happened. Hadn't told anyone, really. I didn't want to seem ungrateful for the opportunity of a lifetime.

But that didn't change the fact that this was a hell of a lot different from I'd thought it would be like.

"Do we need a reason to show a beautiful woman a good time?"

I noticed that he said wo*man* and not wo*men*. "People usually do."

Erik was sitting on the other side of me, and he

leaned close. Whatever cologne he was wearing was absolutely intoxicating. A warm scent that I couldn't put a name to, but that made me want to lean into his neck and fucking inhale.

That wine that I had at the mixer must be kicking in, because there was absolutely no reason for me to feel this way. I didn't want them to have an ulterior motive—I wanted them to not care who I was.

A waitress brought another bottle of wine, opened it, and poured glasses for us. I hadn't even seen them signal for one. But I wasn't complaining. Marius handed me a glass and tilted his own against mine.

Fuck, this was good.

"I don't care who you are," Erik said quietly. "I care if you say yes to dancing with me."

I looked up and found Alexandre looking at me. The combined heat and longing in his eyes made me suck in a breath. No one had ever looked at me like that before. Like they wanted me, and there was nothing in the world that would stop him from having me.

My stomach dropped, a tornado of butterflies appearing. What would he think if I said yes to dancing with Erik?

Tipping the glass back, I downed the glass of

wine in my hand like I was chugging a beer, and Meg started laughing. "Really trying to party now."

"I only had one glass at the mixer. And I need to do it early if I want to be ready for rehearsal."

Tori pointed at me. "You have the right idea."

Now that I had that in me, I looked at Erik. "Okay," I said. He was pulling me up and out of the booth as soon as I said the word.

Meg leaned toward Alex. "Do you want to dance?"

He glanced at her dismissively before his eyes found me again. "No, thank you."

She looked shocked, and my heart dropped. What?

My friend sprang up from the table and came to me. "Give us a second," she said to Erik, pulling me away from him.

"I'm sorry," I said. "I don't know why he did that."

Meg smirked. "You don't?"

"No."

"Girl." She rolled her eyes. "It's incredibly clear that they're all here for you. Even before we left the opera house, they could only look at *you*."

I sucked in a breath. "But there's three of us, three of them."

"There's three of them," she said. "And none of

them have looked at Tori or I for longer than a second. They want you."

My mouth opened and closed. I didn't know what to say. "I'm sorry."

"Why?"

Meg and I had known each other for years, so why did I feel like I was teetering on breaking ice? "Because I didn't agree to come out and party so that you could be rejected."

She threw her arms around my shoulders and yanked me into a hug. Then she whispered. "We're on the trip of a lifetime. One month, and no fucking rules. Three hot Frenchmen want to fuck you through your mattress? Take the chance. Have fun. Let go for once in your life, Christine."

"But—"

"Don't worry about me. I'm in a club full of hot people and I'm a big girl. Why bother throwing myself at someone who's not interested when I'm sure I can find someone who is?"

My heart stuttered, brain stuck on the whole 'three men fucking me into a mattress' thing.

I wasn't a prude. Or at least I wasn't in my own mind. But my friends had always been more adventurous than I was. That possibility never entered my head. But Meg was right. This was France. Everything was looser here. More fluid. Dynamics and relationships and sex. I knew enough French dancers to know that was true.

"Are you sure?"

She pulled back and grinned at me. "*Yes*. I'm serious. It's day one of this fucking adventure we're about to have and I'm not going to get bent out of shape over one guy who doesn't want me. But I swear to god if you don't tell me every delicious bit of this, I know where you sleep."

I laughed, and it was lost in the thumping of the music. "Okay. To be fair, I'm not even sure if you're right."

"I'm right," she said. "Want me to prove it?"

"How?"

Grabbing my hand, she shook it. "Five bucks says that both the other two come to dance with you within ten minutes."

Easy money. "Fine, you've got it."

"Would you like to dance?" A voice drew both of our gazes. A tall blond dressed in all black stood what seemed *way too close* for us not to have noticed him approaching. He was beautiful in a harsh way, but that immediate vibe was off. Like he unsettled the vibrations of the music around me.

Erik appeared at my elbow, and Meg looked at the man. "No." She spun her way back to the table and collapsed next to Tori, laughing.

"I wasn't asking her," the man said to me. "I was asking you."

I gave him a look. "If it wasn't clear already, I already have a partner."

"Sure about that?"

On my lower back, I felt Erik's hand. A subtle gesture. Protective yet confident. He would let me go if I wanted to. But while Erik's hand was something that I wanted to lean into, the thought of this guy touching me gave me chills in a bad way. "Yes, I'm very sure. Let's go."

It was time to dance, and not with that guy.

He guided me with a hand on my lower back, and it was stupid how aware of that hand I was. It was the wine. That's what I kept telling myself. Only the wine. The wine and the fact that I was jet lagged and that these men were so fucking hot that I couldn't breathe. It wasn't anything more than that.

We waded into the bodies on the dance floor together, and like there was a signal, the music changed from the frenetic rhythm to one that was a little slower. More sensual. It was music that rolled in waves instead of hurling itself at you.

Let go for once in your life, Christine.

That was scarier than Meg realized. Letting go right now? That was risky, but *fuck* if I didn't want to.

I glanced around the dance floor. In the darkness of the club and the lights strobing through the crowd, faces were colored swirls in the darkness. No one was looking at me. No one cared. And behind me, Erik touched my arms, asking me to move with him.

So I let go.

How long had it been since I danced at a club without caring?

A long time.

A long fucking time.

I sank into the music and let it take me away. Erik was there with me, our bodies pushing together and then apart again, pure instinct and reaction. His hands asked questions that I answered, flares of light flickering under my skin wherever he touched me. I didn't care if it was the wine that was doing it. I loved the feeling of him.

Spinning, I faced him, locking my arms around his neck so we could dance closer. His eyes were dark. Darker than the shadowy room around them, and it felt like he could see everything. His touch took on an edge—almost sharp through my clothes. It made every point that he was touching me tingle with electricity.

Impossibly, it felt like we'd been dancing together for years. Our moves—our breaths—were in sync, leading somewhere that I couldn't fully name.

Erik bent me backwards, and I trusted him to keep me upright. And he had to do just that when his lips touched my throat, dragging them upward as he brought me back to him. That simple sensation dropped through my body like sizzling waves of light.

Holy shit.

He looked down at me, mouth curling into a slow smile. The way our bodies were locked together made me think of things that were in no way related to dancing. And certainly not to standing upright.

Suddenly, it wasn't just Erik. Another set of hands slid along my ribs, and I jumped, spinning to find Alex behind me, a barely there smile on his face.

Shit. I owed Meg five dollars.

Alex's face was still hard. Intense. An echo of that heat that I'd seen, and his hands on my waist told that story. They clung to me like I was a lifeline. Like now that he was touching me, he had no intention of ever letting me go. Desperate and fierce, and the way he was looking at me made the butterflies in my stomach feel more like a stampede of elephants. I swore that my heart skipped a beat.

Erik was still touching me too, body hard against my back. And I loved it.

I shouldn't love this. I shouldn't—

The thoughts slammed to a stop. *Let go, Christine. Is anything bad going to happen because of this? No. Calm down.*

"My friend," I said, and Alex leaned closer to me so he could hear me over the music. My lips were at his ear and I curled my arms around his neck. The movement pushed my ass into Erik, and I enjoyed the feeling of his hand tightening on my hips. "My friend told me that all of you were here for me, and I didn't believe her."

He was close enough that I felt him smile against my cheek. "We are here for you, Christine."

Like he was conjured out of nothing, Marius was there, and I was surrounded on all sides by hard, hot bodies. It was overwhelming.

"Why?"

"Why not?"

I shook my head. "This isn't a thing that people do."

"On the contrary," Marius said. "This is the city of love. People do what they like here."

Together, they moved, pulling me through the crowd of dancers to the darkest corner of the floor. It was packed here, the mass of flailing dancers pressing in on us. But in the same way, it gave us even more anonymity than being in the center.

Barely any light reached here, and pressed in on all sides by dancers. The three of them were shielding me from anything else.

"Dance with us," Marius said.

I thought I was, until they all started to move, and I realized that they'd been holding back. This? This was everything. It reminded me of those rare times in dance class when we'd improvised and whatever partner I was given seemed to be totally in sync with me.

The way that they moved was fluid, pressing against me and pulling away, touching me with their hands and their mouths, brushing places where my skin was bare. The wine was definitely catching up with me, making me feel like I was floating.

But this wasn't all wine, and I couldn't blame this on being tipsy. It was just them. I was overwhelmed by the sensation as I danced, passing between them as effortlessly as breathing. These men were incredible dancers. And they were on the crew? They might be in the wrong job.

Marius took every last thought I had away when he pulled me back against his body and I felt *everything*. Including the way that he was hard against my ass.

I gasped. All of them. Aroused. Turned on by dancing with *me*.

"This is insane."

We were close to the wall. Without warning, Alex wrapped an arm around my waist and spun me so my back was against it. "It is?"

"Yes."

"When I see something I want," he said low in my ear. "I don't hesitate."

"You want me." It wasn't a question. I could feel the way that he did as he was pressed against me.

"Mmm," his lips drifted away from my ear. "How should we prove it to you?"

He moved me again, spinning me so I was flush against his body while he leaned against the wall. The hard length of him was pressed against my ass, a stark reminder of his words.

Erik and Marius stepped in front of me, filling that space. Need spiraled through my veins. They wanted me, and now that I'd let go, I wanted them. Tonight was one night. They wanted me, and I was going to let them have me.

"If you're going to walk away," he said, accent making everything in my body light up, "do it now."

"What happens if I stay?"

His hands found my wrists, locking his fingers around them. "We show you what we want. We will make you come. Right here. Right now."

CHAPTER EIGHT

CHRISTINE

*M*y whole body was frozen in shock. "What?"

The low laugh shivered across my skin. "Don't pretend that you didn't hear me."

I twisted, but he held me still against his body. "Is this something that you do regularly?" They were so coordinated, it felt like it. And if this was something that they did every weekend, I wanted no part of it.

"Never." That was Marius.

"Then why me? Why now?"

Stepping forward into my space and pressing into me, Erik tilted my face up. Now I was caught between two of them and holy fuck every inch was glorious. "That's the problem with Americans," he said with a smirk. "Always asking why."

"But—"

"Sometimes there is no *why*. Sometimes there is only want. And we want you."

I thought there was something he wasn't saying, but there wasn't a chance to say anything else. His lips came down on mine, and my brain faded into dizzy bliss. Soft lips teasing mine open and tracing his tongue along mine. He tasted like wine too, and my god if I ever thought I'd had a good French kiss? I was proven wrong by kissing a Frenchman.

My whole body felt heavy and hot, pulled downward by the weight of sensation and arousal.

Erik pulled away, only for Marius to take his place. His kiss was softer. More even. But deeper. He pressed me harder into Alexandre's body, and the man holding me captive with his hands had his mouth on my neck.

"Are you going to run away *ma petit e'toile*?"

My little star.

I moaned into lips as Alex slid lower behind me, the sole purpose to knock my legs farther apart. They were serious. If I said yes, they were going to make me come in the middle of the dance floor.

"If anyone sees," I said. "The pictures would be everywhere."

The sound Alex made was closer to a growl than anything a man should be able to make. "I will share with them. I will not share you with the world."

Not an ounce of doubt in his voice. A certainty that was more than a moment. "Then I guess I'm a fallen star tonight."

"Good girl."

Those words unleashed a brand new wave of heat. I'd never understood the appeal of someone saying that until this exact moment. Because holy hell, that made me drown in arousal. It was a living thing that stretched and woke inside me, making me shudder.

This was not something I would ever *dream* of doing in New York. Was this risky as hell? Yes. But I wanted them too badly to say no. Knowing that I was going to be spending my days in the middle of people who hated me?

I needed this.

Alex's hands were still locked around my wrists, holding them down and back by his sides. So when Erik reached forward and undid the button on my jeans, I couldn't stop him. Didn't want to stop him.

Holy fuck, I was really doing this, wasn't I?

The lacy thong I was wearing under my jeans wasn't going to provide any resistance. Thank fuck.

He stepped forward, body nearly pressed against

mine so I was caught between their two bodies. And Erik slid his hand straight down. Beneath my jeans and beneath my thong.

I hadn't realized how wet I was until he touched me, circling his fingers around my clit. My entire body shuddered, the longing for more waking up with the realization that we were still very much in public.

Alex shifted so his arms were fully wrapped around me, pinning both my arms and body in place while Erik moved. Slow circling that wasn't nearly enough. Just gentle teasing. But already, he wasn't someone that was fumbling. He knew what he was doing, and my body was catching up.

A low moan came out of me, and Alex released one of his hands to tangle one in my hair. He turned my face towards his, dragging his mouth around my neck. "If you start making sounds like that, then this will be a lot less private. Even in a place like this"

Erik moved, slipping a finger inside me, and the second moan was louder. I wasn't in control of it. How could I be?

"Marius, keep her quiet." He tilted my head again, and Marius's mouth slanted over mine just in time to silence another moan.

One shift, and Erik slid another finger inside me while the heel of his palm brushed my clit. He leaned hard against my body, pressing me into Alex as he moved. Starting slow with those clever fingers, stroking, reaching, teasing me, finding the places inside that made me squirm and made me wish that we weren't in the middle of a fucking club.

Marius traced his tongue along my lips, wordlessly asking me to open for him. I did. The second glass of wine was hitting me now, along with need that I'd buried. It all felt like starlight soaking through my brain.

Maybe I was a fallen star tonight.

With that thought, the last of any resistance and the need for a *why* and a *why me* didn't matter anymore. I moved my arm, and to my surprise, Alex let me move it. Reaching for Marius, I slid my hand behind his neck and pulled him closer.

I gasped into his mouth, Erik suddenly finding exactly what he needed to. *Oh, fuck.* He didn't stop now, pressing harder into me with both body and hand, fucking me in that one spot that made me see the stars they named me for. As he did it, he ground against my clit with every fucking stroke and I couldn't breathe anymore.

Pleasure pleasure pleasure like honey and velvet and the richest chocolate.

Breaking away from the kiss, I leaned my head back, trying to get air into my lungs. Marius didn't miss a beat, closing the distance and kissing my neck instead.

Heat rolled through me, my hips moving, seeking more of what Erik was offering. All that accomplished was me writhing between both their hard bodies, showing me how much *more* they wanted.

Alex covered my mouth with his hand. "Do you like the way that he's fucking you?"

I nodded, caught between the building pleasure of Erik's fingers and the way that Marius had my shirt pulled off my shoulder, kissing across my collarbone.

"Close your eyes," he whispered. I did. "There's no one in the room but us. Making you feel good."

I heard my own voice leak into his fingers.

"But you have to be quiet," he said, the words so low they shivered across my skin. "Or he's not going to take you all the way."

Marius lifted his mouth from my skin, and then there was a hand at my throat. Almost no pressure, but the feeling of it there. The possession between the three of them. It made me melt into the floor. What the hell was wrong with me?

Now his mouth was at my other ear. "If we were alone right now, my tongue would be so deep inside you that you would never forget the feeling. And then I'd kiss you again to make sure you knew how good you taste."

Light flared behind my eyes. Erik found it. The rhythm that made my heart stutter and pleasure unfurl like a golden wave. My words were muffled by Alexandre's fingers. "Don't stop. Please."

He didn't.

Everything narrowed. It felt like time slowed and the only thing that existed was me and them. Their hands on me. In me. The breath that touched my skin and the way they held me still.

And at once, everything exploded again. One last movement of Erik's hand, and pleasure spun outward. All control was gone. I shook, hips working to take what they needed as I groaned, fingers still muffling my voice. It filled me and took away everything—light, breath, vision—before I collapsed back into myself, my body now weak.

Alexandre's lips were pressed against my ear. "Good girl," he whispered again, and my whole body shuddered.

Erik drew his hand away from me and smirked, meeting my eyes as Alex released my mouth. Marius's hand still rested on my throat, and I didn't know what to do about the fact that I liked it there. Never wanted him to move it.

"Time for clean-up." Erik's fingers shone wetly in

the lights of the club. Shone with *me*. One by one, he slid his fingers into his mouth, cleaning what remained of my orgasm from his fingers.

It felt like he was still touching me while I watched, imagining the feeling of what his tongue would do.

My stomach spun with new arousal. I wasn't sure that I could stand without Alexandre supporting me right now.

Erik reached out and ran his thumb along my lower lip. "Next time, you'll do it."

Fuck.

A flash, bright as day, made the club appear in freeze frame for a second. Like a single strobe.

And then another one.

In the moment it took me to realize what happened, the man with the camera was already moving through the dancers and away. "Oh shit," I said. Now I was dizzy, and not from the fact that I'd just had one of the best orgasms of my life, but because there was a photo of me pressed against Alex with Marius's hand at my throat while Erik's fingers were nearly in my mouth. And by morning, they would be everywhere.

"I have to stop him," I said, shoving them off me. But they were already moving, pushing through the dancers like they were nothing.

Free of the crowd, I sprinted up the stairs. The buttons on my jeans were still open—I couldn't afford to stop and close them.

There. Ahead of me I saw him, the camera swinging off his shoulder as he made his way out of the club. I wasn't going to make it in time.

No.

He disappeared and I pushed myself faster. My lungs burned and my legs shook, my whole body exhausted from jet-lag and alcohol and unplanned pleasure.

I pushed past the bouncer and out the door, only to be blinded by another flash. "Miss Daniels," the person shouted. "Having a good time in Paris?"

The accent wasn't American. Blinking the spots out of my eyes, I held out my hand. "Memory card. Now."

He laughed. "I don't think so. I just got the shot of the century, and you're going to make me rich."

I didn't even see the movement. A blur flew past me, and a fist plowed into the man's face. Now the people who were smoking and loitering outside were looking more than they already were. My borrowed hat was back at the table in the bottom of the club.

Marius was struggling with the man on the ground, who was shouting at me to stop him.

But I was frozen. I couldn't move. People were going to recognize me. And then more people like him would be here.

Arms came around me, moving me quickly, turning me so that I faced the wall of the club near the door. Those same arms now bracketed me on either side while a body pressed into mine. It was Alexandre. Now that my body had been flush against his once, I doubted that I would ever mistake him for anyone else.

I heard footsteps running and shouts.

"Is he getting away?" The misery was plain in my voice.

"No," Alex said. His tone was dark. "They'll catch him."

"If they don't—"

"What did I say to you earlier? I won't—*we will not*—share you with anyone but the three of us. Understand?"

The words rolled down my spine, taking root. They were a comfort, even though the wine was leaving me and the sober part of me was blinking in shock at what I'd done. The risk I'd taken.

And the fact that I didn't regret it in the least, other than the photo.

"You don't know me," I said.

A low laugh. "On the contrary, I think the three of us know you...intimately."

I turned to face him, and he moved with me, keeping me blocked from the people outside the club so they couldn't see me.

"You know what I mean. You don't know me. Why would you go to that kind of length for someone that you don't know?"

In the darkness, it was hard to see his face, but I felt the intensity in the way that he was looking at me. "Because we want you."

"But—"

"You felt it," he said. "Earlier today, when you tripped, and I caught you. I know you felt it."

He didn't have to clarify what he meant, because I had felt it that strange, dizzying pull. "Yes."

"Then what other reason do you need?"

I laughed, the small sound bubbling up. "Because it's crazy."

"Crazy?"

"Not even a day ago I was still in New York. I didn't know you existed. And now we did...*that*," I gestured to the door of the club. "And you're defending my honor like some kind of chivalrous knight. So you can't tell me that it's not a little crazy."

The corner of Alex's mouth tipped up. "So very American."

"That better be a compliment."

He chuckled. "What do they call Paris?"

That wasn't an answer, but I thought about it. "The City of Love."

"People come from all over the world to put locks on the bridges, hoping that it will make their love eternal. I don't imagine there's a cobblestone in this whole city that hasn't heard a proposal or a declaration."

"And?"

"And Paris," he said it in the French way. "Is old. This city is older than your very young country. There are things here that are not meant to be understood. Look no further than the opera house for proof."

I wasn't sure what he meant by that. "Where are you going with—"

His lips came down on mine. Hard. Insistent. Unyielding. Every ounce of that wicked dominance was in his kiss. It spoke of the way he'd held me for Erik and the fact that he wanted to do so much more. Every part of me wanted to yield.

"Busy, I see."

Marius's voice broke us apart. He was standing there, breathing hard, Erik walking back behind him. I didn't even have to ask the question. He held up his hand, and it was there. The memory card.

"Is he?"

"Alive," Erik confirmed.

I blinked. That wasn't what I was going to ask, but that was good.

"Just in case," Marius said. He took the memory card and broke it in half before turning it and hurling it into the river.

Those weren't made of paper. It took some serious strength to crack one of those cards. I'd never seen anyone do that with their bare hands.

"Thank you."

None of them said anything, the feeling hanging in the air that this wasn't a hardship, it was a given.

"Before you kissed me," I said softly. "You were saying something."

Alex looked at his two friends. "There is something between us. You agree?"

They both nodded, and then three gazes were all on me. Whatever sang between us felt like a whole lot more than *something*. My breath caught on the word. "Yes."

"Then it would be a shame to ignore it simply because it's fast. Or untraditional. Or crazy. Any of the things that you've said."

I couldn't argue with that logic. Still, the hesitance I felt...what would people think? Did it matter?

Of course it did, since my life was public consumption. But I didn't want it to. The celebrity I'd gained had given me this opportunity, but it was still my life. If I'd come on a vacation trip to Paris before people knew my name, I would have jumped at the chance to be spontaneous and try this.

Why shouldn't I do that now?

Especially if they were willing to chase down photographers to protect me from embarrassment.

"What are you suggesting?"

The other two closed in, and I was once again surrounded. And it was the first time in a long time that I'd felt truly safe.

Marius was the first one that moved, resuming that same pose we'd been ripped from. Hand gently at my throat and lips at my ear. I was glad for the darkness so he couldn't see the way I shook, and the way my nipples hardened beneath my shirt.

"While you remain in Paris," he said with velvet softness. "You belong to us."

"What?"

"That's what we're...suggesting." The way he said it made it clear that he didn't consider it a suggestion.

I took a single, shaking breath. "What the hell does that mean?"

Erik's turn. "It means that what happened below our feet gets to keep happening. Whenever you want. And whenever *we* want."

"We'll keep you safe," Alex said. "From assholes like that, and anyone else who wants to hurt you."

I laughed once, in spite of myself. "Sex in exchange for being my bodyguards?"

"If that's what you want to call it," Alex said. "But we both know that's not the truth."

"Care to enlighten me?"

Marius's hand tightened. I knew in a place so deep I couldn't name it that he wouldn't hurt me. Not like this. Alexandre came closer. "Because you said yes in the club."

"That doesn't—"

"No." He cut off my words. "Because you loved every second of it, even though we took away your choices. Because you came so hard your panties are still wet, aren't they?"

I blushed. They were. My jeans too.

Every word brought him closer, his voice dropping to that same velvet softness that seemed to make every cell in my body perk up and listen.

"Because your whole body *melted* when I called you a good girl." His grin was wicked, and I wanted to take back my question. Everything he was saying was true, and it was baring me in a way that felt like too much. Too vulnerable.

"Alexandre—"

"You will be silent until I finish speaking."

The careless power that flowed through the words startled me. Made me lean into the hand on my throat and question my own sanity with the way it made me *want* more.

"You want to know what it feels like to be *owned*."

"No, I don't."

"What did I say?"

My breath went short in a good way. He'd told me not to talk, and I had. What would that do? The curiosity that was blooming in my chest was something I didn't understand, and I couldn't even blame it on being tipsy. It was just *them*.

"In spite of all the reasons that you say we can't, you're still here. Letting us touch you. If you wanted to walk away, you would have done it already."

I closed my eyes, wishing he was wrong, and glad that he wasn't.

"You know what that tells us, Christine?" It wasn't a real question. "That you're curious about this. About us. You crave it."

"No."

He didn't reprimand me this time. Just smiled. "Liar."

"What do you have to lose?" Marius's thumb stroked against my skin.

That was a good question. What did I have to lose?

There was a tiny voice that whispered *nothing*, at the same time as another voice whispered *everything*. What they were offering was...tempting. The idea of something daring and different and a fucking adventure. But it was all too fast. Too much. Too far. And it made me unable to breathe.

This didn't feel like an accident. I couldn't quite put a name to why it felt like I was meant to be standing between these three men, but it did feel that way. And part of that was comforting. The rest of it was terrifying.

I wasn't afraid of them, but afraid of how much I wanted them.

Reaching up, I grabbed Marius's wrist. I wanted to see if his heart was beating as fast as mine, but I felt nothing under my thumb. "What do you say, *ma belle étoile?*"

I swallowed. They were so close, and so beautiful, and I didn't want to lose them after something so bright and beautiful. The three of them seemed perfect. A perfect memory on the perfect first day.

93

Meg had dared me to let go, and I had. That was all I had to give.

"No."

Their shocked faces stared after me as I walked away.

CHAPTER NINE

MARIUS

*E*rik snorted, switching over to French. "That went well."

I shrugged, already missing the delicate warmth of Christine's skin under my fingers. "We came on strong."

"I'm not taking it back," Alex said. His voice was deadly quiet, and he stared at the space where she'd been standing before she walked away and left us gaping at the glorious shape of her ass.

"You felt it right?" Erik asked, quiet and awed. "She's our mate."

"*She is.*" The words were practically a snarl from Alex. "And she *belongs to us.*"

A few heads snapped our way, and I put a hand on his shoulder, forcing Alex back into the club. Pierre nodded to us as we entered. "Remember not to say things like that in front of the humans unless you want the police called."

Alex scoffed. "Like Pierre would ever give us up."

The bouncer wasn't exactly human either.

"That doesn't matter," I said. "And you know it."

He turned on me, and the combination of desperation and anger on his face was one that I hadn't seen in over a century. "You know it too. Don't tell me you don't feel that."

"Of course I do." The growl built in my chest. She did belong to us. That fact was rooted in the bottom of my fucking gut. There was a reason that Alexandre had called her a star—that pull towards her resonated like one. A shining bright star that was helping us navigate.

Straight toward everything we'd ever wanted.

"She'll come around," Erik said.

"You know that for sure?" I asked. "How?"

He smirked. "You didn't feel how hard she came."

"That means nothing, Erik." I rolled my eyes. An orgasm wasn't the same thing as agreeing to be with someone. And times had changed since we were created.

"So what do you suggest?"

"We'll show her what she's missing," Alex said.

I raised an eyebrow. "How? Just tell her that she's the mate of three gargoyles? Somehow, I don't exactly see that going over well."

"She thinks we're part of the crew. Keep the illusion. Give her just a taste of what we mean. Sing to her through the stone. Until she realizes that she's made a mistake. Until she understands what we are to her."

Erik rubbed a hand on the back of his neck. "What if she decides to leave when the show is over?"

The snarl that erupted from Alex would have sent the humans running if it hadn't been covered by the music. People around us still looked.

A girl glanced at me suddenly, and I did a double take, realizing that it was Christine's friend. The blonde, Meg, who was wrapped up in the arms of someone just as drunk as she was. I thought that she heard Alex and was about to ask us what the hell was going on, but she just grinned and went back to kissing the fool. A night of pleasure they would both enjoy.

"She's mine," Alex said. "Ours."

"You think I don't know that?" I shook my head. "*Merde, Alexandre.* I want to fuck her. Put her in chains like I know we all want to. Put her on her knees and savor the sound of her voice muffled by my cock. Make her ours in every way that matters."

The tension went out of him. "I know."

I went one step further. "I will fight both of you for the first time in that gorgeous ass." Then I chuckled. "It's not the first fight we've had."

"Nor the last, I imagine," Erik finally said with a laugh. "First, we have to make sure that she actually wants to fuck us. After that—"

Alex said, "She does. She wants it more than she knows what to do with. But her nerves get the better of her."

"In this world, I can't say that's a bad thing," Erik murmured.

"No," I agreed. "It's not."

But we would prove to her we weren't crazy. The connection gifted to us was real. Whole. And entirely too enticing for us to ignore.

"Seems like the kings have crawled out from their shitty throne. How badly did you fuck up Martin?" A voice came from behind me, and I turned to find my least favorite person—gargoyle—in the world. Callum stood on the stairs with my other least favorite people. Sebastian and Witt.

Erik looked him up and down. "I don't know anyone by that name."

"He's very upset that you took his memory card.

Apparently the photos on there would have made him a fortune. Enough to replace the camera that he says you 'tore to shreds with your bare hands.'"

I smiled, tilting my head just enough. "He's lucky that the camera was all we broke."

"Well." Callum looked surprised and amused. "Something's finally gotten to the opera trio. Thought you guys never got worked up about anything."

Pulling my emotions back, I straightened. They were right. Showing our hand right now would only make them more interested in Christine. And if they touched her, I felt as feral as Alex had been when we got there. "You sent the photographer?"

Witt scoffed. "Of course not. But we may have tipped off the press that an international, viral celebrity was at Club Spectre."

Erik's growl was low enough that only Alex and I heard it under the music.

"What interest do you have in celebrities?" Alex asked, hands in his pockets. "Doesn't seem like your thing."

"Nothing," Sebastian said. "Unless they're with you. Makes us wonder what you're doing with her and what she's doing with you."

We all heard the unsaid words. That they couldn't let us have anything that they couldn't have.

Not when they were busy trying to usurp our place. They couldn't have her. She was our mate. Made for us. And she would know it soon.

None of that mattered to these assholes. They would try to take her from us, especially if they knew what she was.

"So what's she doing with you?" Callum asked.

I crossed my arms. "We happen to be quite charming."

Witt snorted, and my jaw creaked as I grit my teeth. Erik stepped forward. "We can have friends. No matter our current status."

"Ah," Callum took a matching step forward. Not quite a challenge, but close enough. "So you think you're owed something when you live in *our* territory?"

I rolled my eyes. "If you got that from what he said, you need your hearing checked. Club Spectre is neutral. You know that. You broke that by tipping off the fucking paparazzi."

His mouth curled into a cruel smirk. "There's nothing neutral in Paris and you know it. It all belongs to me. Besides, who's going to do anything about it?"

Unfortunately, he was right. No one would say anything, especially with the power that they held outside this building. I couldn't wait to feel that power flow in my veins again, so I could protect Christine. Give her the life that she deserved.

"Nothing's changed," Alexandre said easily. "We'll stay out of your way. You give us a wide berth."

"We'll see," Sebastian said. "And maybe we'll see her." The looks on their faces didn't give me comfort, but it was the best we had. All three disappeared down back to the bottom of the club.

"I thought that we'd managed to avoid them," I said. "Hidden her fast enough. That's why I got her behind the curtain and then you took the dance floor."

"Meg pulled her aside." Erik sighed. "He approached them then."

The bass of the music pounded through my body, syncing with my heart. Grounded me. Made me feel powerful. "We'll need to be extra careful. To make sure they don't get to her."

"Agreed," Alex growled.

"Let's get back before we turn to stone in a fucking alley," I said.

"We have hours," Erik protested. "And they're still here where we can keep an eye on them. Why?"

"Because she'll be in her room," I said. "Near the walls. If she touches them even for a second…"

They raced me out of the club.

CHAPTER TEN

CHRISTINE

I texted Meg so that she didn't send out the search parties, thinking that I'd been kidnapped by sexy Frenchmen. But I couldn't go back into that club. Not even for the borrowed hat, because doing that meant that I would come face to face with them again, and I wasn't sure that I'd be able to say no to them another time.

Then I called Raphael. He was already on his way to the street corner where I stood, hiding my face in the shadows. Luckily, with that photographer gone, no one was looking for me. I hoped. Where there was one photographer, there were usually more.

Meg almost immediately sent me a text that was

a video. Of her and someone making out against a wall. She was holding her phone out while she filmed, smiling the whole time. Her way of telling me that she was just fine with me leaving. She was *occupied*.

Raphael pulled up ten minutes later, and I slid gratefully into the back of the car. We weren't too far from the opera house, but exhaustion was starting to cling to my bones, and I was going to have a long day tomorrow.

"Have a good evening, miss?"

"I did," I said. "But I am very tired now."

He laughed. "Not surprising."

Leaning my head against the glass of the window, I watched the streets pass slowly. It wasn't too late. The streets were still filled with people simply living their lives. Both citizens of Paris and the tourists that mingled with them.

What was I?

I guess for the time being I fell somewhere in between. I certainly wasn't a citizen, and yet I felt a deep belonging in this city. It wasn't something I usually felt when I traveled. Just standing on that corner waiting for Raphael, I felt comfortable, even after walking away from them.

While you remain in Paris, you belong to us.

Why the fuck did those words send *good* chills down my spine?

I could see Marius's face in my head as he said it. And there was no part of me that doubted him. Or feared him. Any of the three of them. I knew that they wouldn't hurt me on the same level I felt comfortable in Paris to begin with.

Did I regret saying no? I didn't. Because it was all too fast, and my life was moving fast enough right now.

Belong.

That was the word that sang out of the darkness. A sustained low note, like a cello. It resonated in my chest. That's what I'd been missing for the last six months. Belonging somewhere.

I'd belonged in the ensemble at ABT, and then I was promoted and things got a hell of a lot lonelier. Then the video happened, and everything sped up. You wouldn't guess how alone you became when everyone knew who you were. Constantly surrounded by people and voices, but no one that actually cared about you.

There was Meg, of course, and I had other friends. But the life I had, being able to go out to a diner after rehearsal and sit and laugh...that was gone. It had been gone before I accepted the role of Joan.

The breath from my sigh fogged the glass in front of me, and I tucked my arms around myself. I was lonely. I couldn't argue with that. So why didn't I say yes?

I cracked the window open so I could feel the cool evening air. The scent of the river was on the breeze. Laughter from a nearby cafe. The distant honking of a horn. It helped clear my head. Or at least feel more clear. Because I wasn't clear on anything.

Was I really going to tell them no because I wanted to keep my options open? It wasn't like I was going to be spending a lot of time mingling with Parisians. This was probably one of the few nights that I could actually do that. So the idea of saying yes and having to break my word...

I shook my head. I met them *today*. Today. It was a ludicrous suggestion.

Is it?

Leaning my head back against the car's headrest, I begged the little devil on my shoulder to shut the fuck up. It was hard enough to convince myself that it was a bad idea without that little fucker making me second guess every single thought. She was a bad influence.

Slowing down, I sorted through my emotions. I'd learned to do this recently when things were flying at me too fast. Especially today, when I was exhausted and jet-lagged, and about to have a make or break rehearsal in the morning.

So, the question was, why did I keep coming back to those words?

I walked away. I'd walked away from offers by cast and crewmates before, and I'd survived the awkwardness of being around them during the run of the performance. Something about these men was different, and I wasn't able to put my finger on it.

The pleasure, I had to push aside. What they'd done in the club...I would be thinking about that for a long fucking time. Who was I kidding? I wasn't going to be able to put that aside, but I was going to try.

Was it the fact that there were three of them? And that seemed crazy and unnatural and like someone was playing a prank on me on my first day?

My face went hot, and the world blurred. I blinked back the rush of embarrassed tears before Raphael could look back and realize there was something wrong.

Not that it mattered. We were pulling up to the opera house artist's entrance. "Here we are."

"Thank you, Raphael."

"Anytime, *Mademoiselle.*"

I paused. "I probably won't need you tomorrow. First day of rehearsals and all that."

He smiled in the rear-view mirror. "And yet, if you call me, I shall come running."

"Thanks." I returned the smile as I pushed out of the car.

Raphael waited until I had the door open to pull away. I'm sure that Monsieur Chagny had told him to do that, and I appreciated it, even if I was still unsure about having a driver at my beck and call.

This little back entryway was dark and silent. The complete opposite of the club. Standing in that bubble for a moment, I was able to take a breath. But I couldn't stand alone in the dark forever.

Backstage was quiet. Everyone was either still at the mixer,—if it was even still going—had taken the coward's way out like I had, or was already in their rooms. There was a faint sound of laughter from the direction of the communal area.

Quickly, I stopped by the kitchen and grabbed a banana. And some cereal for the morning. I was blank as I walked around. On autopilot. With my exhaustion, I'd lost the ability to pretend that I was anything but a zombie about to collapse into sleep.

It wasn't until I pushed into the apartment and started to put the food away that I realized my little personal kitchen was already fully stocked. The fridge too. I hadn't asked Anne what the food protocol for us in the apartments was. Did we pull food from the kitchen to restock? Did we make a list for someone?

I shook my head. That was a problem for tomorrow.

Right now my head was too muddled and I was looking at that amazing bed in the corner. The banana disappeared in three bites, and I got ready for bed in record time, groaning as I rolled into it. I didn't care if it made me an old woman. Getting into bed was the best.

There was a window beside it where I put my phone, and it was close enough to my head that I could peek out of it and down to the street if I propped myself up on enough pillows. Would I see them coming back? That was the direction that we'd walked.

Stop it.

I shouldn't even be thinking about them, but the realization I'd had in the car was still there. Still plain as day. The truth was…I didn't believe them.

Only a fraction, I opened the window so I could once again feel the cool breeze off the Seine. I wasn't used to the scent of Paris.

When Alex caught me from stumbling, I felt something. Between all three of us. But everyone here…or at least a lot of people here, hated me. They thought I was just some dancer that got lucky. It didn't matter that I *could* sing, I hadn't paid my dues.

So the idea that three men that looked like *that* not only liked me, they liked me enough to offer to be together for the entire run of the show? After a day? No. I didn't believe it.

It had to be some kind of prank that the rest of the cast and crew had pulled together. Or a joke. Or they wanted to take advantage of my place at the center of the show. It was the only thing that made sense.

Wasn't it?

Wasn't it?

I sank down into sleep almost without noticing, until it was too late, and I was already gone.

Christine.

The voice was a sensual whisper on my skin. A cool breeze in the darkness. That's where I was right now. Rich, warm darkness that felt like velvet wrapping around my skin. That's all there was. My skin. In this reality, nothing else was needed.

Christine.

My name was a song. It split into notes and

melodies and spun around my mind. I wanted to live in the sounds of it.

And that was before the brush of breath on my shoulder. An invisible kiss on my skin. Hands letting me fall back into arms. I was at once floating and heavy. Dancing. Drifting between one set of arms and the next. Touches that left me breathless and wild.

Sing for us.

I couldn't find my voice. Not here. This was a place I didn't have a voice and anything that meant. Here I simply *existed*.

Fingers dragged up my thighs and skated away before tracing up my ribs. Another set of hands. Now there were two, drenching every part of me with touch and softness.

Sing for us.

The music took a slower turn. Sing didn't mean *sing*. I knew it before the third set of hands stroked out of the darkness and drifted lower. And lower still. It was shadows and silk between my legs. Tingles that felt like starlight. Igniting into a different kind of burn.

Every breath tasted new. Blackberries and wine. Honey and vanilla and fresh mountain air. Candy and the satiny taste of chocolate.

Music. A symphony of lips and hands and breath.

The most sacred kind of song. I was dizzy with it. Breathless. A bed of shadows caught us and held us. Let them spread me open and taste me. That first touch was a star in the soft shadows. Still muted, but shining.

Ma petite étoile.

A moan escaped me and I found my voice. For them. The song hit a crescendo and my body arched with the melody. Their hands were there. Everywhere. Holding, stroking, pleasuring, capturing, demanding, *owning*.

It all blurred together into one feeling that couldn't be contained.

The shadow of a tongue between my legs, calling another moan into existence. A finger stroking and sliding inside me, brutally familiar.

Licks of shadow on my nipples. Tongues that felt like flames that I couldn't see consuming me. A kiss on my lips that sank through my whole body with a single ringing note. *Belong.*

They wreathed my pleasure in shadow, fucking me with tongues and hands. Teasing me with aching slowness. Until I was no longer floating. No longer swirling or dancing.

I was at their mercy.

Rocking. Shuddering. Falling. Arching.

Pleading.

And a single resounding word, echoing from my lips and sealing my fate.

No.

A chorus of sighs escaped me as the shadows slowed. I wanted more. I wanted them to throw me over the edge into darkness. I wanted to drown in the pleasure that they denied. I wanted to keep them.

A new song. Quieter. Just for me. This was made of breath, too. Delicate and sacred. It pulled at me. Into me. And that, too, was familiar.

The shadows swayed and began to dance. Asking me to play. I wanted to see them. To touch them. To taste them.

I reached, arms spread wide. My shadow body ached with the need to touch them again. For them to finish what they started. For the spark of pleasure they buried and left to bloom. I wanted it, and I couldn't.

With a running leap, I jumped.

They caught me, and then let me go.

Christine.

CHAPTER ELEVEN

CHRISTINE

a banging brought me awake, and I startled to full awareness, disoriented. It took me three full breaths to remember where I was.

Paris.

In my apartment.

Horny as hell because of the dreams that I had last night.

I was pressed into the corner of the bed, nearly falling into the crack between the bed and the wall. Slowly, I pushed myself away from the cool stone and attempted to blink away sleep.

The banging came again—I hadn't imagined it.

"Open up, bitch, I've got pastries."

I groaned, rolling out of the bed and getting to the door before Meg managed to break it down.

She was already dressed with her make-up done. Rehearsal gear on. There were two cups of coffee in her hand, along with a bag that smelled like chocolate.

"One of those cups better be for me."

"Duh."

Returning to the bed, I grabbed my phone and ignored the million and one notifications that had gathered overnight.

"Meg, it's seven in the morning."

"And?"

I glared at her. "And, we live *in the opera house*, and rehearsal doesn't start till nine. I could have slept another hour, had the longest shower of my life, and still been on time."

She smirked, pulling a *pain au chocolat* out of the paper bag. "But if I'd let you sleep, then you wouldn't be having best friend time with me right now."

"Best friend my ass, getting me up this early," I muttered, taking the cup that she offered. "Where's Tori?"

"Still sleeping off her double hangover."

I raised an eyebrow. "Double?"

"The alcohol and the guy. Plus, as much as I like her, I'm not trying to make us a triad. I just thought

116

it would be good to have at least one other person on your side."

She had a point there. "I appreciate it."

"So?" She sat on one of the stools at the bar.

I looked at my friend, who was *way* too fucking perky this early in the morning. "So, what?"

Meg rolled her eyes and bit into her croissant. "So I want you to tell me what the hell happened last night. The last thing I knew you were dancing with three—*three*—unbelievably hot men, and then suddenly you're texting me about coming back here and they're having a fight alone."

"A fight?"

"Yeah," she nodded. "They were arguing right where I was making out with Phillipe. No regrets about letting you have them, by the way, because my own international encounter was quite satisfactory."

I laughed, and sat down on the other stool, enjoying a bite full of sugar before I delved into the mess that was last night. "First, I need you to promise me two things."

"Ooookay."

"No judgment." Meg snorted, but I kept going. "No judgment, and I also need you to tell me if I'm crazy, I made the worst mistake of my life, or the best decision."

Meg stared at me for a long second, blinking. "What the *fuck* did you do in that club?"

With a laugh, I told her. Everything. Enjoying the way her jaw continued to drop.

"They *said* that?"

"They did."

"And you just walked away."

I rolled my eyes. "Lot of good it did me. The dreams I had last night would make a nun break her vows. You guessed it, about three people. Faceless people, but you can draw the lines there."

"Yeah." Meg was looking down into her coffee. "Shit, Christine. That is not what I expected."

My own coffee suddenly became very interesting.

"Absolutely no judgment. If anything, I'm jealous. But I'm trying to think about the second part of your question."

The last of my pastry disappeared. "I kind of hoped that sleeping on it would help."

"It didn't?"

"I mentioned the dreams, right?"

She laughed. "Okay, so, pros: sex whenever you want while you're here. With three hot men. Who protected you when you needed it last night? Twice? Yes, I'm counting getting you out of that first horrible party as protecting you. You don't have to

118

worry about going out, because the fun will be right under your roof."

I nodded.

"Cons: You don't know them, so they could be serial killers waiting to murder you. Though I don't think the opera would hire those kinds of people, and I'm pretty sure that there's enough people living here right now that if you were getting murdered, *someone* would hear."

"Why do I feel like I can't?"

Meg shrugged. "I don't know. Do you want to?"

"Kind of. Just the way they said it, it felt so...final."

"Okay." My friend brushed the crumbs off her fingers and stood to throw the pastry bag in the trash. "Be honest with me about this. What do you have to lose?"

I stilled. "They asked me that last night."

"And you didn't answer."

No words came.

"Listen," Meg said, stepping towards me. "I know that I'm the one that's always pushing you to be spontaneous and get out of your comfort zone. But you know I would never push you towards anything I thought would actually hurt you, right?"

"Meg, of course."

She blew out a breath. "Then if they still want you, I think you should do it."

"Really?"

"I mean…yeah. Everyone is here, right? We're all here for the same reason, the same thing. To do this show. Living together? You already know that half of the cast is going to end up fucking the other half. And once people see how amazing you are instead of what the tabloids have told them? They're *all* going to want to fuck you too. Women included."

"Meg—" I laughed as she cut me off.

"You already know I'm right, don't deny it."

I wandered toward my still-packed suitcases to start getting my clothes ready for the day. "I most certainly do *not* know that."

"The question I'm asking is, if you're going to fuck someone while you're here, do you want it to be the three hot guys who saw you and said 'absolutely hell yes' from the very first second? Or do you want it to be someone who needed to be convinced that you deserve to be here?"

Crap. She was right. The little devil on my shoulder was doing a little dance, sticking out her tongue and mooning me for not admitting it earlier.

"If it doesn't work out, it doesn't work out," Meg said.

I laughed once. "Alexandre used the words 'belong to them.' I'm not sure getting out of it would be as simple as that."

"You're the star of the fucking show. If something gets bad, you don't think that the problem will disappear?"

"Oh my god, Meg. You want me to get them fired?"

"*No*. I want my super hot, super talented friend to get some excellent dick with relatively low risk. They're French. The whole 'belong to me,' thing is probably just an expression that doesn't translate well."

I gave her a sarcastic look. "You speak French. Wouldn't you know if that's true?"

"I'm not an expert. I caught a little of their argument, and they were using all kinds of phrases that didn't make sense to me. So I'm either rusty or very out of date on the slang."

Pulling out some rehearsal clothes, I glanced over my shoulder. "Like?"

She smirked. "Something about gargoyles and illusions. Maybe they were talking about something for the show."

Sighing, I shook my head. "I don't know."

"I think that this is fun," she said. "That you could have a good time. And that after everything that's happened, you could use some good orgasms as stress relief. That's all I'm saying."

"And when the rest of the cast and crew start

calling me a whore because I'm fucking three men at once?"

Meg's eyes went steely and cold. "Then they can mind their own fucking business, because I guarantee that they'll be doing the same thing. And just because you're the star of the show doesn't mean that you don't have a right to a life. Or privacy." She flicked her pony-tail over her shoulder. "Anyway, I think you should do it. But I think you should make them beg a little more first. Let them come to you. Put them on their knees."

My stomach fluttered. But it wasn't the image of *them* on their knees that was in my head. It was the image of *me*.

"Guess I'll have to see what happens when I see them."

"Hell yes you do. Now don't be late."

There was still plenty of time, but I called after her. "And whose fault would that be?"

Her laugh echoed back before the door closed.

Meg always managed to put my head back on straight. And I'm glad that she was able to, because the last few months I certainly hadn't been able to manage it.

Jumping in the shower, I savored the feeling of the near scalding water. After everything, the fire was delicious. I let it burn away any remaining traces of sleep, and of those fucking dreams that only left me wanting more.

I leaned against the wall, content to soak for a few minutes.

Christine.

My eyes flew open. It was exactly like yesterday when I'd first come into the apartment and was by the window. But also like…last night.

What the fuck?

Maybe I was so focused on the dreams that I was vividly remembering them. That didn't explain why I'd heard it *before* the dreams, but I also didn't exactly have the time to wonder if all of this had made me actually and literally crazy.

My shoulder brushed the tile.

Christine.

I pulled my hand away, and the sensual sound ceased. The second I touched the wall again, it whispered through my mind like perfumed smoke. *Beautiful.*

The water in the shower suddenly didn't feel hot anymore. I made incredibly sure that I wasn't touching the walls as I got out and dried myself, dressing in my rehearsal clothes. I'd been in Paris a full day, and I was beginning to wonder if it had been a mistake to come here. I was caught up in a situation with the three guys, and suddenly I was *hearing things*.

Fuck me.

It was hard to force those thoughts out of my head as I gathered everything, but I did. Désirée was coming out of the door just down the hall. She looked at me for a moment before turning on her heel and walking towards the main theatre.

I grit my teeth and shoved down any anger. "Good morning, Désirée."

Not even a flicker of response.

Of course.

Locking the apartment behind me, I waited until she'd disappeared out of the hallway before following her. I wasn't sure that even a month-long run of working together would fix the fact that she thought I'd stolen this role from her.

I was so overwhelmed by everything yesterday that I hadn't noticed the posters lining the hallway. Old opera posters. I doubted they were originals, but they were old. The designs were easily as old as the opera house itself. Beautiful, ornate gold frames that mimicked the overly gilded front of house.

This one…

It was the poster for *Joan D'Arc*. Was this the poster for when the opera house had burned? Chills ran down my arms. It was a little eerie. I brushed my fingers under the frame, not daring to touch the image itself in case it *was* genuine.

Christine.

I jumped back. Okay, I was going insane. Either I was still hung-over from last night, Meg had spiked that coffee, I was crazy, or the opera house was haunted.

The metal of the spiral staircase rang under my feet. Backstage was busy again. Not as much as yesterday. Or rather, not in the immediate vicinity. I was sure most of the crew were busy in the work-shops, which were further back. Deeper, under where the apartments were.

I kept an eye out for any of them. *Them.* I couldn't even think their names now? But I didn't see them. I managed not to trip over anything, either. So they couldn't appear to save me from my own clumsiness.

In the seats, the cast was milling, waiting for the clock to strike nine. Meg was sitting with Tori, who looked like she was still nursing the hangover. I was glad that I hadn't stayed out later, if only so that I didn't look like that.

"Look at you," Meg said with a grin. "On time and everything."

"I know. I'm very impressive."

There was no point in pretending that we weren't friends or keeping myself distant now.

Things were starting. I'd have to deal with it one way or another.

"But," I said. "I'm pretty sure this place is haunted."

"Well, yeah," Tori said, nursing a bottle of water. "No shock there."

"Really?"

She looked between me and Meg. "You don't know?"

Meg frowned. "Know what?"

"The opera house burned down and all that."

I shrugged. "Yeah, we know that. It was an accident."

"They say that," Tori said. "But there's more to it. Not really a secret—you can find out if you look— but they're not exactly trying to push this aspect of the history if you know what I mean."

I raised my eyebrows, waiting for her to continue.

"Well like…a whole shit ton of people died in that fire. It doesn't surprise me at all if it's haunted."

Oh.

The words hit me and fell over me, not quite processing.

"Shit."

Tori laughed once. "Yeah."

"I kind of hoped that I was making it up."

Both of them looked at me. I hadn't told them *why* I thought the place was haunted. "Every time I touch one of the walls," I said quietly. "I hear voices."

Meg burst out laughing, and stopped when I didn't join her. "Wait, you're serious?"

"Yes."

"Okay. I didn't take you for a method actor."

They said that because Joan of Arc heard voices. Maybe that was true. Maybe it wasn't. But this was very real. Or at least I thought it was.

"I'm not," I said.

Anne walked up to the front of the stage in front of the orchestra pit. "Let's get started. Dancers, you may go to the rehearsal studio downstairs. Chorus cast the other one. Principals, remain here."

Meg and Tori glanced at me as they got up and headed to their own rehearsal with the rest of everyone, the former giving me a look that told me that I *would* be talking to her about it later.

I was sure I would. Because I really hoped that I hadn't flown all the way across the world to lose my mind.

CHAPTER TWELVE

CHRISTINE

I threw my script on my bed with more force than was professional. But then again, I thought the fact that I'd made it all the way back to my apartment without losing my shit on anyone was pretty fucking professional.

Covering my face with my hands, I took a couple of minutes to breathe. That had been…disastrous.

Not as disastrous as it could have been, but it wasn't fucking great.

I had been fine. I knew my parts. It was all that I'd been able to fucking do since I could barely leave my apartment in New York. Hell, I didn't just know my parts; I knew *all* the parts. There wasn't a piece of music in the fucking opera that I didn't know.

But even that didn't seem to impress people.

Sinking onto the bed, I let out a sigh. Not that I needed to impress people. But I was really tired of the stares. These weren't stares of wonder or excitement. They were predatory. Waiting for the moment when I messed up and they'd be justified in their animosity towards me.

It was exhausting.

I hadn't messed up today, but I would. No one was perfect.

So not entirely a disaster. Not by normal standards. Anne, the director, the producers, they were all over the moon. I thought I'd seen Raoul in the back of the house, too.

All we'd done today was music. Making sure everyone knew their parts and getting started on melding everyone together. My throat was shot. Tea. I needed tea. But the thought of sitting still and drinking tea was...

I was too restless for that.

The sun was setting outside the windows, and everyone was probably eating dinner. That was perfect. It meant the studio beneath the stage would be empty. And that was what I needed right now. I needed to move. I needed to dance and not think about everything for a while.

That's what I was. A dancer. There was a reason I'd gone into dancing and not singing at first. I loved it. It sang to my soul.

My suitcases still sat at the end of my bed, full. I needed to unpack and put things away, but the thought of that just made me more tired. No. I needed some time.

I changed into dance clothes and grabbed my toe shoes. My headphones. The big, fat, over the ear ones that blocked out all the surrounding sound. That's what I needed. Just me and the beat.

My slippers slapped softly on the floors as I made my way through the building and down. Down and down. I saw a few people, but like I thought, most people were eating. Mingling in rooms. Going out to explore Paris while we had no evening obligations.

I hadn't seen Alex, Marius, or Erik at all today. The fact that I desperately wanted to...

It brought up the discussion with Meg from this morning. Until I saw them again, it didn't matter. Maybe dancing would get them the hell out of my head too.

The studio was blissfully empty.

My music already filled my head as I laced up my shoes, then warmed myself up at the barre. I wasn't completely out of shape, but I definitely hadn't been able to make it to class as much as I wanted to, having to do it remotely from the small barre in my apartment. It wasn't the same.

But here, by myself, with just me and my body and the music, I finally felt like I was on familiar ground.

The rhythm in my head certainly wasn't classical. The last thing I wanted was anything gentle. Instead, one of my favorite playlists was set to random. Rock and electronic music. Anything that made me *feel*.

It was easy to break away from the barre then, moving any way the music let me. I let my emotions drown in color and pull me every which way they wanted to. Twirling and stretching and doing things that most classical teachers would be horrified to see me do in toe shoes.

The pain in my feet was a welcome relief, and the curtains across the mirrors were pulled, so I couldn't even get sucked into the trap of watching myself and judging my own form.

So I danced.

If I'd never made that video in a studio like this, I wouldn't be here in Paris. I'd be in New York, still a soloist in ABT.

I let the thoughts pour through my own head without any judgment. Right now was the only way that I could do that. Dancing was therapy.

If anyone could see in my head and feel all the doubt in the dread, they'd probably agree with all the people in the cast that I didn't deserve to be here. They were wrong.

Just because it wasn't perfect didn't mean that I didn't want to be here. I cried when I got the call that they wanted me to audition. To sing something from the actual show so that I could have a chance to be a part of it. There were maybe three other moments in my life I could remember being that fucking happy.

I didn't regret it, even if it was hard.

But I did wish that it was easier. Or that it didn't hurt that it felt so alone. It came with the territory, but that didn't mean that it wasn't a struggle.

Never again would I look at any type of star or celebrity and assume that their life was easy. Because it wasn't. *Some* things were easy. The convenience and privilege of money. Of people bending over backwards to do things for you. But you lost a lot of other things. I hadn't been doing this for long, but I wasn't totally sure that the trade was worth it.

I pinned my gaze diagonally across the studio and kept it there, traveling across the floor with full *chaînés* turns. Not stopping. Not stopping. Not stopping. The wall came up fast, and I landed with both hands braced against the walls of the corner.

Christine.

The musical sound of my name echoed through my mind, even over the music.

My breath was short in my chest, that terror racing through me. Was this real? I kept my hands on the walls, trying to focus. This was the first time it had occurred to me to try to talk back.

Who are you?

The silky laughter that came back to me made my hair stand on end. Chills followed, cooling the sweat that I'd built. Suddenly, the peace and isolation of the studio felt more sinister. Because I was alone. With voices.

No more alone than I would be in my apartment, but at least there were people just down the hall.

I removed the hands from the walls, turning, and I jumped. Alex was standing in the doorway, watching me. My headphones had made sure that I hadn't heard him open the door.

"You scared me," I said, pulling them off and leaving them around my neck.

One side of his mouth pulled up into a smile. "*Je suis desole.*"

"I don't get the feeling that you're sorry at all."

"You're right." He stepped into the studio and closed the door behind him. There was a phone in his hand that he slipped into his pocket. "I'm not sorry. You're a beautiful dancer."

"Thank you."

The air spun tight between the two of us. All that happened last night and then the fact that I'd told them—told him—no. But he was still so fucking gorgeous that my stomach tumbled at the sight, and Meg's words were in my ear.

If they still want you, I think you should do it.

I took a breath to speak, and the door behind Alex opened. Suddenly, I was face to face with all three of them. Casual clothes, of course. They'd probably been working all day. That was why he'd had his phone out—texting them.

"You were looking for me? After I said no? I'm flattered."

The light-hearted tone that I was going for fell flat.

"Even after that," Erik said. "We shouldn't have let you walk away alone. We're sorry for that."

"I was all right."

Another silence spooled in the space between us. And I didn't want to face the awkwardness of that conversation. Yet. "What do you do on the crew?" I asked. "Didn't see you all day."

Marius shrugged. "We're not exactly with the show. Came with the opera house."

"Oh." So they were part of the crew that renovated the whole theatre and brought it back to life. "So you know every inch of this place, I'm guessing."

"Yeah, we do."

I leaned back against the wall so I could rest my feet. "You can show me all the secrets."

"We could…" Erik said, leaving that open ended.

But them showing me the secrets went hand in hand with them wanting to be with me. For me to belong to them. Three of them. My stomach flipped and the heat of memory curled through my body. Here, we were entirely alone. Which did nothing to help the need that was restlessly flinging itself through me.

I realized that I was touching the wall, but was hearing no voices. Just in case, I touched my hand to the surface, and nothing. Maybe I couldn't hear the voices when other people were present?

Maybe I could hear what I was saying because I was hearing *voices.*

Something snapped in my brain. Not even a day ago I'd given myself to these men. No matter what, my body trusted them. My mind did too, even if there was still a whisper of hesitation. But they knew about the opera house and its history. Maybe they could tell me that I wasn't crazy.

"Is this place haunted?"

Alexandre moved to the curtains by the wall of mirrors, pulling them back. "Some would say so, yes."

"And what do you say?"

All three of them locked their eyes on me. "Why?"

I swallowed. "Because I'm hearing voices."

Why I would admit this to them, I wasn't totally sure. But if they were pissed that I'd told them no, me looking like I'd completely lost my marbles was sure to send them running.

"What kind of voices?" Marius asked softly.

I stroked my fingers down the wall. "Just my name. And once, they called me beautiful. But only when I touch the walls."

Now Erik was behind me. Not touching me, but close enough that he could. "And you think you're making it up?"

"It crossed my mind."

"Paris, the city, is older than your country," he said again, like last night. "There are things here that are old, and defy understanding. But just because they exist, doesn't mean that they're not real."

I blinked. "So there are actually ghosts in the opera house that are talking to me?"

Alex laughed, but not in an unkind way. "I wouldn't say that, no."

"Then what would you say?"

"I say that we want to show you something."

I sat down on the floor, working to unlace my toe shoes. "Is this the part where you take me to the basement and no one finds my body because I said no?" It was meant as a joke, but none of them are laughing. "Nevermind."

"The roof actually has a beautiful view," Erik said. "If you'd like to see it."

I shoved my feet into my slippers. "That sounds nice."

And if I knew the way to the roof, at least there would be one place that I could go to get away from people if I needed to.

As they led me up the stairs, I dared to say something about the elephant that was walking silently behind us. "I told my friend Meg. About what you offered."

The silence drew tight. I felt their keen interest, even though none of them were looking at me. Finally, Marius spoke. "What did she say?"

"She said—" I laughed. "She essentially said that I was an idiot and that I should have said yes."

I let that hang in the air as we climbed higher. And higher still. Until we reached a door, and I could hear open air on the other side.

They opened it, and the beautiful evening breeze hit me. It wasn't fully dark yet, still light in the sky though the sun had already set. Across the city, lights were starting to pop on, painting a gorgeous panorama. I wished I had a camera.

The roof had several layers, and the top was a maze of pathways between the immense stone carvings—still all originals—that graced those layers and made the top of the opera house seem like a glorious tangle of sculpture. They hadn't been restored yet. You could see the darkness where flames had overtaken them. The cracks and the patina of age.

"This is beautiful."

They smiled at me and gestured ahead. I wove my way through the various creatures and gargoyles all the way to the edge where I could look over the square and the fountain. The Eiffel Tower was visible over the top of the buildings, sparkling, like it did every hour.

From here, the city seemed miraculous. Exactly the kind of city that earned names like the ones it bore. *The City of Love. The City of Lights.*

"Yesterday," I said. "The way you phrased it. It made me nervous."

It was Alex that took the step forward. The dying light of evening caught the pale blue of his eyes, and I swore that they almost glowed. "That you would belong to us."

"Yeah."

He smiled faintly. "I never said that we wouldn't also belong to you."

"It just…" I turned back to face the view. "That sounds so permanent."

None of them denied that. Or made the fairly self-evident point that it *didn't* have to be permanent. We weren't in a Jane Austen novel. I wasn't bound to marry them because I'd let them 'compromise' me on the dance floor. They also didn't make the point that none of this could be permanent. I didn't live here.

The edge of the opera house was a few feet wide. I toed off my slippers and held out a hand to Alex. He took mine as I stepped up onto the wide platform and began to walk.

All three of them watched me carefully.

"Convince me," I said, voice quiet.

"What?" That was Erik, the furthest away now.

Alex's hand tightened on mine, and I quickly switched hands and directions. "You want me to be yours? Convince me."

There was a glimmer of amusement in their eyes now. As if they knew that I'd already decided that I could take this chance. That Meg was right and if there was an issue, it could be fixed. That there were already limits to what could happen. That my stupid, too-careful brain could relax knowing there were safeguards, even though my wild heart was ready to fling myself into something new.

"Convince you?" Alex said.

"Yes."

He smirked. "Along with everything that I already said last night? There's only so much that I can say to convince you while you're up there and we're down here. But there's one more thing that you need to know. Before you say yes. And before we show you exactly how thoroughly we want you to be ours."

I held back my smile at the confidence that I was going to say yes. "And what's that?"

"Come down, and I'll show you."

We'd almost made it to the corner of the building, where one of the snarling statues peered over the corner, looking at everyone that passed below. He was old. I could see the weathering in him. The cracks. How many people had passed below this gargoyle's face? Looked up and took photos?

I smiled as I placed a hand on his head, releasing Alex so I could climb over the statue to the next section.

The sound of shattering reached me too late.

The world tilted. I was falling. *Oh god*. Those were the only words. I didn't have time to scream. All I felt was movement and that interminable moment when I felt the stone crumble and gravity curled its fatal grip around my body.

A scream fell out of my body, and I heard my name shouted.

My arm wrenched in its socket, pain exploding behind my eyes. But my body halted mid-air, legs dangling over nothing.

Long seconds it took me to realize that I wasn't dead. I was still breathing. Hanging.

I looked up.

Alexandre was there, eyes wild. My heart pounded, adrenaline singing. And not just from the fall.

He held onto me, keeping me from plunging to the end, with a hand made out of stone.

CHAPTER THIRTEEN

CHRISTINE

*a*lex looked down at me. Nothing but desperation shone there. I saw his eyes shift to the ground below me before coming back to mine.

"Don't let go," I begged. "Please don't let go."

Something changed his gaze. Hardened. He hauled me upwards like I weighed nothing, and the others were there, helping me over and back onto the roof.

My legs wouldn't hold me. Too much adrenaline and too much fear. I collapsed onto the stone, scraping my knees in the process.

"Oh my god. Oh my god." The words kept

coming out of my mouth like a mantra or a chant. I couldn't fully wrap my head around the fact that I'd just almost died.

Anne had told me that the roof hadn't been restored. I just hadn't thought *that* would happen.

Warmth sank through me, and I leaned into it. That felt good. That felt like safety and happiness.

Marius was sitting on the ground with me—had pulled me back against him so I leaned against his chest. That was the warmth.

Alex and Erik crouched in front of me.

"Christine," Erik said. "Look at me?"

I did. But my heart was still pounding in my ears. The light was sinking from the sky rapidly now, draining everything down into darkness. With it, the air seemed to take on a new chill. Goosebumps ran up and down my skin. The only place that had any warmth at all was where Marius touched me.

There was still enough glow that I could see their hands. All human. No stone.

"Your arm," Alex said. "Your shoulder. Are you hurt?"

It didn't right now, but I could feel the strain under the adrenaline. Later it would hurt.

"She needs ice for it," Marius said softly.

Ice. Yeah. That would be good.

I felt like I was a little outside myself, looking

back. Acknowledging the thoughts as they came through my brain and letting them pass.

Erik reached for me and pulled me to my feet. My knees wobbled, but held. "Let's get her some ice," he said.

Moving to lift me into his arms, I stopped him. "I'm all right."

"You're shaking more than a leaf in autumn."

Still, I felt myself pale. "I can't have people see me being carried. If I fall, you'll catch me."

"Where we're going, no one will see you. Don't worry."

I didn't have the energy to fight him when he picked me up. That weird sensation of your limbs being made of water. Like what happened when you worked out too hard...or had a near death experience.

Down. We wound down through the theatre, lower than the studio level, and further still. Erik was right. We saw no one. But I also had no idea where the fuck we were. The opera house went down this far into the ground?

There was an old wooden door, and Alex was there, opening it for Erik, and I brushed through a curtain into a whole new world.

The space was huge—easily as big as the stage upstairs. A big-ass *crystal* chandelier hung from the center of the ceiling, and it was fancier than the one that was in the lobby. Warm sconces shone and created a cozy atmosphere.

Comfortable chairs dotted the space, and doors— three of them—broke off from the back wall. Paintings decorated the rich, dark walls. A red so deep it was almost black. Like being in a room made of velvet.

A giant TV sat in an alcove along with a wall that was just bookshelves with what looked like an entire library worth. The whole space was as eclectic as it was luxurious.

"What the hell is this place?"

"This," Erik said, putting me down on a large crimson fainting couch, "is home."

I blinked. And again. And again.

Going over what happened on the roof, I hadn't hit my head in the fall. But clearly I had to be dreaming. Or hallucinating. I heard a sound, and Marius closed the door on a freezer in an open style kitchen across the room. He had ice in a bag, and it was bringing it to me.

"You live here?"

I felt stupid. My body was still in the throes of getting rid of all that adrenaline. Definitely wasn't processing everything. I'd thought that Alexandre's hand was made of stone.

"We do," Marius said, gently pressing the ice to my shoulder.

I hissed. It felt good, but hurt, too. "When you guys said that you came with the opera house, you weren't kidding."

Erik chuckled once. "Indeed."

Looking around again, this place could be in a magazine for how gorgeous it was. It was sumptuous and luxurious and also tasteful.

"How long have you lived here?"

"A while," Alexandre said.

That wasn't a real answer.

My whole body shuddered, and I took over pressing the ice to my shoulder. Then I looked between them, my stomach hollowing out. There was something I was missing, and they clearly knew what it was.

"Please tell me what's going on. I feel like I'm going crazy."

Marius, still by my side, gently pulled me against him, and I let him. His lips warmed my temple. "You're not crazy, *mon ami*. You're not."

Alex crouched in front of me and took my hand. His eyes were wary. And hard. Then it wasn't just his eyes that were hard. His hand was hardening in mine. Turning gray. Roughening before my eyes. Getting bigger and growing sharp claws like a lion.

Stone.

His hand was stone.

I wasn't hallucinating when I saw him catch me with a stone hand. "What are you?"

"Monsters."

Erik hit him in the shoulder with a roll of his eyes. "We're not monsters. We are gargoyles though."

I stared at him. "Gargoyles."

"Yes," Marius said.

"Like the statue that just cracked? And almost killed me?"

"Yes."

"Like the children's TV show?"

There was silence at that. "There's a television show about Gargoyles?"

I dropped my head into my hands. This wasn't real, right? Haunted? Yeah, you fucking bet that the place was haunted. With *gargoyles*.

From between my fingers, I glanced at Alex's now-human hand and wondered again if I'd somehow imagined it. He stood abruptly, stripping his shirt over his head.

"What are you doing?"

"You clearly need a demonstration," he said.

"I—" The words disappeared from my mouth as he kicked off his shoes and dropped his jeans to the floor. I hadn't fully registered his body until the jeans came off.

Every inch of hardened muscle that I'd felt pressed against my body last night was now on display. Abs on abs on abs, and everything else was fabulous, too. Then the underwear fell, and even not hard, I had to work to keep my jaw closed. Because holy *fuck* he was big.

Half turning so I could see his ass, Alexandre kept his eyes on me. The raw lust in his eyes was enough to make me lean back. I bumped into Marius and quickly moved away.

The movement caught my eye. A ripple at Alex's feet, his heel darkening. Hardening. Growing. Turning to stone before my eyes. Stretching into the feet of a lion. The transformation rippled up his legs, carving them in graceful lines nearly feline in shape. The tail of a lion appeared, angled as if in a perfect turn.

Everything froze up his ribs and through his shoulders. He moved his fingers at the last moment so they were caught mid-movement when they turned to stone, the tips elongating into those same dangerous looking claws. Beautiful, angelic wings sprouted from his back and looked for all the world like they would lift him into the air.

His face was last. Every human, beautiful thing

about him disappeared. He twisted, face trans-forming into that of a snarling beast. A physical portrait of anger and danger.

But he was real. A gargoyle. Dead as a statue before me. At least three feet taller in this form. "How is this possible?"

"Touch him," Erik said. "Make sure it's not a trick."

I set the ice pack down on the couch and stood, moving slowly. There was a part of me that expected him to move and jump. Terrify me. But he was a statue.

Reaching out, I touched his fingers. They were cold and smooth. Hard. He *was* stone. I pressed against his hand. Touched the snarling face. Brushed my hand over a shoulder and nothing lower—I didn't dare. Alexandre was a statue in front of me.

"How is this possible?" I asked again.

"Magic," Marius said simply.

I opened my mouth to deny that magic existed. But didn't I know otherwise? I was from New York. A hundred strange things happened a day in that city that could be considered 'magic.'

When I knew I was coming to Paris, hadn't I read about the strange and the supernatural? The under-ground catacombs and the fact that this place was old beyond belief, with pockets of strange worlds in it. Didn't I regularly read books where men turned into wolves and monsters?

But it was a whole different thing thinking about the possibility of magic and seeing it right in front of you. "The voices?" I asked. "That was you?"

"Yes," Erik confirmed.

I swallowed. "And the dream?"

"As real as you standing there."

The skin on the back of my neck prickled. I was alone with them. No one knew where I was, and I was with three *magical creatures*. "So..." my words faltered. "I'm sorry. I don't really know what to say."

Erik laughed once. "I'd say you're reacting better than I expected."

Taking a deep breath, I faced the two of them. "Let's put aside the fact that this is a huge bombshell that changes the way the entire world works, and act like I'm not freaking out about that. Because I am."

"Okay." Marius smirked.

My stomach flipped. "Why me?"

"Why not you?"

"Don't deflect," I said, my tone sharper than I intended. "You just saved my life. But it never would have been in danger in the first place if the three of you hadn't taken me to the roof. So I think you owe me a little more than that. On top of everything last night."

They, at the very least, had the good sense not to look amused by that. Gargoyle or not, it would have been easy for them not to catch me.

"We know everything that happens in the opera house," Marius said carefully. "Every person that comes in, every conversation that's had. We hear it all through the stone."

I swallowed. So they'd heard the entire conversation with Meg. And knew that I was inclined to say yes to them. "So you knew I was coming," I said. "You heard all the renovations and the meets about the show and the rehearsals. How does that translate into you picking me?"

Erik sighed, shoulders dropping like he knew that I wouldn't simply agree to something, and looked over at Marius, who nodded. They didn't have a chance to speak.

A growl and the sensation of movement were all I had before Alexandre was there, pushing me up against the nearby wall, hand at my throat. His face was human—beautiful—again, but that feral rage and danger still sang in his body that was partially stone. His eyes weren't entirely human, the pupils spreading out like ink, trying to cover his eyes in darkness and shrinking again as he tried to gain control. The wings flared from his back and the fingers on my skin were hard.

Unyielding.

Claws that could rip me open without a thought.

"Before Erik says another *fucking. word.* to you, you're going to promise to say nothing. To anyone. About what we are or that we're here."

"Alexandre." Marius's voice snapped across the space.

The hand that he had on me wasn't pressing. It wasn't violence that he was projecting, but command. There weren't any exceptions to what he was telling me.

It hadn't even crossed my mind to tell anyone. "Who would believe me?" I gasped.

"You already told your friends about the voices."

I swallowed, and I felt the movement against his stone hand. "I'll make something up. I'll say I was overtired or that it was a pipe that sounded like voices. Something."

The position that we were in was suddenly very clear to me. My thin, skin-tight dance clothes and Alex's nothing at all. It didn't matter that he was half stone and half human. It didn't matter that there was a deeper warning kindled in his eyes. It was still him that had held me last night and commanded my pleasure.

And he was pressed up against me now,

completely naked. How was I supposed to ignore that?

"I don't give a shit who knows about us," Alex said. His voice was a low rumble. "But the more people that do, the more danger there is to *you*." That last word was a growl. "I wish it wasn't true. Yet it is, and I think you'll find that I am *very* invested in keeping you alive and safe."

He dragged his mouth up the side of my neck, and everything inside me melted. There was something feral about him right now. Maybe something about being half-transformed brought him to the edge of being raw.

Behind him, I saw that Erik and Marius were ready to intervene. But they were also completely relaxed. Not worried in the slightest.

"So why you?" He purred against my skin. "Why do you think? Tell me."

My breath went short. That feeling of everything spinning and slowing and connecting that I'd thought that I'd imagined? Not imagined at all. But I had no idea why. "I don't know."

"I think you do. If you still want to say no to us, fine. We don't have to touch you. We both know that's not what you want." Again, there was no room for argument in his voice. "But if you say yes, the three of us are going to spend your free time

154

fucking you until you don't remember your own name."

There was no way to stop the moan that slipped out of me. There was also no way that the three of them couldn't see that my nipples were poking through my thin dance camisole. I was just lucky that they couldn't see how wet I was or the way heat was spiraling through my body without my control.

"And I'll answer your real question," he said, voice now a whisper of breath against my skin. His other hand slid up and into my hair, angling my neck so there was more of it for him to taste. "Why would you belong to us?"

I said nothing. I was already barely breathing. I couldn't spare the extra air. My eyes fluttered closed.

"Because we're not men, Christine. We're monsters. And monsters don't *fucking. Share.*"

They were all there when I opened my eyes. Alex staring into mine, stone roaming over his skin like he was caught between two worlds. "It's not just that," I said. "There's something you're not telling me." There was no way that I would feel like this for nothing. It was too overwhelming and immediate. I'd never felt *anything* like the pull towards these men.

An idea tingled in my mind, and I shoved it away. Because it wasn't…it couldn't. Something else. I needed to ask them something else. Redirect them. My heart was pounding so fast that I thought I might pass out. "You heard—"

"Everything this morning?" Marius laughed. "You bet."

Erik smiled again. "So no. There's no firing us. No going to the producers. No getting rid of us."

Finally, Alex loosened his hand, but didn't remove it from my skin. "But we also have no interest in killing you, as your friend suggested. We want you. Need you."

Marius crossed his arms. "Never fucking doubt that."

I was crazy. I was officially, batshit, crazy. Because all of this made it *easier* to say yes. These weren't human men with human motives. And as absolutely nuts as it was to think about—and I was going to think about it—it made it that much easier to trust them.

What that said about me, I wasn't sure. But all the nerves that I'd had this morning, that hesitance that made me wonder what the hell I was thinking, wanting this? All of that was gone.

"Then I say yes."

CHAPTER FOURTEEN

ALEXANDRE

*C*hristine's throat bobbed under my fingers. The beast inside noticed the vulnerability and wanted it. My mouth had already tasted her skin, and right now, like this, I wanted more.

The line between man and beast was blurred. She'd nearly died. I wouldn't pretend the fact that I'd been able to catch her had been much more than luck.

I could have seen her fall and break on the cobblestones below, and the beast part of me was roaring so loudly at the thought that I could barely hear anything else. Except the fact that she said yes.

Mine.

Mine, mine, mine.

The word pounded through me with a rhythm that reminded me of what it might be like to have a beating heart.

I should step away from her, and I couldn't.

"Yes?" I asked. I needed to hear it again from her lips.

"Yes," she breathed, swallowing again. "But I have some questions."

I could hear her heart. Could scent how aroused she was. If I pinned her to the wall and fucked her now, both of us would enjoy it. But I finally pulled myself back.

Barely. My wings and tail collapsed into nothing as I returned to my clothes. I couldn't be naked when she smelled like that.

"I smell?" Her voice was alarmed.

I turned and blinked.

I'd said those words aloud under my breath.

Erik looked like he was about to burst out laughing, and I was going to kill him.

I zipped my pants and met her panicked eyes, forcing the beast in my mind to fade into the background. "Yes. You smell delicious, and I'm not sure you understand the amount of control it took for me to step away instead of stripping you and showing you what the French kiss was actually made for."

Her cheeks turned pink. "I was hoping you wouldn't know that. I mean, that usually happens in the monster books, but I'm not exactly on my game here, knowing what's real and what's not."

"What do you mean?" Marius asked.

He returned to the abandoned ice pack and gave it back to Christine. That shoulder was going to hurt later, if it didn't already. "Do we need to take you to the hospital?"

"No." she said, too quickly. "No. It's fine."

The others looked at me. We couldn't speak silently in this form, but we knew each other well enough to guess. There was a reason that she didn't want to go, and it had nothing to do with her possible injury.

"I'll see how it feels tomorrow morning, and if it's really bad, I'll go. Promise." She sat on the couch again.

But she'd said yes. So Marius sat with her, pulling her between his legs to sit and took over the icing for her. I didn't think she noticed that his hand and arm turned to stone to protect him from the cold and to make sure that it didn't move.

He distracted her, pulling her back to his chest and kissing her cheek. A flare of combined satisfaction and jealousy rolled through me. Satisfaction because she was here and we were taking care of her. Jealousy that she wasn't sitting in *my* lap right now.

"We'll be making sure," Erik said. And we would. No chance that we let her just avoid doctors if she was truly hurt.

Marius nudged her. "What were you saying before? About how it usually goes?"

Immediately, she was embarrassed again. "Umm... I've just heard things."

"Like?" I prodded.

She swallowed, looking around the room, trying to look at anything but the three of us. Especially me. I got a burst of that mouth-watering arousal scent every time she looked at me.

Probably because I hadn't put my shirt back on. That was very intentional.

"Every...non-human romance novel I've read, they have this amazing sense of smell. It didn't occur to me it would apply to gargoyles." Her voice stumbled a bit on the last word.

She really was taking this well.

"Well," Erik said. "It applies."

"Yeah."

Slowly, Marius curled his free arm around her waist. Like it was the permission she finally needed, she melted against him.

"You said you had questions." Erik said quietly.

"A few."

"Ask them," I growled. "They're the only thing keeping me from spreading you out on that couch and licking you until you scream."

The scent of her arousal flooded the space enough that all three of us knew what that idea did to her.

"You can't say shit like that and expect me to have a clear head for questions."

"Who says that's not part of our plan?" Marius murmured into her neck.

Christine was still flustered, but she smiled. Her body was still relaxed, and I found myself letting my eyes wander over her curves. Those thin clothes could be reduced to ribbons in seconds, and I wanted to see the real curve of her hips. Her ass. See what shade of pink colored the nipples that were like little diamonds through her shirt.

"So…umm, I guess I'll go with practical questions first. How does this work?" She circled a finger at the four of us. "You already heard everything that I said to Meg. So you know my concerns. You also know that I can't just pretend that you three don't exist anymore."

"This—the four of us—works however we want it to work." I said.

"I belong to you," she said quietly. And fuck if

everything about my body didn't harden hearing it come out of her mouth.

"I'm sorry that it makes me nervous."

Erik pinned her with a stare. "What makes you more nervous? That sentiment? Or the fact that you like the idea at all?"

Her squirm told us enough.

Getting up, I moved to the kitchen and poured a glass of water. We'd turned this place into everything that we wanted. After all, we'd had the time. So no, we didn't know things like the cartoon that she'd mentioned. But we weren't trapped in the past, either.

Not with our surroundings, at least.

"Have you done this before?" she asked as I handed her the glass.

She drank the whole thing in one go. Shock would do that to you.

Then she looked up at me with those eyes. A color that I'd never seen another have. The deep blue violet of the hottest flame. Darkened. Deepened. Until it shone within her.

"With someone else?"

I pulled her to her feet. "If you're asking if the three of us have fucked anyone in our immortal lives, then yes. If you're asking if we've ever had this... arrangement with anyone else, then no."

This close, I saw the way her pupils dilated and her breath sped up.

"But what you really want to know," Erik said, "is whether you agreeing to this means that we're going to storm into your rehearsals and demand things of you."

"Yeah."

"Absolutely not." Marius said.

Clearing my throat, "It means what I said. We don't share. And when we're alone, we already know you like what we want from you. You let us fuck you in the middle of a club." She didn't know that it wasn't *all* we wanted.

Christine shuddered. In a good way.

"But it also means that we will protect you."

She laughed. "There's not much I need protecting from. Unless you count assholes like that photographer."

"We do," Erik said.

Christine's phone buzzed where we'd left it by her toe shoes. Then it did again. And again. She grabbed it, the blue glow illuminating her face in the relative dimness of this space.

"Shit."

Marius stood. "What is it?"

"Someone saw me fall off the roof. The police are

here, and they're doing a headcount of the cast and crew to make sure everyone is okay."

We all moved together. She might not know that this was what we meant by protection, but it was.

"Let's go."

Marius grabbed the ice pack, Erik grabbed her shoes, and I grabbed her hand. I would have carried her if she'd let me.

But that could come later.

When she didn't just *say* that she was ours.

She knew it.

CHAPTER FIFTEEN

CHRISTINE

My mind whirled. Not even an hour had passed since I left the ballet studio.

Alex's hand was warm in mine, guiding me up staircases and through passageways that I didn't even know existed. I didn't want anyone to know that it was me on the roof. The production staff would make me go to the hospital. There would be no way to hide that from the press, and then everything about the show would be drowning in questions about my mental health and whether I had tried to jump after only one day of rehearsal.

And of course, there was the other thing.

The gargoyle thing.

Yeah.

I was going to wrap my head around that. But at the moment Alex was here and warm and every part of me knew that they took the *protection* aspect of this seriously.

"I have to be inside," I said. "The apartment. If I come back while they're checking, there will be questions."

His mouth flattened into a line, but he didn't say anything else. I knew that he understood.

The three of them didn't take me up to the residential level. But to the one below. "Where are we going?"

"Getting you into your apartment," Alex said firmly. "You left your window open."

"How do you know that?"

Erik spoke from behind me. "In our gargoyle form, we can sense the building. The vibrations in the stone. It's how we can hear conversations, and feel things like the fact that the window is open."

We pushed into what looked like a storage room. Random set decorations and replacements for the chairs in the theatre. The detritus of renovation and the creation of the next show.

There were two windows on the wall, which was at the back of the opera house. Just like the windows in my room. My heart jumped into my throat. "I can't climb the building. We're too high."

"You're not going to do anything," Marius said. "We'll do it."

"How?"

Alex let go of my hand to open the window and put his head out, looking upward. "Do you trust us?"

"Considering you saved my life? Yeah."

"Then come here."

Again, that tone that offered no room for argument. I was already moving, and he pulled me against his body. "Arms around my neck."

I obeyed.

One of Alex's arms came around my waist, and I gasped at the sensation. His arm hardened and grew. It turned to stone. There wasn't any way for me to move away from him—he was holding me so tight that I couldn't even slip downwards.

There was barely a chance to close my eyes before he climbed out the window with me attached. I didn't want to see how he was climbing so effortlessly with one hand. All I felt was movement, and a whisper of fabric over my skin and my feet were on the floor.

I was in my apartment.

Alex leaned out the window, retrieving my shoes

and the ice pack. "We'll be back," he said. "After they've come and gone."

"You're coming back?"

He raised an eyebrow. "You thought we were finished?"

I rubbed my hands together, forcing the tension and anticipation and anxiety into the movement. "No? I don't know. This is all…new."

So fast I didn't see it, he yanked me against his body, showing me again the way he felt, and now, how hard he was. And what was hard wasn't stone.

"Don't go anywhere, Christine."

I couldn't breathe. "Okay."

There was a knock at the door, and he winked before releasing me and practically diving out of the window. I knew he was safe, but my stomach still swooped.

On the way to the door, I grabbed a sweater from my suitcase and threw it on so it wouldn't look like I was just in dance clothes, and they wouldn't see the bruising that was starting to color my shoulder.

Anne stood there, along with the director and one of the producers. "Anne," I said. "Is everything all right?"

Her steely gaze took in the apartment quickly, noting that nothing was out of place and that I was alone. "There was an incident on the roof earlier.

We're just making sure that everyone is accounted for and well."

"Oh," I said. "That's scary. I hope everyone's okay?"

She smiled then, though I still saw the edge in her eyes. "Of course. My apologies for the interruption."

That wasn't an answer to my question, but I didn't need one. "Not at all."

They headed back down the hallway, heads together in whispers. Désirée stood in her doorway, leaning, watching. The way she looked at me, I wondered if she knew that I'd left my apartment and hadn't come back the traditional way. But if she did, she said nothing.

Instead, she maintained eye contact while she stepped back and slammed the door closed.

Well, crisis averted. It had seemed more intense than it ended up being while we were walking through the theatre. And of course, they would keep looking for whatever happened. There was probably scattered stone outside the opera house where the gargoyle had broken.

If we hadn't done this, though, it would have been a crisis. I was glad that we avoided it.

I locked the door again and leaned against it, wincing at the pain in my shoulder. That was going to hurt for days.

A breeze fluttered over me, the only indication that they were in the room. I didn't have to wait before the ice pack pressed against my skin again. "I guess I'm going to have to get used to you guys being able to do that."

"Yes," Marius said.

I needed to sit down.

The couch—I'd barely even sat on it yet—seemed like a perfect place for me to melt, and to simply exist for a while. With them.

Monsters.

Gargoyles.

Christine would sell her soul to fuck a monster.

That's what Meg said. Was it true? Was that what I'd done?

"Was that statue that broke a person?"

"No," Erik said. "Not every gargoyle is alive."

"Oh." I knew next to nothing about them. Gargoyles. In general.

I laughed. After everything, that seemed like the least important thing that I should be worried about. Gargoyle *lore*. Was this what was going to crack me open? Maybe. "It's too much," I said quietly.

"What is?"

I didn't even register who asked the question because I didn't feel like I was seeing out of my eyes. "Everything. All of it. I want to be here, and I want to be doing this, but my life isn't mine anymore. I can't even go to the hospital without worrying about the fact that people will see it. And that the whole rest of the show will be overshadowed by the question of 'did Christine Daniels try to kill herself?' You hear everything. You say you need me. Want me. Do you even know why I'm here?"

"Tell us," Erik said.

I sat down on the couch and closed my eyes, words bubbling up from my gut before I could stop them. "It was a mistake. Not really a mistake, but it wasn't meant to happen. I was a dancer with American Ballet Theatre, and there were some of us messing around in a studio after hours. We were drinking in there even though we weren't supposed to be.

"Meg knows I love to sing, and she begged me to. I know I'm good, but I wasn't trying to put on a show. I danced, and I sang my favorite aria. *Il Dolce Suono* from Lucia di Lammermoor."

"That's a beautiful song," Alex said quietly.

Somewhere, in a place where I could think, I absorbed that he knew the song and loved it.

"One of them filmed it. My friend Mark. I didn't know that he was filming. We were just having a good time, and then we all went home and that was that. We had a performance the next day."

I sighed, tilting my head back to the ceiling and staring. "The next morning I woke up to more notifications on my phone than I'd ever seen in my life. Mark had posted the video and tagged me. It... exploded. People were asking why I wasn't a singer and why I wasn't performing at the Met? Why didn't I have record deals? Before, I only had a few covers on YouTube and I'd gone to a few unsuccessful auditions.

"That's what people don't realize. Talent is only part of it. There's a whole network of politics below the surface that dictates who gets cast and why. I hadn't broken through that barrier yet. Who knows, maybe I would have been able to do it. Maybe I never would have."

Warm arms came around me, and I didn't resist them. I couldn't stop talking, but I wasn't capable of doing anything else either. So I held on, and let everything pass through.

"But by the time I'd made it to the theatre that night, people knew who I was. There was a crowd of people outside, waiting for me. We sold tickets. Everyone in the company was staring at me—even Meg—and I didn't know what to do. Honestly, I thought that it would go away after a couple of days. It didn't.

"The higher-ups were thrilled with the ticket

sales, obviously. But they weren't happy with the sudden external pressure to promote me when they weren't ready to do that. I went totally dark. Posted nothing, put my head down and waited for everything to go quiet. But it didn't. I left the ballet when, for whatever reason, someone managed to break into the dressing rooms, trying to find me. I don't..."

I faltered, swallowing. "I don't think they wanted to hurt me, but I didn't want to take that chance of anyone else getting hurt because of me. A few days later I got the chance to audition for this, and I *wanted* it. In spite of all the crazy I knew that it would bring, I wanted to sing Joan. I've always loved her story and no matter how it came, I knew that it was an opportunity that might never come again."

Warm scent wrapped around me. Like freshly baked pastries. *Pain au chocolat*, and fresh coffee. Things that smelled like comfort.

"And with that announcement, it felt like the world went crazy. I don't think there are many people who can realize what it's like suddenly to have *everyone* recognize you. I went on TV shows remotely from my apartment, but I couldn't go outside. The show had to hire security for me. So I just...stayed inside and read books and learned my lines and my music and hoped that it would all be worth it. But it feels like nothing ever stopped. Like the second that video went viral, no one cared who I was anymore.

"I'm just the ballet singer girl. Christine Daniels, surprise talent. Only Meg stayed normal, but she still has her life. Rehearsals, even though she took a contract for this. Everyone else? It's not about me. It's about who I am or what I am or what happened to them because I'm here. And now I'm pretty sure that all the pressure has cracked my brain because I'm sitting here with three gargoyles—*gargoyles*—who want to fuck me and that's only something that I could have made up in my head. You're too gorgeous and it's too good to be true."

All the words went out of me then. I'd never said all of that at once. Not even to Meg. Maybe it was the after effects of the fall. Maybe I was in shock. Maybe I'd just finally cracked and couldn't do anything else than get it *out*.

I finally took stock of where I was, lying on the couch, my back pressed against skin. Marius sat in front of me on the floor, and Alex leaned against the wall by the electric fireplace. So Erik was holding me. That was his warm scent that seemed to have notes of sugar and pie and frosting along with bread. Was that a gargoyle thing?

Marius was smiling. It didn't fully meet his eyes. "You're not crazy."

"If you're figments of my imagination, of course you would say that."

He raised one eyebrow. "Did figments of your imagination meet your friends and finger fuck you in a club? Save you from falling from a roof? Carry you through a window."

"It's possible," I muttered.

Marius chuckled. "Then you have a very good imagination."

He wasn't wearing a shirt. Alex had never put his back on, and I felt bare skin behind me. None of them were wearing shirts, and the miles of muscled chest and arms were enough to keep my eyes busy.

Small silver studs protruded from Marius's nipples. There were bars through them. "Like what you see?" He asked.

"How does that work with your transformation?"

"No one's looking closely enough at a gargoyle to see piercings," he said with a laugh.

My head was pillowed on Erik's arm, and slowly, he moved his fingers through my hair, dragging them along my scalp until he could grab my hair in that delicious *give me more* way. And then he did it again.

"But you have piercings," I said again. "It didn't occur to me."

Erik moved his hand again, gripping my hair

and tilting my head backwards until my face was far enough to see his. His grin was feral. "We may be monsters, but we do like to play. Like the night club. Like piercings. Like tattoos. Like sex." He kissed my cheek. The only place he could really reach. But that arm under my head moved, shifting so it was across my chest and holding me in place against him.

"Tattoos?"

"Tattoos," he confirmed. "Among other things."

I glanced at Alex and froze. He had my naughty book in his hands, complete with the bare-chested man on the front. A slow grin came to his face. "If you read these, then you should never have had to ask why you."

"What do you mean?"

He tossed the book onto the nearby chair and stalked over to me. Erik didn't relinquish his hold on me, instead standing, pulling me with him so that I was pressed between them. A familiar sensation now, and one that I didn't mind in the slightest.

Something curled around my calf, and I looked down to find a stone tail there, curving from behind me. Reptilian and scaled, Erik's tail rippled as it moved. Alex's hands turned gray, those deadly claws lengthening as they drew up the sides of my body. But I wasn't afraid. Not of them.

Marius stood, and then there was a complete triangle of them surrounding me.

"You know why," he said. "Say it."

That was what I was afraid of. The idea that was tingling at the edges of my consciousness. Those words and acknowledging that any of it could be true. "I can't."

Erik's tail tightened. Those claws pressed gently, threatening to tear my clothes into shreds. Another slithering feeling of a tail. Marius, the spiked tail of a dragon curling around my hips. I was tangled up in them, and there was no way that I could break free.

I closed my eyes and let myself fall into it. Into the reality that I couldn't believe but also couldn't deny. That I'd fantasized about and chastised myself for wanting something so far from reality. To belong with and to someone on such a deep level that there wasn't a way to escape. To have something that no one could take away.

"Say it," Alex said again. His forehead pressed against mine. The gesture was gentle, but his voice was anything but.

Marius's tail stroked down over my hips, daring to twine between my legs and make me think about the possibilities of that tail that was both hard and soft.

"I don't know how," I said.

One hand moved, a single claw slipping beneath the hem of my shirt and tearing upwards with steady, deliberate precision. Baring me to them. "One little word, Christine."

My camisole tore apart, leaving nothing but skin. Alexandre consumed me with his eyes, the color darkening so close to black. A void. The eyes of a monster. "Why you? Because we need you. We *waited* for you. Felt you the moment you stepped out of your car here. Knew that your voice lit us up like lightning. But I also knew the second you fell into my arms that you were *mine*." His tail—the third, and the shape of a lion—joined the others. This one slipped around one wrist and pulled it to my other arm, effectively binding them together. "We're more beasts than men. And you know from your books that beasts don't need time or space to know that something belongs to them. You're ours."

It wasn't real. It couldn't be real. But it was. They were real.

Let go for once in your life, Christine.

They were right. I felt it that day. The way that the world spun out between us and told me something had happened. Something deep that I didn't believe. But they were right.

I belonged to them. So I smiled.

"Prove it."

CHAPTER SIXTEEN

CHRISTINE

*E*rik growled behind me. "Baby girl, you are going to regret saying that."

"Am I?"

"Don't you know?" Marius asked, stroking between my legs with his tail again. "Don't taunt the monsters."

"But I thought you liked to play," I said.

"Mmm," Erik's mouth pressed against my neck. "She's going to use our words against us. Maybe she should learn a lesson for that."

Alex was still staring at me, more of his body transforming as he let me see the monster. His voice was like gravel, and at the same time, it caressed my skin like the gentlest breeze. "I'm still waiting for her to say it."

It was an impossible task, to say it out loud. Once I said it, it was real, and then the whole world changed.

"Whisper it if you need to," he growled. "But we are not moving from this spot until you do."

His teeth were at my throat, followed by a kiss and a lick and those transformed fangs. My entire body was still, held by all of them. Sharp points grazing my skin sent my heart racing, my body panicking and sensing the predator. The monster.

My stomach swooped, and I swallowed. The whisper I managed was barely audible. "I'm your mate?"

The growls from all three of them rippled through me, causing my knees to give out. Their arms and claws and tails were the only thing keeping me upright. "That's *right*," Alex said, the transformation completing. Somehow he still moved as stone, slow and steady, lifting me and carrying me to the bed. "You're our fucking mate."

Erik's tail curled around my ankle, and I saw his wings grow out of his back. The wings were shaped like that of a bat, the upper tips curving into their own set of claws. His eyes were black, the tips of his fingers sharpening into the other set. Not for a second did it make him less beautiful.

Now that I could see him, the dark tattoos that curved around his ribs and disappeared beneath his jeans caught my eye. I wanted to see where they went.

Alex barely let him take his place. Three dominant monsters wanted me, and they were going to fight over me at the same time as they shared me. I still wasn't entirely sure that I wasn't crazy. But if I was, then I would embrace my fate.

"See?" Erik said, hovering over my body and consuming every bit of bare skin I had with his eyes. "You already belonged to us, baby girl. We just needed you to see it."

"I didn't know gargoyles had mates."

Marius laughed behind the others. "If that's what you're concerned with at the moment…"

"I have so many questions. Why do you have mates? How come it's all three of you? What happens to the mates? How did you feel me? You're okay with all having me?"

He smirked. "Do you want us to answer questions? Or do you want us to fuck you?"

"Both."

Marius pulled Erik back, replacing him, drawing a still-human hand down the center of my chest.

Fingers slipped into my tights and pulled them down and off. I was almost naked with them, and I wasn't embarrassed. I wasn't hesitant. It felt right.

I was lifted from the bed for a moment, Marius draping me over his lap and spreading my legs over his knees. "I'll answer one. Yes, we're all fine with having you. And we have every intention of helping each other take you. In as many ways as possible."

His legs under mine turned to stone. I couldn't close my legs, draped as I was. Completely exposed to the two monsters in front of me. Heat flushed up my body until I was entirely pink. The way they were looking at me made me squirm. Writhe. Try to do anything to relieve my building arousal.

Marius wrapped his arms around my chest and transformed them, trapping me further. Panic and lust twisted through me at the same time. "I can't move."

"Mmm, exactly." His voice in my ear sent goose-bumps rippling over my skin. "You asked us to prove it. We're going to do just that."

In front of me, Alex was stripping again. I'd already seen him once, but it was different now. His body was still a man, and he was hard. Thick and straight—ready to take me and prove to me what I'd asked them to.

But he didn't fuck me.

Alexandre knelt between my spread thighs, drawing sharp claws along that exposed skin. Not hard enough to hurt. It grazed my skin and made everything tighten with need. I *needed* more of that sensation. Claws.

Marius groaned. "Christine, you're going to be the death of us if you keep doing that."

"Doing what?"

"Getting wet when all I've done is touch your thighs," Alex growled.

I blushed. They didn't need to know the truth. It didn't matter.

A soft laugh, and I glanced at Erik, eyes now entirely black orbs. "I don't think it was her thighs. Was it, Christine?"

"No," I managed to say. He stared at me until I kept going. "Your claws. The feeling of them."

I felt Marius stiffen in the same way I saw Alex do it. The latter tilted his head, so still that it was clear he was no longer fully human. "More claws, you say?"

One lone talon drew a line from my knee towards my core. It was everything I could fucking do not to move and beg for more—try to fight Marius's stone embrace to try to get closer.

"Do you know how sharp they are?" Alexandre whispered. "Almost nothing in the world is that sharp." The tingling, barely there scratch reached my clit and grazed it. Teased it. Circled around it. I knew that Alex wouldn't hurt me. My body didn't. And that made it so much better.

I spun between pleasure and the feeling of being touched and the fear of that sharpness. That single point of contact made me crave *more more more.*

"Fucking hell." Marius murmured into my neck. His arms tightened around me more, locking me against his chest. And Alex kept touching me. Tracing my swollen clit with one claw and then another, watching the way I was shaking and writhing like he was figuring out exactly how to tease me.

I needed more. "Please."

Alex's black eyes flicked to mine, and that mouth —just on the border of transforming—smirked. "Since you said please."

Claws pressed to my thighs, he leaned down and licked me. I swore, light flaring behind my eyes. That one movement—that sensation—was enough to convince me that magic was real. This wasn't my first time, and never in my life had a single flick of a tongue made me feel like I was being fucked.

He pressed deeper, licking into me and over me and all around me. I was falling into an ocean of glitter. Stars and sparkles and the slow, luxurious sensation of being enjoyed.

Pleasure built in the deep center of me. That rich, slow kind of pleasure that could be set off by the smallest flicker once it burned bright enough. The kind of pleasure that I'd only felt by myself and never with another person.

Erik drew my attention, and the fact that he distracted me at all from Alex sealing his mouth over me was a statement about what I was looking at. He popped the buttons on his jeans, dropping them and then his underwear. The sharp and strange lines of his tattoos resolved into lightning bolts and storm clouds that flowed over his hips and fading over his thighs.

They looked nearly silvery on his skin and matched the silver on his cock. He was huge—thicker than Alex. Probably the thickest cock I'd ever seen, and it was his human form. But the silver—studs lined the top of his shaft in two rows, all the way along it.

I'd heard rumors about piercings like those, but I never thought that I'd see one. Or have the opportunity to feel one. If I would even be able to fit him inside me.

The image of Erik stretching me open sank through me, melding with the pleasure of Alex's mouth. Pleasure flashed through me, bright, fierce and fast. I arched against Marius's hold as much as I could—which wasn't much—*begging* for more of it.

Alex growled. The sound rocked through my body. It wasn't a human sound. He was entirely a beast. A monster. The creature in front of me was stone, wings flared, rough stone lips still locked to my skin. The tongue that stroked over my clit fluctuated between what felt like smooth, slick marble and something coarse that nearly made me moan with the new, strange sensation.

The next growl had him rippling back into human skin, mouth still on me, still drinking the orgasm that he brought out of me. My body relaxed, melting against Marius. His cock wasn't stone, but it was hard under my ass. Every part of me expected for him to let me go so I could see him.

He didn't.

Erik stepped forward. "Make room."

Marius widened his legs, spreading me further apart. The gasp that pulled from me made him chuckle, and he widened further. "I felt you dance earlier," he said. "I know *exactly* how flexible you are."

One more movement, and my legs were stretched to their limit. There was no hiding anything, and I didn't realize what was happening until Erik hit his knees in front of me alongside Alex and leaned in.

Neither of them hesitated. Both tongues were there. Licking me. Consuming me. Stroking both sides of my clit with tangled licks that brought brand new heat racing to the surface. I didn't recognize the sound that came out of me. Desperate and feral. Like the three of them together had brought out the animal side of me.

They were the predators to my prey, and the deepest part of me knew it. Yielded. Recognized those words, that I belonged to them.

Erik dipped low, fucking me with his tongue while Alex swirled circles around my clit. "Oh, fuck. Oh my god. Oh *fuck*." Those were the only words that existed. I'd lost the ability to speak.

I lost those words two when they both licked me again. Nothing existed but light between my eyes, every muscle taut and straining as the wave hit me and carried me away. I was diving in a sea of golden light. A shower of breathless sparks. Every nerve overloaded. Perfumed with ecstasy before fading away into a pleasant, heady haze.

Marius did release me then, transforming his stone limbs and cradling me closer, kissing my neck. Erik's claws grazed down my leg. "Christine, you taste like heaven."

My words weren't fully formed, but I knew what I wanted. "Someone needs to fuck me right now. Right now."

My back hit my mattress, Marius climbing over me. "Oh, we're absolutely all going to fuck you," he said, eyes dark. "Unless you've changed your mind."

"Don't you dare," I shook my head. Maybe it was the remaining adrenaline from the roof. Maybe I was going into shock. But I felt drunk without drinking. The idea that they would stop touching me was fucking unthinkable.

Warm light cast us in new brightness. The light outside had died entirely while they tasted me. Now I could see Marius above me, sharp green eyes close and darkening. My own eyes were drawn to the bars in his nipples that I'd seen earlier, and lower to the bar through the head of his cock. The silver bar peeked out from under the shaft that curved upward. Longer than the others. He was going *deep*.

A laugh burst out of me. "I'm sorry," I said quickly. "This isn't funny. I just thought about the fact that I didn't think to bring condoms, and if I had, I would have never thought about gargoyles using them."

Marius's cock brushed over my clit, making me shudder. "No need. We're not human, so we can't get you pregnant." His eyes heated. "Though the thought of you pregnant with one of our children makes me harder than a rock. And there's nothing else that you'd need protection from. I promise."

He was pressing against my entrance, and I nodded my consent. My next thought was that I hoped they insulated the walls. Or else Désirée was going to get an earful. Marius slammed home, and I almost screamed. He was deep. All the way deep. Hitting a place with his cock and his piercing that I wasn't sure I'd ever felt. And *fuck* it was amazing.

The balls of his piercing slammed into me with every thrust, which shoved sizzling pleasure through me in waves. I couldn't do anything but feel. Paralyzed. Fucked.

I needed to move and help. If I stayed still the whole time, what would they think? Twisting, I tried to shift us so that I would be on top. Marius didn't move. My strength was about as effective as pushing on a rock.

One eyebrow rose, and he slowed, teasing me with shallow strokes. His eyes were no longer green, the black eyes of a gargoyle looking down at me with wicked amusement.

"Yes, Christine?"

"You don't need to do all the work." They'd pleasured me at the club. They'd just made me come twice, and this was the first pleasure they'd taken. There wasn't balance.

I shifted my hips again, and he growled. He grabbed my wrists and pinned them to the bed, and suddenly his teeth were at my throat. There wasn't any break in the rhythm of his slow, deep thrusts.

"Christine." That was Alex's voice. Crouched by the bed. "You're our mate. You agree? You accept that?"

"Yes." The scrape of Marius's teeth over my pulse made me gasp. He wasn't going to bite, but he was holding me in place, making sure that I didn't move while he fucked me. Steadily. Thoroughly.

Alex's hand covered mine where it was pinned to the bed. "There may be a time when you can ride us to your heart's content. Take charge and command us in your pleasure. But now? In the beginning?" His words were backed by a low growl that was almost a purr. "Our monsters are at the surface, and they need to claim you. Until they know you're ours completely."

"But—"

Marius's growl cut me off, and I heard the smile in Erik's voice from the other direction. "I told you that you'd regret telling us to prove it. My inner beast loves a challenge. Now, are you going to be a good girl and let us fuck you? Or do we have to tie you down while we make you beg for us to do it?"

Arousal swept through my body in a fucking tidal wave. It was like opening myself to them and admitting the impossible unlocked parts of myself that I'd never wanted to admit to. Those deep fantasies that I craved but was afraid to let myself experience.

Being tied down and made to beg sounded like the dream that I'd had last night. Now that I knew it was them. Until I said no, and they'd disappeared, respecting that wish. I was glad I hadn't said no again.

They knew. The thoughts made me wetter. They could probably hear my heart. Scent my new arousal. But their hands covered my wrists with Marius's hold. Their hands reached my ankles. Imprisoning me and holding me down.

But they didn't have to make me beg.

Marius *fucked*.

My whole mind blanked out. His scent wrapped around me, running through the woods and fires between the branches. Flashes of starlight burst behind my eyelids, where his piercing dragged and pressed. Harder and deeper.

And then a different kind of hard. His cock stiffened, smoothing out and growing thicker. Turning to stone for brief moments. So different. The texture and temperature and shift in weight made me shake.

It was magic. They were magic. It was the only way—the only reason I was on the edge of a third orgasm. It was real and it couldn't be real and somewhere I heard my own voice begging in echoes and heard the slap or bodies together.

Marius ground down, dragging his hips over my clit. It set me off like dynamite. The explosion had nowhere to go, held as I was. It spun and collapsed through itself. A black hole at the center of me that was pleasure and pleasure and pleasure.

Somewhere in between the waves of bliss, he came. Roaring and shaking, fangs and claws pinning me in place. My body was in total shock. Small spasms around his cock and all over made me feel like I was flickering.

It was long minutes before Marius relaxed, releasing the place where he'd nearly bitten my pulse. One lick soothed the skin, and a kiss warmed it. When he pulled back to look at me, his eyes were human again. "Did I hurt you?"

I shook my head. "No."

He smiled slowly, licking the spot on my neck where his teeth scratched. "And you took *all* of my cock."

"I think tomorrow this will seem more real. After

I wake up and realize that this isn't a dream. Or the afterlife of me falling off the roof."

They chuckled, and Marius moved slowly, pulling out of me slowly enough that I shuddered. He hadn't driven deep at the end, and it was still fucking perfect. "Whatever it takes for you to believe it."

Erik leaned over the bed, a bandage in his hands. I hissed against the cold of the ice pack that I didn't notice him holding. He was wrapping it around my shoulder. Even glancing at it out of the corner of my eye, I could see that there was swelling and bruising. But it could wait. "What are you doing? Two of you still have to fuck me."

Hands pulled me back across the bed so I was flush against Marius. He moved me exactly where he wanted me, arranging me over his body so my shoulder could rest easily with the ice.

"You need to be able to walk and rehearse," Erik said.

"I'll be fine."

Alex drew a hand down my spine, settling behind me. "Don't be so sure. Not to mention that you need your voice, and I like it so much that I want to wear it out."

My whole body tightened, at once aroused and relaxed by the hands now actively soothing me. I absently realized they'd pulled the bed away from the wall. I didn't need the wall now, since they were here with me.

A tail curled around an ankle, and I felt new hands stroke my legs. I was already beginning to tell the difference between their touches. Erik was there, tracing patterns on my calves.

"I still have so many questions," I said, but the words were slurred. I felt fuzzy with exhaustion from the adrenaline crash and the best sex that I'd ever had in my life.

Tomorrow I'd deal with the reality. I had mates. Three mates. Mates were real. Magic was real. And I still had the eyes of the entire world locked on me.

CHAPTER SEVENTEEN

ERIK

I watched Christine sink into sleep—the ever so subtle softening of her muscles and deepening of her curves. She was pale and beautiful, her shoulder and wrist coloring where Alex had yanked her back to safety. Even her ankles were still pink from us holding her.

None of us could feel what she felt, but it didn't seem to matter. Her taste. Her scent. The smallest expressions on her face told me what she was thinking and feeling. And the second we made it impossible to resist, her mind opened up and she let us in. She didn't realize how deeply yet.

Alex stroked his fingers down her spine to the

curve of her ass. She was so fucking beautiful. The heartbeat of *mine, mine, mine,* inside my head made me want to drive into her. Make her scream loudly enough for the whole opera to hear.

But there would be time for that.

"She took that well," Marius said so quietly that it would never disturb her.

"Your cock? Or the fact that she's our mate."

He chuckled softly. "Both."

"Almost too well," Alexandre said.

"Why?" I shrugged. "She's our mate. Whatever magic it is that makes these things happen, I doubt it would choose someone who would be completely opposed to believing it."

Alex smiled, and his glance flickered toward the book that he'd found. "You're probably right."

We'd switched back to French in our casualness, and I was glad when he finally spoke again. "I almost didn't catch her."

"Don't say that," Marius answered.

He insisted. "It's true. She was almost gone."

The deep, feral part of me shook itself free, ready to destroy anything that was a danger to the sleeping woman in front of me.

"You did catch her. We can't protect her from other things by focusing on the things that almost happened. Only on the things that are going to happen."

Like making sure the whole world didn't think that she'd tried to throw herself off a roof, or Callum and his band of idiots.

"You saw Callum ask her to dance last night?"

They shook their heads. They'd been at the table. We hadn't had a chance to talk about it until now. That, and their little threat. "You think they'll try to take her?"

Marius's eyes promised death even as the rest of him remained gentle and soft for Christine. Off the bed, away from her, his tail flicked back and forth, agitated. "Yes. I do. You know why."

One more stroke down Christine's calves and I stood, unable to keep the nervous energy from skittering under my skin. Mates were precious and rare, and incredibly vulnerable. Red flared across my eyes.

"*Erik*." Alex's voice cut across my thoughts. I hadn't realized that the growl was building in my chest.

Christine stirred and settled again, tucking her face closer to Marius's chest.

Our mate. Pure and impossible and so fucking precious. So fucking *rare*. If someone besides us touched Christine—harmed her in any way, or worse—we would go mad. The pain of it would cause us to destroy ourselves.

If Callum knew what she was to us, he wouldn't leave her alive.

"We're still bound to the opera," Marius said. "Would he go that far, knowing that we're essentially powerless?"

I snorted. We were far from powerless, but I knew what he meant. We were a long way from what we'd been. The power to command and shape stone. For other gargoyles to bow simply because of who and what we were? That disappeared that night. I'd inked it on my skin so I'd never forget.

As if every day that we lived wasn't a constant reminder of what had happened.

"For the knowledge that he would never have to worry about us breaking away from here and that he wouldn't be challenged? Yes, I think that he would. And all he has to do is take her one step beyond our circle, and we won't be able to get to her."

"We shouldn't have taken her to Spectre," Alex said.

"They would have figured it out, anyway. They have eyes watching us. All they would need was to see us together once, and they would suspect. It's only to our advantage that they don't know what she is. Right now, all he thinks is that we're interested."

Marius lifted Christine higher on his chest, her face fitting perfectly into the hollow of his shoulder. I saw the way his fingers tightened on her. "We have to find a way out now. For her. She can't stay here forever. We can't keep her here, and we can't protect her if she leaves."

It had been two-hundred years, and we were no closer to breaking the tie that melted us to the bones of the opera house than we were the day it happened. Until two days ago, we thought we'd had all the time in the world, and time itself had less meaning.

Now every second that passed was another of Christine's life passing.

Gargoyles were made. Not born. Not transformed. We only had so much time with her, and I wasn't planning on wasting a second of it more than necessary. Especially if anyone was going to harm her.

Alex stiffened, moving swiftly and smoothly off the bed and to the window. I heard it a second later. Intentional footsteps scraping on stone. I flicked off the lamp we'd turned on, dousing the room in thick blue darkness. It wouldn't do much if they'd already seen, but we wouldn't take that chance.

I crept closer to where Alex was flat against the wall and peered out of the window at the street below. Callum, Sebastian, Witt, and others were outside. Prowling. Looking up towards the windows and the roof like they'd find us there.

"They can't know, right?" I murmured. "What she is?"

"No," Alexandre said. "But it doesn't matter. They saw us with her, and it's enough for them to want her. To spite us."

"I've never wished for less power more in my life," Marius hissed behind us.

He wasn't wrong. If we weren't who we were. If our making hadn't made us strong—the strongest gargoyles in an age—then they wouldn't hate us. And wouldn't want to destroy us by any means necessary. Though they'd already done enough by contributing to the face that we were trapped here.

"Have they seen?" I asked Alex.

"No."

But they were still walking towards the building, aiming to circle around it. They wanted us to see them, no matter we were.

"We'll need to watch when we leave," I said. "To make sure that they don't know."

They walked around the building and disappeared. None of us moved or breathed until only the normal silence of the city remained.

"We need to tell her," Marius said. "If she's going

to leave the opera house when we can't. She needs to know."

"We'll tell her," I said. "And answer all her questions. Everything. She's all that matters now."

I didn't need to be in my stone form to hear their complete and total agreement.

CHAPTER EIGHTEEN

CHRISTINE

*C*hristine.

I snuggled closer to the sound. Now that I knew what the dreams were, I didn't want to wake up. But this seemed more insistent. "Christine."

Hands dragged over my skin, and I slowly realized that I wasn't fully asleep anymore. A blanket was sliding up my body, and I opened my eyes to Marius looking at me. My apartment was dim. Morning.

Marius's hand was beneath my neck like he'd just finished laying me down. "We have to go."

"No," I said quietly. "Don't."

"We have to, baby. The sun is almost up, and as soon as the sun touches this building, we're stone."

Visceral disappointment spun through me, unfiltered because I wasn't quite awake. I felt hungover. Addicted to the feeling of them and their touch.

Marius knew. Somehow, he knew. Leaning close, he pressed a kiss to my temple. "We'll be listening to you sing."

Right now I didn't want to sing. I wanted to be held. Which he did for a moment longer before pulling away and letting Erik take his place. "Good morning," he whispered.

I wrapped my arms around his neck like it would keep him from having to leave. "Morning." My words were a mumble against his skin.

"I need you to do something for me today, okay?"

"Does it involve getting fucked by three gargoyles?"

He laughed, slanting his mouth across mine. "Later, it does. But I need you to stay inside the opera house today. Don't leave without us."

I found my smile. "First I'm your mate and now I'm your prisoner?"

He wasn't matching my smile. "We're going to answer all your questions. I promise, *mon étoile déchue*, but this is important."

"Okay. I have rehearsal and then some interviews

later today. I think a photoshoot too, but it's all here."

Gently, he unwrapped the bandage that was attaching the now melted ice pack to my shoulder, and I winced. It was swollen. I would have to be careful today. "Then we'll see you after that," he said. "And if you ever want to talk to us, now you know how."

"I can talk back?" I'd asked the voices who they were in the ballet studio—I hadn't realized they answered.

"Just think of all the naughty things you can say to us that we won't be able to do a single thing about until this evening."

"I will think about that." Thinking about that was making me squirm and want to pull him down for something else. But I let him go. Alex sat down beside me and handed me my phone. "It's early still. You can sleep longer."

Turning on my side, I curled around where he was seated and closed my eyes. "Big scary monsters my ass. Taking care of me like this."

In a second flat, I wasn't curled on my side. I was pressed down into the mattress looking into Alexandre's black gargoyle eyes, and I grinned. I knew what it would do to him. "Wicked," he said quietly. "Trying to trick me."

"It worked, didn't it?"

He smiled. It had an edge. "It did. Probably would have been better if you hadn't shown us exactly how much you like us to be *big*, scary monsters."

A shiver ran down my spine, and all three of them laughed.

"Now promise me you're going to stay inside like Erik said, and that you're not even going to think about touching yourself after we leave just because we can't stay."

I pouted. "That's not fair."

"I never said it was. But if I smell that delicious cunt on your hands later, I'll be jealous. No telling what my beast will do."

"Is that a threat or a promise?" The low growl made me smile, and every part of me tightened. "I promise."

He leaned down, purring in my ear. "Good girl."

I moaned. "You saying that to me isn't helping me keep my promise." There wasn't any doubt that they could scent the way those two words made me wet.

"Keep your promise, mate." The words weren't human.

"Okay."

Alex kissed me one more time, long and deep, tracing my tongue with his and letting me feel his own tongue turn to stone briefly. "Sleep more. You'll need it later."

One more stroke of his hand over my hair, and he stepped away. All three of them were gone in moments, out of the window and up to the roof. They'd pulled my bed away from the wall, but I could still reach it.

I brushed my fingers across the surface and tried pushing my thoughts to them. *I want you to come back.*

The low laughter felt like tingles across my skin and through my mind. Silvery tendrils of sensation like they were reaching out for me too.

Soon, mate.

That was Marius's voice. I could tell the difference now. And Erik. *Sleep.*

It was like a caress inside my head, and I went back to sleep.

By comparison, waking up to my blaring alarm a couple of hours later was far from pleasant. I would much rather be woken with gentle kisses. My hand, fingertips still brushing the wall, let me hear the gargoyles' amusement.

Easy for you to say, I complained.

We'll make it up to you.

Turning off the alarm, I checked my phone. No messages from Meg or anyone else, so at the very least we'd avoided the suspicion of the rooftop. That was step one. Step two was making it through today.

I dragged myself out of bed and started the coffee, showering while it was brewing and intentionally *not* touching the walls. Because if they wanted me to keep that promise about not getting myself off, then I couldn't be listening to their voices while I was naked and wet.

I put my coffee into a travel mug so I could have that along with my water. Hell, I felt more hungover today than I had yesterday, and last night I hadn't had a single drink of alcohol.

There was the fact that I almost died, and the incredible sex, but my brain wasn't used to thinking of sex as a hangover. Since I'd never had sex like *that*.

Turned out that Meg was right. If I'd known that it would be like that? I definitely would have sold my soul to fuck a monster. Luckily, I didn't have to.

Meg waved me over as I entered the house. "You okay?"

"Yeah," I said, sinking down next to her and lowering my voice. "Thanks for the heads up last night."

"It wasn't you, right?"

I swallowed. "It was, but it's not what they think. I'll tell you about it later." There was some kind of explanation that I'd be able to give her. I had to. Meg was the one person that I couldn't lie to, and it wasn't like I could act like I never saw the guys again. She thought they were a part of the crew. But I needed to talk to them about it first.

"You look tired," she said at normal volume.

Opening my mouth to tell her that it was just jet lag, my words got taken out of my mouth. "I imagine that she's tired, based on the sounds coming from her apartment."

Désirée sat behind us, smirking. Enjoying the way that everyone was now looking at me and evaluating me. There were two options here. I could stay silent. Let them think what they thought and ignore them. Or I could show them that I wasn't just a pushover.

This morning, I wasn't in a mood to let them mock me or the happiness that I'd found.

Mates.

Fuck.

I was going to have to get my head around that one later today.

Taking a sip of my coffee, I looked away from Désirée. "I didn't hear anything from your apartment. If you wanted to join in, you should have just asked."

Meg was taking a sip from her water bottle and nearly choked. Around me, there were a couple of gasps and whispers.

Christine, one. Désirée...she still probably had more points than me, but I felt good about that victory. Meg elbowed me in the side. I could see her grin out of the corner out of my eye and kept just as silent as the glacial quiet that was building behind me.

Rehearsal was called to order, so there wasn't any chance for her to strike back. Yet. "I'll see you later," Meg whispered.

The dancers were rehearsing in the studio again and would be joining us later as we started to put everything on its feet. The faster the show integrated all the moving parts, the faster it got better. It was always like that. Always.

It meant that today would be hard, but hopefully easier after. Already I felt better, because the anger I'd felt yesterday was eased with what I'd just said to Désirée.

All of it was easier. My voice was stronger, and everyone seemed more motivated. The show was shaky, but we had the general shape of our move-ments by the time rehearsal was over. I was hungry, and tired, but nothing was over yet. My shoulder ached. There was nothing torn or broken, but I needed to ice it again later.

Anne waved me over. "Ready?"

"No," I admitted with a laugh. "But let's go."

She gestured towards the lobby. "We've set everything up out here. A set for the interviews and then after we'll take some photos with the necklace."

"The necklace?"

"Would you like to see it?" I turned to the excited voice and saw Monsieur Chagny holding a black velvet box. The kind that you saw in movies when they opened it and it was filled with diamonds the size of a bird's egg.

"Of course."

"This necklace," Anne told me, "was one of the only things to survive the fire two hundred years ago. You'll wear it for the gala, and a replica for the court scenes in the show. And the finale of course. Since it's so valuable."

Raoul smiled. "Anne thought that using it would be good publicity, and she was right. It belongs to my family, but has been on display at the *D'orsay* for as long as I can remember. It will be returned there after the show closes."

He opened the box, and my jaw dropped. It was pearls. A whole string of white pearls as big as my thumb. And from the bottom of that strand, a pink stone hung, encircled by more pearls. "Is that—?"

"A pink diamond? It is."

"It's beautiful." And more than that, I nearly felt drawn to the stone. A magnetic feeling. I wanted to touch it.

Gently closing the box, Raoul smiled again. "I'm glad you think so."

"Let's get you into make-up," Anne said.

They'd set up a station outside a false interview set with black curtains like a series of rooms. The other principals would be interviewed as well. Désirée and the others were already sitting, getting made up. She had a blonde man standing near her that seemed vaguely familiar.

The make-up station was in a section of the lobby which was marble. Once my artist got started, there wasn't much talking to be done. I toed off one shoe and my sock, pressing my foot to the stone.

Hello?

Purrs erupted in my head. I jumped, startling my artist, and she blinked. "Sorry. Got a chill."

She just smiled and went back to putting on my foundation.

Are you all right? Alex's tone was calm. Too calm. There was something wrong.

I'm fine. Why?

No reason.

I sent the equivalent feeling of me making a face that I didn't believe him. *We'll tell you soon.*

You sounded beautiful today, Erik whispered, causing me to blush. If the make-up artist noticed, she said nothing.

Thank you.

Marius's voice was smooth and teasing. *Could I get you to sing like that while I fuck you?*

Holding back my laughter, my toes curled. *I don't know that even I would have the breath control for that.*

Maybe it would be a good challenge.

And give Désirée more ammunition to use against me? I asked. *No thanks.*

Erik laughed. *I thought your response was perfect.*

I promise that if you were in our place downstairs, no one would hear the singing. Alex said, voice caressing through my mind like velvet night. *Or if they did, they'd think it was a ghost. An echo of an echo.*

The sound I sent back to them wasn't one that I could make out loud right now. *If you guys keep going the only thing that I'm going to be able to answer in these interviews is how badly I want to be having sex and nothing about the show.*

Good. The word was tripled.

Anne came over to me, and they silenced. "Christine?"

I didn't move, as the artist was currently dusting a shimmering shadow onto my lids. "Yes?"

"You're going to get questions about last night."

"Did you find out what happened?"

She shook her head, and I noted that she looked troubled. "One of the statues appears to have shattered. There was a report of someone hanging from the building, but there was no evidence of that."

Thank fuck. "What would you like me to say?"

"Laugh it off. The roof hasn't been fully restored and we're working on securing any loose statues so that there will be no danger to the public. Just an accident."

"Okay," I nodded. "I can do that. Anything else?"

"Just be your normal, charming self."

"I'll try." Already I felt the exhaustion that would come later from smiling and nodding and paying attention like I spoke fluent French until the interpreter could finish.

How long until you're free? I asked.

We are free as soon as the sun is no longer hitting the opera house. Soon.

So the sun didn't have to be fully set. The relief that brought me was enough to let me relax.

I'll see you soon. Those were the last thoughts I pushed to them before I lifted my foot from the stone. I wasn't sure how much they could sense of my passive thoughts, and there were things that I needed to think about. Like the fact that they were my *mates*.

Mates.

Like the books that I read.

Like *fiction*.

And yet I didn't doubt it. It made too much sense. The feeling that yanked me toward them the first time that I'd encountered them. The fact that I trusted them enough to touch me the first day we met when I hadn't been able to trust anyone in months.

The fact that I'd said *no*, and they'd let me walk away even though they knew that we were meant to be, anyway. I was a little surprised that I *wasn't* more freaked out? Maybe before all of this, I would have lost my mind. But the fact that I was here in this role already felt like magic. Essentially conjured out of nothing.

So maybe magic wasn't as strange to me now. Or maybe because I'd been so isolated and lonely these last few months that I wanted it to be real. People had said over this whole viral journey that I was the main character of some kind of fairytale. For the first time, I actually felt like it.

The natural next questions about what happened when the show was over hovered at the edge of my mind. Yet I didn't want to think about those yet. For a couple of days, I wanted to fall into the luxury of being the mate of delicious monsters. Monsters that made me shiver and moan. They would be waiting for me.

"All done," the make-up artist declared. "Perfect."

"Thank you," I said. It was perfect. I looked and felt more alive than I had in weeks.

They ushered me into the interview space, and I was relieved that I wasn't dreading it.

CHAPTER NINETEEN

CHRISTINE

"*I* think we got it," Anne said, and I relaxed.

The photoshoot that I'd done before—the one that had resulted in that airport billboard—felt easy compared to this one. They'd hustled me in and out of four different costumes, and then some clothes. Vogue-like dresses and a suit that looked like armor.

The necklace was far heavier than it looked, but was gorgeous, the pink diamond glittering in the bright lights that they'd set up for the photos. More than that, like when I'd first seen it, the necklace pulled at me. The diamond almost seemed to hum when it touched my skin. Probably simply the awareness that I was wearing one of the more famous diamonds in the world.

Still, I liked the feel of it and the way it was alive. The rest of me was tired.

I was sure that the photos would be great, but I was dragging. My shoulder hurt from lifting the sword over and over again. When was the last time I ate?

The costume assistant had looked at the bruise on my shoulder, but said nothing, thankfully. She unpinned the dress that I was currently wearing and I slipped back into my own clothes. It felt a bit like I was putting my own skin back on.

"Anything else you need from me?" I asked Anne.

"No, Christine. Thank you." She put her hand on my shoulder. "Excellent work today."

"Thank you."

Like the connection between us was a physical thing, I felt him. Alex stood at the edge of the lobby, near one of the hallways that wove around the theatre and could lead backstage. It was an effort not to run.

He was leaning against the wall like he didn't have a care in the world, and I slipped into his arms like we'd been doing it for years and not days. His lips warmed my hair. They were so much taller than me. So much bigger. I already wasn't tall, but they made me feel absolutely tiny.

"*Bonjour, mon amour.*"

"That took way longer than I thought," I murmured, voice muffled in his shirt. Where did they get shirts? Where did they get money? I wanted to know everything.

"Let's go," he said quietly. "Or whoever's left in this lobby is going to get an eyeful of me kissing you."

"I don't care."

He laughed. "I don't think that's true." All at once, he stiffened, arms coming hard around me. His voice was identically hard. "We need to go. Now."

"What's going on?" I glanced behind me and saw Désirée with the blond man that I'd seen earlier. Who was now staring at me. Chills ran down my spine. A bad vibe. I knew that feeling. "I've seen him before."

"Yes, you have."

"Care to enlighten me?"

His hand tightened around mine. "We'll tell you together."

This time I paid attention as we wound through the backstage and through a hidden door that you could barely see and down into the bowels of the theatre. To their front door. "Well, now I know how to get here."

"The door will always be open for you."

The heavy curtain inside the door brushed over my shoulders, and I was back in their warm, luxurious space. Erik was waiting on the couch, Marius was nowhere to be found.

"You're still alive," he said with a smirk.

"The camera didn't steal my soul."

I slouched down onto the couch next to him, immediately wincing when I leaned against him on my right side. "Ow."

"Sounds about right," Alex said, heading for the freezer.

"I'm okay."

"You will be," he said. "We're making sure."

I blinked. "How?"

"Do you trust us?" Erik asked.

"Of course."

He slung an arm around my waist, easily rearranging me so that I was laying out on the couch next to him. "Marius will be here soon, with a friend. He's one of us, but a doctor. He is very discreet."

Panic immediately gripped me, and I pushed it back. It was just an instinctual reaction at this point. "I assume he doesn't want anyone to know that he's a gargoyle any more than I want people to know that I almost died."

Erik smiled before he kissed me. "Exactly."

This morning, and all day, I'd thought I'd see them and jump into bed right away. This, though, the warmth of being held, was intoxicating.

"Here we are," Marius said.

I was lifted back to sitting, across Erik's lap. This kind of closeness had never been comfortable to me. But right now it felt like the most natural thing in the world. I leaned back into him, and he tucked an arm around my waist.

The man with Marius looked like them. Big, tall, and handsome. Like them, he looked late twenties, maybe early thirties. He was carrying a bag, dressed in a black shirt with long sleeves. Honestly he looked...normal.

He spoke in French, asking Marius a question.

"*Oui*," Marius said, switching to English. "This is Christine."

The doctor crouched. "Hello Christine. My name is Laurent." His accent was thicker than my mates.'

My mates. Warmth flooded me. There must have been a change in my scent because all three of them turned towards me with wide eyes. I kept my eyes on the doctor. "Hello."

"Marius told me what happened. I think you are very lucky."

"Yes." And not only about the fact that I wasn't splattered on pavement.

He set down his bag and pulled out a stethoscope. "May I touch you?"

I nodded. He listened to my lungs and took my blood pressure on my good arm, not seeming to mind that Erik and I were attached at the hip.

"Okay, I'm going to examine your shoulder," he said gently. "You tell me if it hurts."

I took off the sweatshirt I had on over my rehearsal clothes so he could see it better. It didn't *look* good, that was for sure. Slowly, he touched my shoulder, probing the skin. It was still swollen, and it did hurt, but no more than a bad bruise. "A little."

He raised it slowly and rotated it. It did hurt, but nothing compared to what dancers normally went through. Based on this pain, it would be okay in a couple of days. "No more pain?"

"It aches," I said. "Sore. But it doesn't feel like there's anything wrong."

Laurent nodded once. "I agree. You are very lucky. I can't confirm there are no tears without a hospital, but—" he cut off and broke out into French.

Marius translated. "He suspects that if you'd actually torn something that you'd be in far more pain, and that if something feels worse or strange, we're to call him right away. Keep icing and take some painkillers."

My nerves eased. "Thank you."

More French was spoken, but I was relaxing. Alex brought me water and a couple of ibuprofen for me to swallow.

Laurent didn't leave through the opera entrance. I didn't think that he'd come in that way either. "Where did he come from?"

"This connects to the catacombs. The monsters in the city use them often."

"He's a gargoyle?"

"He is."

I laughed. "Guess if I have a problem it will have to be at night."

Erik blew out a breath. "No. That won't be a problem with Laurent. He's not bound the way we are."

The sound of a door closing distracted me. Marius reappeared without the doctor. "What do you mean? I thought all gargoyles were nocturnal."

"No. Only the unfortunate ones," Alex said. There was sadness in those words, deeper than I could describe.

"Okay," I said. "I'm torn between asking you to explain that and all my other questions, going to the kitchen or my apartment and grabbing food because I'm starving, and asking you to fuck me."

The sadness in Alexandre's eyes disappeared as he laughed. "What do you want to eat?" He asked, eyes darkening. "My mate being hungry is unacceptable."

My stomach growled in response. "I would kill for some pizza. But I doubt they're serving that."

Alex stood and walked in the direction Marius and the doctor disappeared. "Where are you going?"

"To get you pizza."

I stared after him, mouth open, until Erik laughed. "Why are you so surprised, *cherie?*"

"I don't know." I slipped off his lap, but kept my legs slung over his so we were still connected. "I'm surprised by all of this."

Erik leaned in and brushed his mouth over my bruised shoulder. "It is a hard thing to describe, the instincts that we have. You are the only thing that matters."

I scoffed. "That's not true."

"It is for us. The second your scent found us on the breeze, everything changed. Marius nearly tore himself from the building in his need to get to you."

My eyes widened. "When was this?"

"When you arrived at the opera house."

In my chest, my heart stuttered. That was only

days ago. "And before you knew about me? About this? What was important to you then?"

I was pretty sure that gargoyles were immortal, and none of these men seemed like the kind to sit and wait, content to do nothing. Hell, they'd created this entire place down here. I didn't even know if these rooms were a part of the original opera house or if they excavated them.

"Getting free of the opera house." Marius said, appearing again. "I heard we're getting pizza."

"Apparently," I smiled when he sat down on the other side of me so I was tucked between their warmth. It was comfortable, and my body relaxed even more, feeling that kind of safety. I leaned my head on Marius's shoulder. "Explain what you meant by 'getting free.'"

"What's your favorite stone?"

I blinked. "What?"

Marius laughed softly and turned his head to kiss my temple. "I promise it's relevant. Like a gemstone."

"Probably sapphire."

"Like your eyes," Erik said, running a hand along my jeans.

"Like my birthstone."

One side of his mouth ticked up into a smile. "Noted."

"Stones carry energy," Marius said. "Vibrations.

Like the way we can talk to you through the stone, that's using the energy. Your favorite stone usually indicates that the vibration is close to your own energy."

I smirked, snuggling down into them further and enjoying the way they let me. "Then can I choose *you* as my favorite stone?"

"You're not far off, actually."

"Really?"

He laughed. "I'm getting ahead of myself. Stones' energy can be changed. Temporarily or permanently. And that's what happened to us. The night of the famous fire, there was actually a thunderstorm."

I'd known that. The lightning from the storm set sparks that floated through the doors and after that, there was no controlling it. Then the opera had been little more than a stone husk until they started restoring it a year ago.

"There's a lot of history, but we were…fighting other gargoyles. Retreated to the opera house to regroup when the lightning hit. We were close enough together that it ran through all of us. It changed our stones' resonance to match the opera house. When that happens to a gargoyle—and it doesn't always happen through lightning, though that's common—we can only go as far as we can feel the resonance of *that* stone through the ground. And we become exactly what all humans imagine. Stone during the day and men at night."

That wasn't what I expected. "So if you weren't connected to this building, could you like…go out in the sunlight?"

Erik burst out with a laugh. "Yes, *cherie*. We're not vampires."

"But why do you have to be stone in the daytime?"

"The sun is more powerful," Marius said. "The energy it gives to the stone is stronger, and it forces us into that form. At night it doesn't hold that power."

That's why they said as soon as the sun stopped touching the building and not after the sun set. That made a weird kind of sense, at least.

"Even when it's cloudy?"

"The sun still shines, even when the clouds are there."

Annoying, but fine. "And what about me? Why was I right?"

Marius curved an arm underneath me, lifting and scooping me around until I straddled his legs and our faces were so close I felt his lips against mine. "That's the reason mates are so rare. Their energies are an *exact* match."

Oh.

"So I sound like the opera house? Energy wise?"

"Actually," Erik said, startling me with how close he was, "you're a match for the gargoyles we were. Before we were struck."

"All three of you?"

He laughed. "You do have a lot of questions."

"I warned you."

Marius kissed me, pulling me in and running his tongue along mine. It danced and plunged and stroked—very similar to something else of his. If Alex didn't hurry up with that pizza, I was going to move on to the fucking part of the evening. Because that was happening either way.

"We were made from the same stone. At the same time. Our energies matched from the start. In case you were worried. You were always meant to be ours."

My body shuddered involuntarily. When they said things like that, it crashed through me how deep it was. How vast and permanent. And how I didn't mind for one fucking second. It also made sense on more levels than I could process—the reason I seemed to let myself go and have those fantasies that I'd never let myself have with anyone else. That I trusted them before my mind thought I should. My body *knew*.

"So can we just get you struck by lightning again and get the hell out of here?"

He kissed me again, harder, like he was trying to distract me again. "If we're struck by lightning again, our vibrations would change so much that we would shatter."

"Fuck." I leaned my forehead on his shoulder. "Yeah, that was stupid. If that was the solution, you would have done it in the two-hundred years that you've been here."

His hands ran down my spine and back up again, over and over. I sank into the movement, wilting until I was boneless against his body. "Not stupid. It seems like it would be the way to go."

"I just thought if you could like...ground it to something else. Channel it like a lightning rod. But I guess stone isn't a great conductor."

Marius murmured. "Unfortunately. Maybe if we had something that matched us exactly, but finding something that matched our current energy *exactly* would be impossible."

"I match you."

He chuckled. "I'd rather you not die of electrocution."

"I'm guessing you don't know how to break it, then?"

"No."

I looked over at Erik. "Then I can't be the only thing that matters. Because I can't have mates that are stuck here."

He grinned. "My thoughts exactly. We have much better motivation to figure it out."

"I'm starting to need you more than I need pizza," I said.

"I'm going to fuck you last," Erik said.

"Why?"

That wicked smirk was enough to make me writhe, that now familiar heat licking down my spine. "Because you need to be *thoroughly* warmed up before you take me."

Warmth blazed across my cheeks. He wasn't wrong. Erik's cock was huge, and with his piercings? If I wasn't warmed up, it might hurt. There was an echo of an echo in my brain that wondered if the bite of that pain would be worth it.

"You're starting without me?"

I turned my head to find Alex with several boxes of pizza, smiling. As soon as I saw the pizza, my body forgot all about sex. "Yes. But now I'm going to consume an *ungodly* amount of pizza, and you're going to answer the rest of my questions. Then we'll start again. And you better be prepared to see me put away this amount of food."

"You're our mate," Marius said. "You are perfect,

no matter what percentage of pizza your body is at any given time."

"Good." I stood off his lap and retreated to a single chair so I wouldn't be distracted while I ate. "Because you've never seen a New Yorker eat pizza."

CHAPTER TWENTY

CHRISTINE

"Okay, let me get this straight," I said, pushing the empty plate onto the coffee table between us. It was littered with pizza boxes, plates, and drinks. I was pleasantly full.

The pizza itself wasn't as good as New York, but that was almost a given.

"You're connected to the opera house. Stuck during the day, and can only go so far at night. On the full moon you're not stuck, but you're a little closer to in-between forms because moonlight is sunlight—which is kind of werewolfy to be honest. You guys were powerful as fuck, and basically royalty until you got stuck here, and I'm your mate because my spiritual, essential, *soul* energy is an exact match for yours. We can make the mating thing almost physical by you guys going vampy and biting me, and you're all three totally okay with sharing because it's meant to be. There are more creatures than gargoyles. Pretty much every mythological creature is real. Did I get everything?"

Alex laughed. "I think so."

"Oh wait. You guys don't have a pulse?"

Marius shook his head. "Nope. Rocks don't need a heartbeat."

"But you're human too."

"It doesn't matter."

It was still weird, but I filed it away. "Okay. I only have a couple left, I swear."

Standing, Alex pulled his shirt over his head. My mouth went dry, and the words in my head went blank. He said something, and it was just fuzzy noise in my head. "What?"

"I asked if you had to sit alone for those questions."

I shook my head.

"Good."

He lifted me out of the chair like I was nothing, carrying me back to his own and arranging us together. I'd never been with anyone that did that—

let me sit on them and with them, tangled up. But now that I'd had it, it was all I wanted.

There was the tiniest relief when they were touching me that I now knew was because our energies matched. I loved that. Alex's scent was cool. It reminded me of the fresh air at night that swept off the rivers back home. Sometimes all the way from the ocean. It wrapped around me along with his arms, and I laid my head on his shoulder so I could see the others.

They told me about the connection mates could have after being bitten by the gargoyle, and had all said that we should wait. The mating frenzy was intense, and with the show, I couldn't afford to be practically chained to a bed for endless bouts of sex.

Though that sounded kind of nice.

"What are they?"

"Huh?" Just touching them distracted me.

Alex slowly kissed my cheek. "Your questions."

"Right." I cleared my throat. "You're…immortal, right?"

Marius said. "Yes. We can be killed, but we won't die."

Anxiety suddenly burned in my chest. I knew it was the part of my brain that was still in awe that this was happening and thought it didn't make sense to be talking about forever after such a short time. "So, what about me?" I asked softly.

I knew the answer before they said it. The regret and sadness was in Alex's eyes. He shook his head. "I've never heard of a human, immortal mate."

My heart sank. "That's it?"

"Of course not." Erik's voice was dark. "We're finding a way out of this building, and then we'll find a solution for that. The world is full of magic, Christine. We exist. The world may not have found that answer yet, rare as mates are."

"But," Alex said gently into my skin. "If we can't, it doesn't mean that we'll love you less."

I gasped at the word love. That's what this was, right? Impossible, beautiful love that's effortless. I didn't know that I could say it yet. But it was there, beating under the surface of my skin like my pulse.

"I'll get old."

"All humans get old," he said. "We've been alive a long time, Christine. We're not unfamiliar with people aging."

"Yeah." It seemed silly to be so sad about some-thing that would be years from now. But it also felt like just when they'd found me, I'd lost them.

"Don't worry about that tonight," he whispered. "I have too much fun planned for you for that."

I would try, but the heaviness still sat in my chest.

Shaking my head, I reached the last question. "Why couldn't I leave the opera house? And why did you pull me away so quickly?"

"I told you we were fighting other gargoyles," Marius said, leaning forward on his knees. In the warm light of the lamps, his hair shone a gentle gold. He'd pushed the sleeves up on the shirt he was wearing, and any woman that said that built men's forearms wasn't porn was flat out lying. "And that we were...powerful. Gargoyles almost never remember the moment of their creation, whether it was intentional or an act of wild magic. None of us know what creates the power that we have."

While I was face deep in my pizza they'd explained their power. Not magic in the traditional sense, but a connection to the world. They could go further from the opera house than others might be able to. And when gargoyles roamed freely, their power fell into a natural hierarchy.

My mates had never encountered someone more powerful than them. Paris had been their territory, functioning almost like Alphas of a wolf pack, until they were bound to the building.

"Right."

"The ones who took our place," Marius said carefully. "They don't want to risk that we'll ever come back to power. They want us to stay here."

"Did they have anything to do with you being bound here?"

A low growl shook beneath it. "We can't prove it, but we believe so." Then he sighed. "We're afraid that they'll use you to get to us. Speaking of mortality. If you die, even before we amplify our bond, it will be...unbearable for us. Could break us."

I knew when he said break, he didn't mean emotionally. He meant that their physical stone form could break. So when they told me not to worry about me getting old... "Even if I die of old age?"

"Yes."

"That sucks."

Alex smiled at that. "I would rather have a life with you, and follow you into the afterlife, than to be immortal alone. The others feel the same."

They confirmed it.

He turned my face back to his, and Alexandre's eyes were fully black. His hands were lengthening into claws. "But I will not let you be in danger because there are monsters in this city that hate us. They will kill you to hurt us and make sure that we never find a way to break our connection to the opera."

"Christine," Erik said. "The man who approached you at Club Spectre when I was taking you to dance."

"The blonde guy that gave me the creeps. I remember." And suddenly I understood. He was the one in the lobby, and the one who'd been with Désirée. "That's him? He was here?"

"His name is Callum. He's the current top gargoyle, along with his friends. None of them know that you're our mate. But if they find out, they'll try to get to you. Even without knowing, we think they'll try to get to you if only to hurt us."

"And you didn't want me to go outside so they couldn't try anything. But he was here. With Désirée."

"He's not going to touch you." Alex's voice was pure monster. Feral. "I will kill him."

The fact that the man who's lap I was sitting in just threatened to murder someone for me bothered me less than I thought it would. And the looks on both Erik's and Marius's faces told me they felt exactly the same. "I can't just stay inside, though," I said. "I know there are some things that I'll have to do for the show. Press. I'm pretty sure they want me to do some TV interviews."

"As long as you're not alone," Alex said. "Or without your security. Anything that the show has you do, they're not going to risk your safety."

I stared into the distance for a second. "I was going to ask you this anyway, but it's relevant now.

What do you want me to tell Meg? Tori, I'm not worried about. I don't think she even knew that the three of you wanted me in the club the way that Meg did. And if she asks, I can get out of it. Meg is a different story. Plus, she could watch my back, if she knew."

"How do you think she'll react?" Erik asked.

A laugh burst out of me. "She'll be over the fucking moon. I know you heard her. She already thinks it's my destiny to fuck monsters."

He grinned. "If she can keep the secret, I have no problem with it."

"But not tonight," Alex said. "Tonight, I think there's been enough talking. You're mine."

I smiled at the others. "Just yours?"

"Just mine."

Erik winked. "Remember what I said."

"I do." That he was fucking me last because I needed to be warmed up.

Alex stood, keeping me in his arms, and striding for the center of the three doors along the back wall. Inside was…everything I expected and nothing I expected too. The walls were rich and dark, like the living space. Alex flicked on a lamp, and the room was bathed in a golden glow.

A bed dominated the space. Four iron posts with

connected bars across the top. "I honestly didn't expect a bed. Do you guys sleep?"

"We don't have to as often as humans—and it's easy to nap when you're a statue—but beds are useful for all kinds of things. And I won't lie and say that I don't love a good nap in my human form."

"My kind of man."

"I'm about to be your kind of monster," he said, laying me on the bed. "You're all right being alone?"

I was distracted by the fact that he was peeling off his black jeans and that meant that I was treated to all that gorgeous skin. Unlike the others, he wasn't tattooed and pierced. It was just him, and he was beautiful.

He'd asked me a question, and I was just staring. "Obviously, all of you is great. But if every night was like last night or more, I think that you'd probably kill me with orgasms."

Alex crawled onto the bed, over my body like the predator he was. "There will be more nights like that. And nights with *more* than that."

I shivered. "All of you make me…" hauling in a breath, I laid back beneath him, letting him pin me with his stare. His body hovered inches above mine, and I could almost feel him, like we were magnets. "Last night when you held me down."

The sound he made was half way between a purr and a growl.

"It's like the things that I never let myself think about or want...the three of you bring them out of me."

A slower, sensual growl. "Because we want the things that you want. We're the same."

He stroked one set of claws up my side, and I arched into his touch. "If you keep tearing off my clothes, I'll have to buy new ones," I warned him.

"Or you'll simply be left with no clothes. Then you can stay in our beds." His wings grew and flared, heavy and wide. But he sheathed his claws long enough to yank my tank top over my head and toss it aside. My pants too.

"What do you want?" I asked. "If we're the same?"

Alex's eyes turned black, the color overtaking the whites of his eyes. The stare left me breathless. "I want to claim you."

"I'm already yours."

A snarl that had arousal twisting through my core. His hand touched my throat, claws tickling the sides of my neck. "I want to let the beast *out*, Christine."

I tried to disguise the fact that I was already breathless. "Then let it out."

"You don't know what that will mean."

"Am I your mate or not?"

His hand turned to stone against my skin. "Just because I'm your mate doesn't mean I can't hurt you. If I let the beast have control, I can't stop until he's finished."

"You won't hurt me," I said. My heart pounded in my chest in need. In anticipation. "Does your beast know who I am?"

"*Fuck yes.*"

"Then he won't hurt me either," I whispered. The space between us went tight, and for a second, I swore that I could feel him. His thoughts and need and the beast he was barely holding back. I didn't know where the words came from, but I didn't hesitate. "Take me, Alexandre."

He threw himself away from me, and the lamp went out. There was nothing but rich, velvet blackness, and the rumble coming from his chest. I felt him in the dark, watching, suddenly realizing that he could see me even when I could see nothing.

Claws dragged up my legs, bringing a gasp from me. I hadn't realized he was so close again. Those claws kept going, barely scraping my skin as he teased my breasts. The pin pricks grew heavier, from ticklish brushes to deeper. Riding the line of pain without crossing it, and I moaned.

My voice sounded loud in the dark until it was

met with a purr so deep the vibration alone made my eyes roll back.

His claws tightened again, testing me. "Please, Alex," I said.

I was a ballet dancer and convinced that you couldn't be one without liking some pain. It was too brutal a discipline for me to believe otherwise. And I was meant for them and they were meant for me… then it made sense for me to like that edge of pain. To *crave* it the way I craved the rest of them.

He was still holding back, but I felt the beast staring at me in the dark. "Tell me yes, Christine."

One final chance for me to say no. No chance in hell. "Yes."

His smile was audible. "Good girl."

The beast was unleashed. Stone claws on my thighs, shoving them apart to make way for the roughness of his tongue scraping over my clit. Softening. Warming. The incredibly talented tongue of a man before it petrified once more.

That same dark purr ran through my body. "Fucking delicious." Something made of stone shouldn't be able to move the way his tongue did, curling under my clit and circling, dragging pleasure out of me without remorse.

I forgot to ask them if being with them just made everything better. That was the way it felt. He dipped his tongue low, fucking me with it, deep as he could before dragging it up and around my clit once again.

A coil of pure heat wove through my center, gathering and growing. And it shattered into dust when he pulled away. "You'll come on my cock."

There wasn't any room for argument. Those words were law. Alex's tail slithered around my waist and lifted—*lifted*—me. A shriek of surprise came out of my lips, and I dropped to the bed on my stomach, only to feel him. All of him stretched along my body. Every piece of him was heavy. Solid. Delicious. Stone rough against my skin, cock cradled by my ass. Even the tips of rough feathers brushed my hands.

Fingers and claws wove through my hair, pulling my head back so his mouth—and those stone fangs —could reach my throat. "Who do you belong to, mate?" The rocky gravel of his voice matched the friction of his tongue on my skin.

Fuck.

I moaned, shoving myself up and back, trying to get him to move faster. Take me. It was starting to feel like last night, where if I didn't have him inside me I was going to lose my goddamn mind.

"Answer me."

Oh god. That was the voice of the monster, and I

shuddered. Pleasure washed over me, golden fire-works behind my eyes in the darkness. His voice nearly made me come. It was dripping down my thighs, and it wasn't nearly enough. "You," I managed, voice muffled in the soft comforter. "I belong to you."

The answering growl nearly made me come. "That's right. Now take me as I am."

Cold, hard cock at my entrance. He was stone. Fuck. So much bigger in this form than he was as a man, and in his human form he was still bigger than any other man I'd ever been with.

He pushed into me, and we both groaned. The cold only lasted for seconds, cock warming with my body. The shock of it only added to my pleasure.

In and in and in, slow, slick pleasure until he was buried deep, and his hips were flush with mine. My breaths were shallow, fighting the feeling of being so full. "Fuck," the word was the only thing that I could think. "Fuck."

Alex laughed, low and rich. "As you wish." His tongue dragged over the skin of my throat again before he moved his mouth to the place where my neck met my shoulder. "When you take my bite, it will be here."

His teeth closed over the place, hard enough to feel, not hard enough to break the skin yet. It was all

I could do not to beg for him to do it now. Bind me and make me truly his. I already was.

Again, I felt that sensation of predator and prey, and wanting to be caught. I savored the feeling of being conquered and taken. That's what he did.

The hand in my hair pushed my head further into the blankets as he began to move. Fucking me. There was no easing into it. He wasn't fucking me and then he was, every stroke heavy and hard. *Claiming.*

I couldn't move, held in place by his claws and teeth and cock and even his tail curling around my leg, spiraling to my ankle. Everything was Alexandre. Raw and feral, the beast taking what was his. Even his scent was stronger. Overwhelming.

It shouldn't feel this good—couldn't. It didn't seem possible that this level of pleasure could exist, but it did. Alex drove into me, every thrust ramming to the hilt and filling me over and over and over and hitting places inside me that made stars come to life.

There was no going back from this. Having mates could only be forever. I already knew that I was ruined for anyone but them. *Nothing* would feel like this.

Alex's tail slid off my leg, curling underneath me and finding my clit. The stone tip of the lion's tail teased me. I was so swollen, so sensitive that it was a match to my fuse.

Blinding ecstasy exploded. I screamed into the sheets, the slapping sound of his body in mine somehow in harmony with my moans. It drove him on. Everything was *more*. He fucked me harder, body lifting off mine to press me down further.

He growled, and I knew it was pleasure. Somehow I knew, and it shut my mind off. I now only existed in a haze of being fucked. Alex's tail writhed under my clit like a tongue, wringing more waves from my body.

Another orgasm was building under my skin, and for a second I thought it might kill me. In the next moment, I didn't care, because what a way to go. Alex moved faster, grinding with every thrust. Rough stone scraping, somehow transforming into a perfect storm that taught me what it meant to belong to someone.

It felt like his cock was getting bigger, if that was even possible. The sounds from him and the sounds from me were in sync. There was no control in my screaming, just pure need as every thrust felt like a new, smaller orgasm leading up to the tidal wave.

Alex's snarl ripped through me. *"Mine."* His teeth closed over that same spot, the scrape of pain heightening my pleasure to its peak.

I broke.

My throat would be raw in the morning from that scream. I fought him, my body taking what it needed. Thrashing and struggling for any way to get one extra fraction of him inside me. I was blind and deaf, the world narrowing to the point where we connected.

He jerked, rhythm faltering for a single moment, before he came with a roar. One mighty thrust, so deep that I was sure we were fused, and he stopped. His cock pulsed, filling me with heat, and then swelling larger at the base. It wasn't my imagination. Larger and larger, stretching me to the point of aching. Exquisite aching that had me gasping for more. There was no way that I would be able to get him *out* of me.

I shuddered, trying to catch my breath. He was still as only a statue could be, the only movement, tiny pulses of his hips, reminding me how thoroughly I was his. "Mine," he said again, but it was softer. A caress along with a kiss on the back of my neck.

"Wow," I said, breathless. Spent. I was empty of anything else.

Squirming, I tried to move, and was met with a low, warning growl. Almost a purr. "My body will release you when it's ready."

I moaned, aftershocks from still being stuffed full of him making me shake. "What does that mean?"

Slowly—so slowly, he scooped an arm under my body and moved to the side so we were laying connected, on my good shoulder. Claws gently stroked up and down my skin, soothing and arousing all at once. Instinctually, I squeezed down on his cock and moaned. It was too much. Too big. I knew that if I kept doing that—kept squeezing him —I would come again.

That I might not actually survive.

When he spoke, his voice was less monster and more man. Parts of him were warming and soft-ening to flesh. His chest behind me. The arm under-neath me. His cock was not one of those things.

"My soul is that of a monster. A beast. No matter that we're made of stone, our bodies and instincts are the same when I fuck you in that form. That includes my cock making sure that my cum is *deep* inside you as long as possible." He kissed the back of my head. "You know what they call that in your dirty wolf books?"

I sighed, smiling. "I'm never going to live that down, am I?"

"The fact that you read those and loved them made you believe us faster. I'm not shaming you for it. Please read more and tell me all the ways the characters fuck so we can try it."

I flushed, curling my face towards the bed. Not in embarrassment, but at the simple acceptance. Such a small thing. I was used to having to explain or justify. "Thank you."

His chest hardened enough that he could release a low, comforting purr. "But you know what they call it?"

I swallowed. "Knotting."

"Mmm. You feel good around mine."

There wasn't a chance that I could verbalize what I was feeling. Any time I moved, tingles of pleasure moved outward, begging us to start all over again. My needy body aside, it was the feeling of complete, utter contentment and safety.

It did feel like a knot. A thickness that I never thought would fit, let alone feel like this. Did he feel the same? I wiggled my ass, and the purr stopped short in a warning growl. "Baby girl, don't you dare move like that again. Or I will fuck you again, and harder."

"Hardly an argument against it," I muttered.

"If my knot doesn't ease? It gets bigger," he murmured into my neck. "And bigger. Takes longer for it to release. It's already reluctant to let you go. If you want to be able to go to rehearsal tomorrow, don't test me."

I tensed, still deciding whether to do it. The hand on my stomach shifted to claws that were now grazing my throat. "When we have you alone for days on end and there are no consequences for keeping my cock sheathed in you for indefinite amounts of time, I will fuck you until my knot is so big you'll think it will never come out. Since the entire world will notice if you're missing in the morning, you will stay still. Do you understand?"

"Yes." I would never get tired of that tone. Silk and velvet layered with a dominance that my entire being responded to.

A knock on the door sounded and Marius pushed into the room and turned the lamp on. I blinked, even the calm glow bright after the intense darkness. "I'm jealous," he said with a grin. "If I knew that's what you'd sound like, I would have knotted you last night."

"You'll have your chance," Alex growled. I felt the way he was fine with Marius's presence, but his beast was still on edge and possessive.

My other mate sat on the edge of the bed. "Your clit is swollen beautifully."

I squeezed Alex involuntarily and moaned.

"I wonder what would happen if I sucked it? A needy thing like that belongs in my mouth."

"Marius." The words were a warning. He was barely holding himself back. In the corner of my eye, I saw his tail flickering in irritation.

Marius laughed and Erik shouted from the other room. "Stop teasing them like you'll feel any different."

"Fair enough," he said, smiling at me. "I only came in to see how beautifully wrecked you look, mate. You sounded delicious."

I carefully reached out with one hand, letting him take it. "How long do you think it will take before I'm used to all of you saying things like that?"

"Hopefully never." He stood again, smirking at the way our bodies were locked together. "Let me know if you need anything."

The door closed softly behind him.

"It feels strange," I admitted, barely a whisper.

"What does?" Every part of his body was human now except for his cock. Still hard and thick—knotted—inside me. The rest of him had curled around me now, cradling me into his body.

I closed my eyes and breathed in the scent of him. "How everything is different," I said. "Just... instantly. One minute I'm walking backstage and the next second I have *mates*. Not only that, but it feels like the thing that was missing. What if this had never happened? This show. Or what if I never went viral to be in it? I never would have met you."

"But you did meet us," he said. "And I've never been happier."

My heart stuttered in my chest, butterflies flickering in my stomach. Everything was comfort, the crash from all that pleasure catching up with me now. "Don't want to fall asleep," I said. "Just want to be here."

Alex pulled me as close as he could. "If you weren't tired after all of that, I would think that I didn't fuck you hard enough."

"Definitely did."

I sank down into sleep, feeling the vibration of his laughter in my chest.

CHAPTER TWENTY-ONE

_____

CHRISTINE

"You're fucking kidding me." Meg said, completely ignoring the fact that she just spit water all over herself. "What's the punchline of this joke?"

"No punchline," I said. "Turns out you were right about the fact that I'm a monster fucker."

Telling her was going well so far. And my mates had no qualms about me sharing what had happened between us.

Alex had woken me early in the morning, our bodies having slipped apart in the night. I was barely conscious as he wrapped me in a blanket and carried me back to my apartment. No one saw us. It was the middle of the night, and I noticed that he was able to be silent more than I believed possible.

He held me in the shower, washing himself off my skin before putting me to bed. "I need to tell Meg," I whispered before he went to the window. "She's going to ask where I keep disappearing to. And she'll probably want a demonstration."

"We can do that."

"Not a naked demonstration."

He kissed my forehead. "That's only for you *mon amour*."

Rehearsal had been even better, the first few days of jitters wearing off and people becoming more confident in what they'd learned while in our separate preparation phase. Now Meg and I were in my apartment, taking a coffee break before we both had evening costume fittings, and I'd told her.

Luckily, the coffee was still brewing, so it was water and not coffee for the unexpected spit take. "Christine...*what*? Is this about the haunted voices you've been hearing? Cause I love you, but this sounds a little..." she paused. "I don't want to use the word crazy, because you're not. But you know how this sounds, right?"

Pressing my lips together, I flipped off the coffee

pot and grabbed mugs for us. "I'm very aware of how it sounds, believe me."

"Okay. Good. Good. And this is not a joke?"

"It is not a joke." I glanced at the time. The sun should have slipped off the building by now. "Any of you nosy eavesdroppers want to come back me up?"

Meg stared at me, and then jumped as the window creaked and Erik slipped inside. "What the fuck?"

"Nice to see you again," he said with a grin.

Alex and Marius slipped in behind him. The three of them together made me wish that we were alone. I locked eyes with Alex. "You were right, she needs a demonstration."

Erik reached out to shake her hand, and she took it, then immediately jumped back when his hand shifted to stone. "Oh my *fuck*."

"It was me on the roof," I said. "The four of us were up there talking, and I leaned on one of the not-alive gargoyles. It cracked, and I fell. The reason I'm alive is that they were able to catch me with stone hands."

It had been hard enough to say the gargoyle thing out loud—I hadn't been able to get the part about us being mates out. That probably would have been a few steps too far without seeing it for real.

"I have no words," Meg said.

I snorted into my coffee. "That's a first."

She glared at me, but the corners of her mouth twitched up.

Alex stepped around the others, coming to me and making sure I set down my coffee before wrapping me up. "How are you today?" The words were soft enough that Meg couldn't hear, but that didn't stop the blush as he kissed me. I was *so* good. Amazing what a couple days of excellent sex could do for your mental health. Now I didn't give a shit about the way Désirée glared daggers at me and mumbled when I walked past—or any of the cast and crew that had silently chosen sides between us. Because it didn't matter. Not when I had this with them.

That wasn't what he was asking. He was making sure that he hadn't hurt me. "I'm good," I said against his lips. "I'm not even sore."

It was the truth, even though I didn't know how it was possible. I'd ached between my legs from far less impressive sex. But with the three of them, my body seemed to be saying that it wanted everything and more.

"Fuck, you're cute." Meg said.

In the moments that he'd kissed me, I'd almost forgotten that she was here. And I realized that my feet weren't touching the floor. Alex had lifted me off them, and my arms were around his neck. This time, the blush was different.

I looked at my best friend as he put me down. "Surprised?"

"Yeah," she said. "I really am."

"But you're okay?"

A high-pitched giggle escaped her, and she clapped her hands over her mouth. "I mean...yeah? I'm the one who told you to go for it with them, right? If I told you no now, I'd be a bit of a hypocrite."

Erik pulled me back to his chest, wrapping his arms around my waist. "Please don't tell anyone else. It could be dangerous."

She looked shocked. "How?"

I let them explain the asshole who'd approached the two of us in the club and why he might want to hurt me.

"Wait," Meg held out a hand. "Mates. You're fucking *mates*? My god, you fucking lucky ass bitch."

"Told you she'd be fine," I said.

"And yeah." She waved a hand while taking a sip of coffee. "Of course, I'll make sure that she doesn't get grabbed by the evil gargoyles. That does *not* sound like a good time. But, if you happen to have any gargoyle friends that would like to have some fun with an American, by all means let them know."

Marius leaned against the bar. "I'm sure we could think of someone."

"So," Meg said, a gleam in her eyes. "Since you're mated and cozy and shit, I'm assuming she's told you about the dream."

"*Meg.*"

She rolled her eyes. "Don't '*Meg*' me. You're going to stand there and tell me the dream is not about them now?"

I couldn't say that it wasn't about them. But I couldn't say that it was, either. "It's just a dream."

"I'd like to hear about this dream," Erik said, not disguising the fact that my body was hiding his hardening cock.

"Should I let you tell it?" Meg asked. "Or should I do a dramatic retelling?"

"Aren't you late for your fitting?"

Pulling the phone from her pocket, she glanced at the time. "Not even a little. But I have a sneaking suspicion these three will be more effective at getting it out of you if I'm not here. Oh," she pointed at my mates. "Don't forget that she only has after-noon rehearsal tomorrow so she can sleep in. I'm borrowing your mug. See you downstairs, BYE!" She practically skipped out of the apartment, leaving me gaping after her.

"Traitor!" I called after her and heard the laughter in response.

"A dream?" Marius asked.

"It's nothing," I said. "Just a recurring dream that Meg won't let me live down."

Erik spun me so my back was against the bar, crowding me. "She was right about one thing though. I'm sure that we can get it out of you."

"It's nothing."

Alex chuckled, crossing the room and helping himself to coffee. "Your scent tells us that you're lying."

"Shit."

They laughed, and Erik pressed himself harder into me. "Are you embarrassed?"

"Maybe."

Marius reached out, rubbing my shoulders from where he stood behind the bar. "I bet we could get it out of you if you were screaming. Should we test it?"

"I mean yes, but I have to be downstairs soon."

"Sounds like you should just tell me," Erik said.

I reached for my coffee and managed to grab a sip even while his body was distracting me. "The three of you are relentless. You know that?"

"Yes," they said at the same time.

"Okay." I closed my eyes. If I really didn't want to tell them, I knew that they wouldn't force the issue. It wasn't that I didn't want them to know. It just felt so vulnerable. But if I couldn't be vulnerable with them, then who? "In the dream, I'm being chased. But not like a dangerous chase. I never see who it is, because it's dark. Yet I always know that when I'm caught, they're not going to hurt me." I swallowed. "They're going to fuck me. I've never made it that far in the dream. It always ends just before they catch me. And I usually have to take matters into my own hands."

No one spoke, and my stomach twisted. Erik was entirely still against me. That monster stillness. I opened my eyes to darkness. Erik's eyes were completely black, filled with enough heat to set me aflame. "You want to be chased, baby girl?"

My mouth went dry. Did I want that? "I keep dreaming it."

"That's not a yes or a no." He leaned down to whisper in my ear. "Because I can make that happen."

It was hard to pretend that my heart wasn't pounding in my chest and that I was having a hard time breathing. Another fantasy that I'd shoved aside because it wasn't 'normal.' Because it was on the darker edge of things, and there was no way to do it safely.

But with them...

"How? If Callum and his friends are looking for me, anywhere we go would be dangerous. And it's not like you can chase me through the opera house with hundreds of people living here."

He lifted me so I was sitting on the bar, standing between my legs. He was so tall that he was pressed against me *exactly* where I needed him. "You let me worry about that. All you have to do is say yes, if it's something you want."

"And what about you?"

One eyebrow raised. "You feel my cock? I am barely in control of my beast at the thought of chasing you." His voice dropped into a lower register —the gravelly, rocky sound of the gargoyle. "Hear your heart pounding and feel you underneath me on the ground. Making you *mine*."

I didn't let the relief show—that they'd reacted that way. It was the same with Alex's comment about my books. Things that I would half to get used to being open about, and not worried.

Like he knew exactly what I was thinking, Alex came for me, reaching around me and sliding a hand into my hair. Erik stepped back and let Alex step forward. He tugged, tilting my head back so I could look nowhere but at him. "We match you," he said. "There is nothing that you can tell us that will shock us or make us think less of you. It doesn't matter how dark or how dirty you think it is. You are *ours*. Your deepest, blackest desires were made to mirror us. You want to run? We want to chase you. You want to let us tie you down and fuck you with our tongues and tails until you forget the power of speech? It would be my pleasure." That last word turned into a purr that reached into the center of me and *pulled*.

"So there will be no more hiding things that you think are embarrassing, or worry that we're going to think something other than the fact that you're our mate, you're the most beautiful fucking thing we've ever seen, and that every second we're not touching you is driving us to madness. Do you understand?"

It was the same tone as last night. No room for argument. "I understand," I said. "But I can't promise. It'll take me time to…unlearn it."

Alex smirked, grip tightening ever so slightly in my hair. "If you need to have it spanked, sucked, or fucked out of you, I promise you none of us will care about giving you the reminder."

"Noted." I didn't doubt it for a second, and I also didn't have the time to tell them that spanking was another thing on that list. But we were going to have time for all of it. "I have to go to my costume fitting."

"We'll see you when you're finished."

Yes. Yes, they would. I forced myself away from them and out of the apartment before I actually was late.

The costume section of the opera house was huge and *packed* with costumes for everyone. Despite being the title character, I actually only had a few. The chorus members and dancers like Meg had far more.

She was still waiting in line when I arrived, and her smile was bigger than the fucking Cheshire Cat. I held out a hand and lowered my voice. "Not here."

Meg pounced on me anyway, hugging me around the shoulders and spinning me around. "I'm just so fucking happy for you. Seriously. It felt weird to say it in front of them. But it's amazing."

"I knew you'd be happy, but not *this* happy."

"Girl," she sighed, pulling back and moving us away from the other gathered cast. "Ever since the whole video thing happened, you haven't been happy. I mean, you were excited about this and the opportunity, but you weren't happy. That night when you sang in the video you were bubbly and happy and *free*. I haven't seen that girl since then. Except just now. With them."

"Really?"

She made a face. "Do you have any idea how wide you were smiling when that man picked you up? *Off the floor?*"

I smiled as she said it, but I honestly hadn't realized. At the time, I'd been too wrapped up in Alex to notice, and that was exactly her point. "It doesn't feel real."

"I'm not gonna lie. The whole *gargoyle* thing is going to take some getting used to." She whispered the word.

"For me too."

"But I am going to need to know every fucking detail of that kind of sex."

I flushed and looked around. "Maybe I'll tell you when we're not in a building where they can hear every conversation thanks to the vibrations in the stone."

Meg's eyes went wide and then she covered her face with her hands. "Wow. Okay, yeah."

"And only maybe."

"Come on," she whined, bouncing up and down. "You get monster dick and I can't hear about it?"

"Oh my god," I laughed. "*Later.*"

She moved back to her group. "Fine. But you are so not off the hook."

I rolled my eyes, but I was smiling as I went

further down the costume space to where the leads were being fitted. Far less crowded, there wasn't a line to enter the shop for our costumes, and I pushed open the door, and froze.

Sitting on a chair, waiting in front of the pedestal where Désirée was being fitted for a gown, was Callum.

CHAPTER TWENTY-TWO

MARIUS

*A*lex finished the coffee he'd poured in Christine's apartment before we thought about leaving. It was nice to be in her space—surrounded by her scent—even when she was away. "We should have gotten actual jobs on the crew," I said. "So we'd have a reason to be seen with her."

"I don't think that would work, since we could only show up at night," Alex pointed out.

"Still."

Erik was pacing slowly around the space, arms crossed. I could practically feel the tension in him, though we weren't connected in this form. He noticed me watching. "I want to take her to the park."

There was a relatively large park on the very edge of our range, away from the opera house. It would be perfect for what Christine admitted that she wanted. Good-natured jealousy sprang into my chest. I wanted to be the one to chase her, and one day I would be. But Erik deserved his moment with Christine. He was the last one to fuck her—for good reason—that didn't mean I still couldn't be jealous of the fact that he was going to be buried inside her again.

Now that she'd had Alex's knot and welcomed it, I needed her to have mine. I wanted to be locked to her body for hours. Days.

"So take her to the park," Alex said, shrugging.

"It's a dangerous idea. So close to the edge of our territory, and them looking for her."

That was a good point. "The catacombs?"

"Still dangerous."

Any place outside the opera house was danger-ous. They would have to be crazy to try to take her directly from here while we were in the building. If Callum, Sebastian, Witt, or any of the others that ran with them touched Christine, they would die. It was that simple.

An idea came to mind. The Tuileries were close

by. Not the park that he was talking about, and not a place you could go for what he wanted. But there were also tunnels all over Paris. Not just the catacombs, but a network created by monsters and creatures who needed to travel through the city without notice.

Beneath the gardens, there was a section of those tunnels that was open and excavated. There, the city had begun to carve out the space for an underground mall and then abandoned the effort.

Right now, it was dark, empty, and damp because of its proximity to the river. "I have an idea."

"All ears," Erik said. He'd switched back to French, which we often did out of habit. Eventually, Christine would absorb the language through our connection, and we'd be able to speak in either language.

"That space under the Tuileries. Do we know any river nymphs who owe us a favor?"

He looked at me. "What do you mean?"

"Turn that place into a garden. Or whatever the hell you want it to be. It's close, it's surrounded by stone. There's only two entrances. Alexandre and I could each watch one. We'd know long before they arrived, if they did."

"That's not a bad idea," Alex said, washing out the

271

mug that he'd used. "We can keep it that way. Use it for more than you playing hunter as well."

Erik scrubbed a hand over his face. "It's been a while since I talked to Penelope."

She was the ancient river nymph that watched over this section of the *Seine*. Grumpy most of the time, she could be bribed for favors. Plus, she liked us since we took pains never to pollute the river. She remembered those who did.

"Better get over there," I said.

"Right." He went to the window. It was faster, and the likelihood of being spotted was actually lower. Especially now, compared to what it used to be. The age of smartphones was excellent for monsters—people looked up much less.

Alex placed his hand on the wall and grinned. "Her friend is more excited than she showed."

"Think Laurent would be interested?"

"Maybe."

I made a note to ask him if he was looking for anything the next time that I saw him. "Have you thought of anything new?"

"No."

None of us had come any closer to figuring out what would sever our energy from the building without killing us. Lightning was too much. We'd already tried things like guns and magnets. The effect on our chemistry just wasn't enough. Not like the way lightning completely went through you.

Even simulated lightning would be more likely to crumble us into dust than help. The fact that we were stuck here grated under my skin like a visible thing now that it was keeping me from Christine.

"But we'll think of something." His voice was soft and spoke to the doubt in my head. That after so long, we *wouldn't* find anything.

He still had his hand on the wall and went still. "What?"

"Listen."

I pressed my hand to the stone. Christine's voice called me immediately, jumping out from the rest of the jumble. "I don't want him in here."

"You don't get a say in that. Just because you're Joan doesn't mean you get to all the shots. Callum is my guest, and I want him here."

Everything went silent in my head. Callum was here. In the building *again*. In the same room as my mate. Alex and I were moving to the door in unison. Nothing mattered except for her. Not the potential appearance of two men coming out of Christine's rooms. Not the fact that if enough people kept seeing us in the opera house they would start to ask questions. Nothing except for her and the fact that she was too close to that monster.

We were entering the costume loft when Callum came striding towards us like he hadn't a care in the world.

"Get the fuck out." My voice was a snarl that I was holding back, along with my gargoyle form. It was barely beneath the surface, waiting for this asshole to give me a reason.

"I was invited," he said lightly. Then he sniffed, and his eyes went dark. Too dark for a human. "Oh, my. This just got far more interesting."

Fuck.

He could scent her on us. Scent *us*. And the way we were connected.

"What are the chances that the three of you would find a mate? I guess I underestimated her at Club Spectre."

Both Alex and I stayed silent. We were on a hair trigger as it was.

"I think I'll be going."

We followed him all the way downstairs and out through the lobby. The fact that he knew where he was going so easily put me on edge.

Callum turned on the steps of the opera, the sky fading to full dark. "She's pretty, your mate. If I'd known what she was then, I would have shown her how much better life would be without you."

Alex straightened, looking him straight in the

eyes. "You outnumber us, with all your little follow-ers. All this time, you've hated us and feared us, and yet after we were bound to the opera house, you never came after us again. You know what I think?"

He rolled his eyes. "I'm dying to."

"You either think that you can't beat us, or you know that the knowledge that you were the one that 'beat' us, keeps your power strong."

Alex and I both knew there were gargoyles of similar power to Callum. Close enough that he could be challenged for this territory. Paris was coveted for the amount of old stone and statuary here. Ideal for creatures like us.

"Imagine how people will look at me once I'm the one that killed you. And if I didn't even have to fight you? That story would fuel me for more than two hundred years. Paris would be mine for a thousand."

I sighed. "Until some gargoyles just like us came along and simply took it from you because the world beneath your feet recognizes that they're more than you."

Callum bared his teeth. "When I get my hands on her—"

There was no breath between the seconds that I was standing away and then in his face. "If you want to declare war, Callum, do it. But know that the second any of you set foot in our territory, or touch the stone of the opera house, we can and will kill you."

He stared at me, like he was weighing up whether I was joking. Then he curled his mouth into a smile. "No war. Not yet. I like that woman's pussy too much to bar myself from this place."

We watched him walk away down the rest of the steps. I considered doing it now. Ending it. But that would start a war that we couldn't win, automatically turning all the gargoyles of the city against us out of sheer instinct. If they came to us, it was just Callum and his band of lost boys.

Hesitating, he turned at the bottom of the steps. "I was content to let the three of you rot in that crusty shell of a building like you deserved. But now you have luxury, and a mate. Things you don't deserve." A mocking grin. "I'm just returning things to their natural order. Your mate will be mine, one way or another. And I will make sure that you watch her die."

Alex's hand flattened to my chest, holding me back from taking another step towards him. Only Callum could make that kind of threat while not actually declaring war.

We watched him disappear across the square, hands in his pockets, and I could hear the fucker whistling. I clenched my jaw so hard that it creaked in protest. Imagining the snap of his neck was so satisfying, I did it three times before I was able to move.

"Let's get back to her," Alex said. The same tension was in his voice. But for now. In order to keep Christine alive, we couldn't touch him.

CHAPTER TWENTY-THREE

_____

CHRISTINE

"You are not welcome here," I said to Callum.

Désirée turned to me, rage on her face. "He's with me."

Straightening my spine, I focused on the head seamstress at the far end of the room. "I don't want him in here."

"You don't get a say in that. Just because you're Joan doesn't mean you get to all the shots. Callum is my guest, and I want him here." Désirée turned back to the mirror like it was final.

"If you want to give your 'friend' a fashion show,

do it on your own time. I don't want to be fitted for my costumes in front of strange men."

"Strange? I'm wounded." Callum stood, and I just stared at him. He just chuckled. "Seems my presence is no longer desired, my love. But I shall see you later, and I look forward to a private fashion show."

Now that I knew what he was, I could see the signs. Tall enough that Désirée didn't have to lean down on the pedestal when he kissed her. Kissed her in a way that would make me blush in front of other people. She just smirked at me when she pulled away with smeared lipstick. "Fine."

Callum winked at me as he passed, and I hated the feeling that I got. If my energy was an exact match for my mates, it was the opposite of Callum's. Just being in his vicinity made me feel on edge.

I glanced at Désirée as I passed. Did she know what he was? I didn't think so. She wasn't discreet, and it seemed like the monsters in the city—I had no idea how many there were—thrived on that secrecy. Obviously, since nobody knew they existed.

The seamstress—whose name was Anna—smiled at me. We'd talked quite a bit over the last couple months between measurements and being shown the sketches of the costume. I was even sent muslin mock-ups to try.

"It's nice to meet you in person," I said.

"You as well, Christine. Let's try the gown first. That is the one that needs to be the most precise."

"Okay."

The dress was beautiful, a pearly off-white that shone in the cool lights of the studio. "This is beautiful."

Anna smiled, but her mouth was full of pins. I let her focus, instead looking at myself in the mirror. The large bell sleeves fell to my fingertips intentionally. It was tough to resist spinning or twirling my arms to see them move.

The hem was too long, and Anna pinned her way around it before helping me delicately take it off. The undergarments for underneath the suit of armor I was going to wear were nearly perfect, and comfortable. The armor itself wouldn't be ready until next week.

My last costume was the shift in which Joan of Arc was burned. It didn't have to be as perfectly fit. I was obviously supposed to look disheveled. Anna pinned some alterations anyway. She was quick and efficient, and in less than an hour I was slipping my own clothes back on.

Anna disappeared into the back of the workshop, and at the next set of mirrors, where I'd first passed her, was Désirée. She finished with her costumes a while ago. Glancing behind me, there was no sign of Anna, and I sighed.

We were doing this, then.

I almost made it past her before she grabbed my arm. "You are an ungrateful little bitch."

"Take your hands off me, Désirée."

"You're lucky this is all I'm doing after what you pulled. That role should be mine. If you had any respect at all, you'd walk away."

Looking over, I shrugged off her hand. "What the fuck is wrong with you?" Her eyes went wide, and for a second I thought she was going to slap me, so I kept going. "You know damn well that I didn't ask for this. And if you had been in my position, you wouldn't have said no. So, by all means, be a bitch to me. Keep your feelings hurt and turn half the cast against me. It's not going to change anything but the way people look at *you*."

All of that wasn't what I'd planned on when I opened my mouth, but it felt good to get it off my chest.

"You don't think that Anne and Raoul and literally everyone in the cast see how you're reacting to this? It doesn't matter if you feel it's justified. You know this industry as well as I do. People will remember you like this. So feel free to hate me. I'm sure that you do. But know that I don't give a shit."

I was at the door when she called after me. "I'm your understudy. You know that, right?"

Closing my eyes, I stopped and took a breath. It would be so easy to say something sassy that would piss her off. But I took another breath, and another. I had to live by my own advice if I was going to say it to her. So I turned and smiled. "I know. Thank you. I appreciate it."

The gleam faded from her eyes, and that was way more satisfying than anything else I could have done. Her eyes were on me until I disappeared. I sensed them.

Instead of going back to the apartment, I went downstairs. The apartment meant I might run into Désirée again, and it was better if she didn't see me for a while.

"Hello?"

The curtain inside the door barely brushed aside before Marius had me up against the wall inside the door. "Did he touch you?"

Callum. He was talking about Callum. "No," I breathed. "He was barely there. Left when I made a fuss."

"Good," he barely managed the word before he kissed me. "Good. Otherwise, I would have been pissed that I didn't kill him."

My stomach flipped. "You saw him?"

"We made sure that he left the fucking building," Alex said.

That was a relief. "He feels wrong. Whenever I'm around him I swear our energies clash."

"They better," Marius growled.

I almost teased him about being jealous, but there was no humor in his face. That wasn't funny to them. Hell, it wasn't funny to me. "I'm okay." The words were gentle, but they snapped a measure of life back to his eyes.

"Yeah. Sorry. I just—" His jaw worked, and glancing at Alex showed pure, unadulterated rage on his face.

"What happened? What am I missing?"

"He knows you're our mate."

I bit my lip. "That's bad, right?"

Alex inclined his head. "Yeah, it's bad."

I didn't ask how bad. Right now, I didn't want to know. For the night, I wanted to be done with the outside world. Twining my arms around Marius's neck, I smiled. "It's a good thing I have the three of you to keep me safe."

Marius leaned his forehead against mine, and I couldn't help but feel the sadness in that motion. Quiet desperation.

"Where's Erik?"

That made them smile. Or at least it lessened the

intensity of their instinct to protect. "Making a surprise for you. We're going to take you to him."

"Away from the opera house? But you just said about Callum…"

Marius released me from the wall and took my hand. "We're going through the tunnels, to a place that's controlled and within our reach. You'll be safe there. Alex and I will be watching the entrances."

"While I?"

He just smiled.

Across the room, there was a door hidden in an alcove. Barely visible. Alex opened the door for us, and we stepped into blackness. "I can't see anything."

"How unfortunate," Alex said, stealing me from Marius. "I guess I'll just have to carry you.

My legs were swept out from under me, my squeak echoing. "Oh my God we're actually in the catacombs."

"Technically, the catacombs, as most people think of them—with skulls in the walls and such—are a little to the south." Marius's voice echoed in front of us. "But there are tunnels like this all over the city."

Where anyone who knew about them could access them. "Alex, are you carrying me because it's dark? Or because if you sense something wrong it will be easier to run with me?"

He lifted me higher and unerringly kissed my temple. "Why can't it be both?"

They were thinking of how to protect me even when it was just darkness they were protecting me from.

Occasional spots of light peaked through the darkness, but the black remained remarkably consistent. "I have a question," I said. "But it might sound silly."

"What is it?"

"In the middle of…everything last night, I wanted to ask. Does being your mate make things feel better? Or is that just a gargoyle thing?"

Alex laughed wickedly. "As much as I'd like to say that it's a gargoyle thing, it's a mates thing. Our energies resonating."

"Okay, so I'm not imagining that you guys touching me feels better than anyone else I've ever been with."

"You are not imagining," Alex said, voice dropping. "But I will ask you a favor."

"Mm?"

He tightened his grip. "While my beast is so close to the surface, don't mention your previous lovers. When all it's thinking about is the threat on your life, it doesn't distinguish between those threats. Even men who I'm well aware you don't care for."

Suddenly my body couldn't move. "He threatened me?"

Alex slowed his walk. "Yes."

"Why didn't you tell me?"

"Because we're not going to let it happen," Marius said in the dark.

I placed a hand on Alex's chest, drawing him to a stop. "I know that. I don't doubt it. But if someone threatens my life, I deserve to know about it."

The darkness filled with a tense silence.

"Say something, because I am completely serious."

"All right," Alex said.

We started moving again slowly, a tinge of awkwardness still in the air. But Alex moved his thumbs back and forth, stroking my skin in apology. A few minutes later there was light in the tunnel. Faint, but growing. They both stopped, and Alex set me on my feet.

"I am sorry." Alex stroked a hand down my arm, holding my hand.

"Thank you."

One kiss brushed across my lips. The brief connection released the lingering tension.

Marius turned me to him. "*Je suis desole.*" He just held me, tucking my head beneath his chin, so tall that he had to lean down to do it. "I mean it. I'm going to keep you safe, no matter what."

"I know." I whispered it into his shirt.

"I'm interrupting something?" Erik asked, appearing from the direction of the light.

"It's all right. I'm sure they'll tell you later."

He looked between Alex and Marius before focusing back on me. "Ready for a surprise?"

"Sure." I still felt a little awkward and tense, but it was also the first time we'd had any kind of disagreement. It wouldn't be the last.

Regardless, I was glad they would be close by. Having them far away after that felt strange. I knew they wanted to protect me—that the monsters that they were wouldn't allow anything else. In practice, that was going to take some time to work out.

"Are you all right?" Erik asked quietly.

I nodded once. "Yes. Or I will be."

He looked at me, but didn't press. Either they would tell him or I would tell him later. But he'd gone to the trouble of making some kind of surprise for me, and I wanted to honor that.

"This is going to sound strange. But I need you to take your shoes off. Socks too."

"You're right. That does sound strange."

What little light there was danced in his eyes. "I

promise I'm not going to feed you to sharks feet first."

My laugh echoed off the damn walls. I toed off my shoes and slipped my socks inside them. Whichever of my mates was guarding this entrance could keep an eye on them. I left my keys too.

"Close your eyes," Erik said, stepping behind me to put his hands on my shoulders.

"That kind of surprise?"

He laughed. "I want the grand reveal."

The light got brighter behind my eyes as he led me the rest of the way down the tunnel. "Step down."

I did.

"One more." It was a bigger step this time. "Open your eyes."

My jaw dropped.

We were standing in the entrance of an underground space easily the size of a football stadium. The walls were ragged, some of them looking like they'd been abandoned in the middle of being carved. Vines and moss cascaded down those same walls, creating a softness that looked like velvet.

Trees and grass—an entire woods spread across the room. Tangled and messy and wild. Like someone had planted this a hundred years ago and we'd just found it.

And the light...there wasn't any true light. But

there were things that glowed. Plants and trees, flowers and moss. It was a dim glow, enhanced by the damp fog in the air.

"This is amazing."

"I'm glad you think so."

I glanced at Erik before continuing down the steps to the bottom. Soft, spongy grass lay under my feet. I wiggled my toes in it, glad that he'd had me take off my shoes. "You just knew this was here?"

"No." He rubbed a hand on the back of his neck. "Its only existed for about an hour."

My jaw dropped a second time. "You *made* this for me? How?"

"I didn't make it," he said. "But I talked to a friend. A nymph. And she agreed to help me."

"I hope you didn't sell your soul."

"No. She's partial to shiny things. A few diamonds did the trick. This is under the *Tuileries*. Over there, if you take those stairs, you'll come out by the river, which is the edge of how far we can go in this direction."

"Diamonds? Where the hell did you get diamonds?"

He grinned. "We can sense other things in the ground besides just sound. And if they're close enough, we can pull them to us.

Oh my god, that was something that I would

have to come back to. That was so fucking cool. "Why?" I asked then. "It's beautiful, but why did you make this?"

Erik cleared his throat. "This morning, when you told us about the dream. It wouldn't be safe to take you to a park with Callum looking for you. And I didn't want to chase you through the tunnels. We needed somewhere we could be safe."

My heart rate picked up. "You want to chase me?"

Erik's eyes spiraled into black. "I do."

"Well," I swallowed. "I love it, thank you. And it's a good thing you made it. Callum was at the opera house, and while I was in my fitting I guess he threatened me. That's why it was awkward back there. They didn't tell me about it until Alex mentioned it by accident."

He went deathly still. "What?"

"You deserve to know as much as I do, or I'd be a hypocrite." The look on his face told me that he was thinking of dragging me out of here and back to their rooms below the opera. But I didn't want that. "Which is why this gift is absolutely fucking perfect."

"We should go back. This changes things."

"Is it still controlled?"

"Yes."

I smirked. "Are my other mates watching and protecting us?"

"Yes."

"Then nothing's changed." I twisted my arms around his neck, pulling myself up so I could almost kiss him. The confrontation with Désirée, the thought that someone was trying to kill me, and the worried tension in my chest that I wanted to erase— all of those things made me bold. Erik gave us a gift. I wanted to use it. I whispered. "Come on. Play with me."

His response was immediate. The attention focused on me sharpened like a knife, and I felt Erik take a step back and his gargoyle take a step forward. Telling him about Callum would only make the monster that more feral, and I wanted it. I *craved* it.

Fingers fisted in my hair, pulling my head back so I was looking at him. "You want this?"

Heat rolled through me. That tone did things to me that I would never be able to explain. "Yes."

"Watch." Erik's free hand grabbed my arm, and with one flick of a claw, scratched me. One motion lifted the scratch to his mouth and ran his tongue over it. It healed before my eyes. "If you get scratched, don't worry. And if you need to stop—"

"I won't."

He paused. "If you need to stop, say my name."

"Got it." My voice was only breath. Say his name because he would be buried beneath.

"I'll give you five minutes." His voice was low. "And then I'm going to hunt you."

I shivered, goosebumps running over my entire body.

"You know what happens when I catch you?"

Not if. When.

When he caught me, he would fuck me. And I would love every second. "Yes."

"I want your permission, Christine. When I catch you—and I will catch you—you're mine. I'm going to hold you down and fuck you until you scream. It will not be gentle."

The arousal that swirled under my skin was intoxicating. I pushed aside the voice in my head that told me that I shouldn't want this. That it was fucked up. Maybe it was. I still wanted it. "I give you permission," I whispered. "To fuck me like you *don't* have permission."

The monster's black eyes took on a feral gleam, and he smiled, releasing me. "Run."

My hesitation only lasted for a second. Erik pulled his shirt over his head and tossed it aside, chest transforming and wings appearing. My monster.

I ran.

CHAPTER TWENTY-FOUR

CHRISTINE

*T*he woods were foggy, the air thick with water. And more than that, they were *silent*. No animals lived in these woods. The only sounds that I could hear were the occasional dripping of water and my own breathing.

Inside the trees it was darker, the luminescent glow filtering through the fog. My heart pounded, and more. This was like my dream.

Had I been dreaming of him? I didn't know.

"Three minutes." Erik's voice echoed.

I wasn't going to make it easy for him. He wasn't going to make it easy for me. The sense of danger made me focus, and the fact that it was Erik made me calm. This was my mate hunting me. A game for us to play.

He could scent me. That was going to make it almost too easy, unless I did something. To confuse the beast.

I sprinted away from where I knew he was, dodging the trees, and I took my shirt off as I went. I ran until I reached the other side of the woods, dropped my shirt, and retraced my steps before branching off and creating a different path.

Doubling back one more time, I broke off the path one more time. It wouldn't slow him for long, but he wouldn't be able to walk straight to me. I hoped.

"One minute."

The far corner. That's where I wanted to be. It was an obvious place, to be as far away from him as possible. Maybe that would make him question.

A group of four trees clustered together creating a little hollow, and I slipped into that, crouching. The dim twilight was eerie, as I tried to see through it, wondering if he'd moved closer or started earlier.

I forced my breath to slow and become more even. I would need to run again, and I needed to be able to breathe when I did it.

"Where are you?" He called, voice almost a singsong.

Pressing my lips together, I tried to breathe as little as possible. I wasn't sure how good gargoyle hearing was, but if it was like the rest of their senses, even the slightest sound would give me away.

"You can't hide from me." The voice seemed to come from everywhere in the mist. Hair prickled on the back of my neck, everything in body tightening. My nipples were as hard as if I were outside naked in winter. And between my legs...

A branch snapped.

Adrenaline exploded through me, freezing my body into absolute stillness. I was a rabbit being hunted. A bird about to be flushed out and shot down. Every sense that I had was sharper.

There.

Movement through the trees. A shadow of a shadow of a shadow. Maybe simply a shift in the fog.

Low, wicked laughter crawled across my skin. "Clever girl, trying to trick me." He'd found my split scents then. "That won't keep me from finding you."

I saw him. Through the fog, form fading into silhouetted reality. Wings spread like a dark angel, the movement too smooth, too practiced to be human. I heard him inhale, searching for me. He was still a small distance away. I held myself still against the urge to run *now*. If I moved, he was close enough to hear and see me.

Erik walked right, disappearing from my field of view behind the trees. No more words, just that utter, close silence. Even echoes were dampened in the fog.

If I didn't know better, I would say that I was alone. Everything was calm and quiet. Peaceful if it weren't for the frenzy in my brain.

Behind me, awareness prickled. And then the soft, almost peaceful sound of a purr.

I bolted, flinging myself out of the trees. There wasn't time to try to trick him. The roar behind me told me that. Heavy stone footsteps that shook the ground. He was so much more powerful—so much faster. I shouldn't have run.

An arm looped around my waist, and I gasped, my whole body slammed back into a tree. It scraped my skin and was thick enough that I couldn't use it to twist away from his grasp. He had me.

Erik's hand was at my throat. This wasn't a gentle threat. He squeezed slowly. Just enough to send brand new fear and arousal through me. My hands grasped at his arm anyway, even knowing it was useless against that kind of strength.

"You know how I knew which trail was real?" He leaned close, dragging his tongue up the side of my throat, just outside his hold on me. "I followed the scent of your cunt that was the freshest. Let's see how wet you are for me, knowing that I'll catch you every time you run."

His free hand opened the button on my pants, pushing his still-human fingers down into my thong and up into me just like he had that night at the club. The sound that came out of me wasn't a moan, it was a whimper.

"Take your pants off," he said. Or he would do it for me, his tone said.

I waited for him to release my throat. He didn't. His hand squeezed tighter, and my body clenched around his fingers. The world was even more dim now without a full breath of air. "No no. Take them off. I'm not going to move. You're a dancer. Use that flexibility."

Fuck.

His thumb brushed over my clit, moving in slow, deliberate circles. The three fingers inside me were pumping into me with steady ease. The comfort of a predator who liked to play with its food.

He was going to consume me slowly.

That thought alone drenched his fingers all over again, dragging up embarrassment and shame and all the things I'd thrown away the minute that I'd said yes.

Erik laughed, the sound slithering through the

trees. "You like when every choice is taken from you."

Gasping for more air, I brought my leg up, grabbing my jeans at the ankle and awkwardly pulling one leg off. The movement changed the way those fingers felt inside me. Slick and sliding. Delicious, even if a poor replacement for what they represented.

The other leg gave way, and I tossed the pants aside. Still pinned helplessly, his hand fucking me not for my pleasure but to remind me exactly where I was and how he held every ounce of power.

"I'm taking a piece of clothing every time I catch you. And when you have none left, I'm taking you."

The bark of the tree scraped against my back, and the scent of water and sex was everywhere. Surrounding me.

Erik pulled his fingers out of me, wings flaring wide. "Open."

I didn't. Defying him was insane, but I did it.

The grip on my throat shifted, hand moving to press the sides of my jaw. "I said *open*, so you can taste your needy cunt." It worked. My mouth opened and he slid his fingers in. He dragged my own arousal over my tongue and painted it on my lips. Marking me.

I flashed back to that night in the club, under the

lights, when I was still gasping in pleasure and him telling me that next I would be the one to do it.

This was the next time.

His breath was hot in my ear. "Sixty seconds, Christine. Don't let me catch you."

Then he was gone. I tumbled to the grass, barely catching myself, and he was nowhere. He'd disappeared into the fog. Blind, animal panic fell into place, the primal fear of being stalked awakening.

Sixty seconds. I launched myself off the ground, tripping over my own feet before I managed to gain some speed. He was going to catch me again. Of course he was. The abstract shapes of trees lurked in the gloom, startling me if I came too close.

Sweat clung to my skin, making my hair stick to my neck and face. My lungs were working overtime with so much wet air, and I was blindly pushing through the woods, following my instincts to where I felt safer.

This was the dream.

There were different forms of it—not always woods—but this was the feeling. The faceless predator always following, always gaining, ready to take his pleasure from me.

It was fucking exhilarating. New energy flowed into my legs, and I ran faster, now zigzagging through the trees.

Time was more than up. I felt it. He was after me again. I had to be nearing the midpoint of the woods. They felt huge. Were huge. I was in an unfamiliar maze the size of a football field, a monster hunting me down to claim me.

A flash of movement to my left sent me reeling to the right. I should stop, find another place to hide. Not that it had worked last time. My instincts said to keep running, and so I ran, even though my lungs burned.

Where was he? Panic started to seep through me again, and I held it back. He could be anywhere. Setting a trap to make me feel safe or cutting me off. There was no way to know.

My ankles slammed into something hard, and I fell face first into the grass. It felt like my scream went nowhere, dead in the watery air. That hard thing wrapped sinuously around both my legs and yanked me backwards. Flipped me over so I could see him.

He melted out of the fog, gargoyle shape peeling back to reveal an Erik with wings and tail, and the onyx eyes of a monster. The shape he cut was pure power, every hollow and muscle highlighted in the hazy dimness. The lightning tattooed on his thighs looked real.

And he moved faster than I knew that they could.

I was on my knees in seconds, that same tail curling like rope around my wrists and holding them tight against my spine. It bent me backward just enough that I had no leverage. I struggled against the hold, but I couldn't move stone.

Claws flicked through the band of my bra, reducing it to nothing but fabric tatters. "One more piece left."

Just my soaked thong—barely able to be considered clothing.

Erik's hand dropped to his cock, the thickness of it plain even in the dimness. One stroke, and another. The studs in his skin shone softly.

Fuck, he was so big already. When he shifted, his cock would grow even further. I wasn't sure that my body could take him. And I was equally sure that, right now, he didn't care.

"Don't make me open your mouth again."

Rebellion welled up in me. I wanted to hurl words back at him, but I didn't have any words right now. I was still gasping from my run. Bound and exposed. So I opened my mouth.

His cock filled me instantly, my jaw stretching to try to fit the thickness of him more than an inch. The first set of studs pressed into my upper lip.

"Another day I'll wreck you, just like this. You'd

be beautiful, covered in tears from trying to take my cock down that pretty throat."

There was no way in hell I could take him in my throat. I shivered in delicious, dark anticipation because his voice told me that he would make me try anyway. Until I *was* tear-stained and wrecked and begging.

I had no resistance left to those thoughts. Not when I was like this. At his mercy and savoring every second. Exhausted, with no way to escape what he chose. And I wanted that image that he'd planted. I wanted to be taken and used like a monster's plaything.

No matter what anyone else would think of me for it.

Erik's tail moved, pushing me upward and deeper onto his cock. The taste of him was warm and lightly sweet. Like the way he smelled. Comforting even though his actions were anything but. Baked things and coffee in the air. Mates must taste good to each other too, because I could drink in that flavor.

The tail tightened, forcing my back to arch higher. My knees pressed harder into the grass, rooting me down. The way I was bent—helpless—he towered over me. A dark monolith, with his cock the perfect height to take my mouth.

He fucked deeper, pushing the first set of studs

between my lips, and then the second. I hadn't reached the third when he was as far as I could take him. My body jerked, trying to get him out, and I was held still by his tail, and now, his hands.

One on either side of my face, holding me steady while he thrust his hips. My jaw ached from the size of him. World going dizzy with my need to breathe. He didn't let me. "You have a mouth made to be used," he growled.

It was like he read my mind, and pleasure curled through my core. He would scent that too and know that I loved this. My body and my mind at odds, both fighting for different things.

Deeper. He pressed deeper, holding me still even though I fought. Cutting off the last of my air. It was his choice whether I got to take a breath. His choice to take pleasure or ease my suffering.

He chose his pleasure. The thick head of him hit the back of my mouth. Again. Again. He fucked my mouth with ruthless efficiency even as my vision faded, dimmer than the already subdued light swirling around us.

"One last chance." I was released all at once. The world came slamming back into me with fresh air, and I nearly choked on it. My limbs shook from all the adrenaline, skin chilled from water condensing on my skin. I was weak now. "Run."

I ran. After this, he wouldn't hold back. That deep knowledge that the game was coming to a close sang inside me. He would show me no mercy and I didn't want any.

The monster hadn't broken me yet.

Not nearly as fast. I wasn't nearly as fast as I was when we started. I felt the scrapes on my body from the tree and the ground. New branches slashed over my skin, dragging cuts across my ribs as I fled. Soon I would have more from his very skin.

I could still taste him on my tongue, mixing with the flavor of me that he'd painted on my tongue. It was like a tether. Even if I managed to escape, I would be bound to him like that.

There was no escape.

But I had to try. The deepest, wildest part of me wasn't going to surrender. He would have to fight me to take me.

He was behind me. I heard him running. Gaining ground. I pushed myself faster. There was a small clearing ahead—no trees to get caught against there. Everything burned. I surrendered all my energy to running. Escaping. The last bit of reserves that were a last resort.

It didn't matter.

The monster caught me halfway through the clearing, leaping from behind me and landing, rolling us together. The second we stopped, I fought him. Shoved. Kicked though it would leave bruises on me. Screamed even though my voice was raw. There was nothing I could do that could hurt a monster like him, but I would never give up.

I was playing the role now. Screaming and clawing as he managed to grab one wrist and pin it wide, and then the other. His knees pinned my thighs wide, so I was spread open like a sacrifice.

The tips of his wings came down, pinning my wrists so his hands were free. And he didn't show me mercy. His hand came around my throat again, claws teasing my neck at the same time his other hand shredded my panties.

I could breathe. Barely.

The head of his cock pressed against me, and I groaned. He was so fucking big. The stretch was half pain and half pleasure. But Erik didn't stop. He pressed and pressed and pressed, working me with his hips, forcing himself inside me. Taking me. Just like he promised.

I was so wet—so aroused from everything—that friction was not a problem.

"I don't care if you have to work for it." His words were a snarl of rumbling boulders. "You're going to take every. Single. Inch."

That cock was still flesh. Hot and hard, and

filling all the space that I had. His piercings dragged inside me and my eyes rolled back. Light, golden pleasure—everything that was the opposite—blasted through me. It wasn't an orgasm. Not yet. But fuck, it felt good.

It hurt.

There wasn't a second that wasn't both, and I loved it. My mind surrendered before my body. I pushed against his hold, arching my hips and squeezing him, trying to force him out. He pushed in further. All the way. His hips locked against mine, balls pressed against my ass.

He was in me, and I hadn't thought that it was possible. "Oh my god."

The growl shredded the air. "Did I say you could fucking speak?" The hand on my throat tightened, and he pulled his cock far enough back to slam into me. Hard. Painful. Exquisite. "I didn't hunt you down to hear you talk."

He showed me exactly what he'd hunted me for.

The monster took me.

One stroke after another. All the way out and all the way in. Savage. Brutal. Feral.

I came, screaming, on the first cruel thrust. The pleasure itself tore me open with claws and fangs. It shredded me open and left me wanting. I'd never felt anything like this.

There was no fight left in me. I was his to be taken and fucked. Used until he was finished with me. The stone monster above me smiled, knowing he'd won. And he was relentless.

He was ruthless. Merciless. Remorseless and wicked as he punished me for running from him. Each thrust into my body taught me that pain and pleasure could be so tangled that you didn't know the difference. And every time he ripped another orgasm from my body, I surrendered pieces of myself I hadn't realized were left. Until I was blank. A vessel for his wrath and pleasure.

The monster's slave.

Puppet.

Plaything.

There was no part of me that was not theirs. And there was no coming back from that.

He came with a roar, driving himself so deep that I saw falling stars. Was the falling star they nick-named me. I thought I heard my scream echo off distant walls, but I was too gone to be sure.

The only part of him that had been left flesh was his cock. No longer. It swelled inside me, hardening and stretching me wider. My body fought, and he snarled, forcing his hips down into mine. The deepest he'd been. That swollen knot that locked us together at the base of his cock pressed exactly where I needed it. Suddenly, my clit felt like a soft breeze could send me over into oblivion one more time.

He was utterly still, the monster looking down at me. Still and beautiful. His hand released my throat, but I was still pinned like a butterfly for his pleasure.

One single claw scratched, tracing around my nipple. Erik lowered his mouth and licked the small cut, healing it. "Mmm. I should have put chains in these woods so I could keep you here and make this cunt mine whenever I like. Over and over again."

Arousal, hot and thick like honey, spread through me. The image of being his slave did things to me that I would flush to speak about in the light of day. Here, in this dangerous twilight, I reveled.

Again, he did it, scratching slowly and drawing blood only to heal those cuts. They were small enough—my senses still tangled enough—that it felt like he was slicing into me with a knife made of pure ecstasy. Cut me open and drown me in the sensation.

A longer cut that started at my throat and dragged down between my breasts. I moaned, managing to wiggle my hips a little around him, wanting another spark for all that bliss that was zinging under my skin.

Erik licked up the cut, erasing it from existence,

before his face hovered over mine, dark and dangerous. Fire lanced through my breast as he slapped it, leaving fiery marks that stung. He slapped the other side. "I told you to be quiet. The only thing your mouth is good for is choking on my cock when I give you the privilege."

Claws raked down my ribs, shallow slices that burned. He didn't heal them. And further, down to my swollen clit. I wasn't allowed to move or make a sound, and yet if he touched me, I was going to.

The monster smiled. He knew it too.

He licked his thumb, and it was too late to realize why. His claw dragged down my clit. Pain and gossamer, glowing pleasure exploded outward. I screamed, fighting all over again. That thumb that he licked soothed over my clit and healed the cut, and I was still coming. My mind clinging to the last shreds of the orgasm I knew I was going to be punished for.

"I thought you'd learned your lesson."

I knew better than to speak.

"You don't move. You don't speak. You don't take pleasure that isn't yours."

He moved, thrusting though he was still knotted inside me. I moaned again, and just barely managed to keep myself from begging with my mouth and body.

"And you know what happens when I fuck you when your cunt has a knot in it."

I did. Alex told me that it would get bigger, and take longer to release. The raw quality of the words had my body squeezing him, and the answering snarl was too much. I couldn't help myself. My body arched, and he slammed his hips down.

"Fine. Disobey. I'll happily fuck you until you understand."

And he did. He fucked me with stone, burying himself deeper because of the knot. His piercings in gargoyle form were rougher. Adding texture and friction every time he moved. The wet sound of him fucking me, grunting with each brutal stroke. I would remember that sound.

"Every time you defy me you make me harder," he growled. "Every time that greedy cunt steals pleasure from me, you deserve to be taken hard. Until you understand what you're good for."

My mind faded into the fog. I no longer recognized the orgasms. It was just pleasure. Sapphire mist that floated in my brain and behind my eyes.

The grass beneath me was damp, my entire body covered with sweat and sex, Erik's knees still pinning me open where he wanted me, even after knocking them wider.

When he finally came, the knot expanded inside

me, and I saw fireworks. I was made for this. No one's body could take this and live. And yet, I was. And I was desperate for more. An addict to this feeling.

So much better than a fucking dream and a vibrator.

"What did you say?"

Fuck. I'd said those words out loud.

"Keep going," he dared. "My knot will never leave this delicious cunt of yours."

He fucked again. Never stopping and never slowing. This time, when he came, I came with him. And it was finally too much. His knot swelled a third time, and I heard the sound of my frantic, pleasured screaming even as I was fading into the dark.

CHAPTER TWENTY-FIVE

ERIK

*C*hristine lay underneath me, still and perfect. She passed out, and the moment she did, my monster receded.

I was knotted in her so deeply that it would take hours to release. We couldn't stay here for that. But I allowed myself a moment, sagging, resting my forehead against hers.

That was…

There were no words to describe it. Everything that I wanted and more. Everything *she* wanted. But I still felt the recoiling of my human mind. It wasn't an easy thing to do that. For either party. To yield completely to baser, darker instincts.

And until she woke and I could see clarity in those gorgeous eyes of hers, I knew that I wouldn't be fully settled.

Regardless, I knew the truth. In those moments I savored her fear. Craved her panic. Loved the way she took every ruthless punishment. The fact that she took *all* of me, and a knot that was bigger than it had any right to be, was so fucking unbelievable. She was made for me. For us.

And there was no question that I loved her.

I heard footsteps through the trees, Alexandre appearing. "Is she all right?"

"Yes."

"Are you?"

Was I? "I will be when she wakes."

"Marius is grabbing what's left of her clothes. Let's get her back. She'll be cold."

"I want her to be in her own bed."

He looked at me. "We'll wait for the humans to sleep, and then we'll go."

Slowly, I lifted myself and folded Christine's legs around my hips, and her arms around my neck. My tail helped keep her upright, still locked to my cock like a vise.

"I didn't expect to feel nervous," I said to him.

"You gave her a word to stop. And you would have, right?"

Horror struck me like ice. "Of course." There was no part of me that was so far gone, even with my beast in control, that I would truly hurt my mate.

"Then don't feel nervous. But I understand. Hearing her scream like that wasn't the easiest thing, though I know Marius and I would both happily play the game if she asked."

We walked towards the entrance towards the tunnels slowly, so I could keep an easy grip on her limp form. "She told me about Callum."

Alex scrubbed a hand over his face. "I want to kill him, and I'm the one who had to hold Marius back. He told us, to our face, that he's going to try to kill her."

Feral rage sprang up inside me—entirely different from the animal instincts that I'd just harnessed. This was unstoppable instinct. To protect the most precious thing that I'd ever been given at any cost.

My senses swept outward, searching for danger, and I found nothing. Only the distant but approaching sound of Marius. "Anything approach?"

"No. Completely silent. Except for the two of you."

Good. That was good.

Marius was equally wary when he joined us. But he smirked at me. "Are you going to be able to

317

get out of her before you need to be back on the roof?"

That hadn't been my main concern, swept up in it as I was, but I thought so. The idea of danger and hearing about Callum was making it shrink a little faster; my body recognizing the need to be mobile in order to enact the protection of my mate. "Yeah, it'll be okay."

"She passed out from?"

I chuckled. "Either an orgasm or the triple knot. Not sure."

Alex grabbed Christine's shoes from where she'd left them, and we moved as quickly as we could through the tunnels back to the opera. It wasn't late. Still early evening. It would be awhile before we could safely move to her apartment.

Instead, I settled on the couch. It was perfect for the way she was draped over me. Alex handed me a blanket, and I draped it over the both of us.

"So earlier," I said to them. "The tension? She mentioned you didn't tell her what Callum said."

"It wasn't a conscious thing," Marius answered. "The two of us didn't confer and decide not to tell her."

"I just—" Alex growled. "I didn't want her to have to worry about that. And then I was an idiot and mentioned it in passing. She's not wrong. It's her life, and she needs to know if she's in danger. At the same time—"

I held out a hand. "I know."

The protective instinct was the strongest. And it overrode everything. Common sense. Reality. Laws. Whatever was in the way. Nothing would stand in the way between us and Christine's protection and safety.

Curling my arms around her back, I held her closer, savoring the feeling of her body cradling mine. Warm, delicious, and perfect.

Her hair was damp and clinging to her skin. I gathered it, twisting it over her shoulder so she'd be warmer, and a wave of her scent washed over me. Lilacs in the summer. Like color had been taken from the flowers and placed in her eyes. Tangled with her scent.

"If something happens to her while we're locked on the roof..."

"Don't say that," Marius begged. "Don't even think it."

The ache of that thought pulsed in my chest. We would do absolutely anything to prevent that from happening, but the idea of her pain was my pain.

Christine's body was warming up now, and I was relaxing with her. Strictly speaking, we didn't need to sleep. Not physically. But it was nice at times. I moved my mate's head so her face tucked into my neck and I could feel the slow, steady ease of her breathing. Then I closed my eyes.

Alex's hand on my shoulder woke me. The lights in our home were lower, the chandelier barely glowing. It felt like hours had passed. My knot was smaller. Not small enough for our bodies to release, but getting there.

Marius inclined his head toward the door. Time to go.

I managed to get the blanket around both of us so that we were shielded. If all went to plan, no one would see us, but this was part of protecting her, too. It didn't just apply to her body.

In the middle of the night, the opera house was deathly silent. Before they started to restore it, Marius had spent a lot of time wandering the ruins, seeking the quiet he couldn't find in his mind.

Strangely, now that it was restored, it almost seemed emptier. Because the absence of people was far more obvious.

We saw no one. There was the sound of sex from some of the rooms where the majority of the cast and crew were staying, but other than that, it was like walking through an abandoned building.

On the stairs, I paused. "Where are her keys?"

"Here," Alex murmured. "They were with her shoes."

Marius slowed when we passed the doorway of her castmate. "You think he's in there?"

I raised an eyebrow. "Why would he be?"

"He's fucking that one," Alex said under his breath. "And if he came back into this building so soon, he has more of a death wish than I thought."

He unlocked the door, and we got inside. "What the hell did I miss there?"

Marius started to transform, rage starting to make him shift. "We asked him if he wanted to declare war. He wouldn't, because he doesn't want to lose access to her." He nodded behind him towards the other apartment. "But I think it's because he knows he has access here. Christine's name is on the fucking door."

"From now on." I crossed to her bed and laid down with her. "She sleeps downstairs with us, or one of us is here with her."

"Or all of us are here with her," Alex said.

That had its benefits, too.

Marius smiled grimly. "Agreed."

Christine stirred a little, and all of our focus shifted to her. But she settled again, pressing closer in her sleep. Those small movements were everything. Satisfaction rippled through me, knowing that after everything, she felt safe enough to bring herself closer to me in her sleep.

"I can't wait to bond her," I said quietly.

They agreed, not having to speak to do so. I wanted that closeness. The sensation of feeling her at all times. The frenzy that came after when all of us would lose ourselves in each other and pleasure. Maybe we could take her to the woods again. Not to chase her, but to drown her in love.

"How much time do we have?"

Alex smiled. "A few hours."

"Good."

Regardless of the fact that we were still knotted together, I wasn't ready to let her go.

CHAPTER TWENTY-SIX

CHRISTINE

I was warm. Comfortable. Sated and soft. Tired in the way you were when you pushed yourself to the physical extreme. Where was I?

Slowly, I blinked my eyes open.

My apartment. It was dim, but a different kind of dim than had been in the woods. This kind of light heralded the earliest light of morning when the sky was just starting to lighten.

I was on top of Erik, cock still inside me and knotted. But it was almost gone now. Inhaling deeply, I stretched, feeling the aches from running and being chased and tackled.

Under me, the softest purr started. "Good morning."

I lifted my head to warm brown eyes staring into mine. His hand was low on my spine, drawing little circles. There was worry in his eyes.

Cradling me, he reversed our positions so he was over me, taking care to be gentle and conscious of where we were connected. Being under him was visceral. I loved that feeling. Safety. Protection. A different facet of who I'd been pinned under last night.

I'd been safe then, too.

He leaned down and pressed a lingering kiss to the center of my forehead. My stomach tumbled into butterflies.

Erik moved so his cheek was pressed to mine, lips at my ear. "Are you all right?"

"I'm great," I whispered back. "Did you think that I wasn't?"

He pulled back just far enough to see my eyes, nudging my nose with his. "It's not an easy thing, what we did. And the human part of me needs to make sure that my mate is okay."

I reached up and ran my fingers through his dark hair. "Not the monster part of you?"

"My monster will protect you at any cost." The answer was immediate. "But he also savored the fear in your eyes and the way your heart pounded. It loved driving you wild with those words. *Loved* taking you without any mercy."

A shiver ran through me.

"Still, it was real. And if I went too far, or if you were truly afraid of me…"

"No." I shook my head and placed my other hand against his chest. "I knew that it was you the whole time. And I loved all of it. I'm not afraid of you. Please don't think that."

Tension that I hadn't noticed drained out of his body. The kiss he dropped on my lips was soft and sweet. The antithesis of everything we were talking about. I smiled through the kiss. "I love this, too."

His knot eased, and our bodies loosened. We both groaned, the strange loss that was in my chest from no longer being connected and the relief of being able to move.

Erik pulled out of me slowly. I was definitely going to ache from this, and I didn't care. It wasn't something that I could do all the time, but I definitely wanted to do that again. "Maybe next time," I whispered. "It can be all three of you chasing me."

"Yes." Alex's voice came from across the room. It startled me. They'd been so quiet I hadn't realized they were here with us. I could barely see an arm flung over the end of the couch when I looked.

Marius sat in one of the armchairs, reading my werewolf romance.

He looked up. "Absolutely."

"And you?" I glanced at Erik.

"Yes," he said, purr rolling through me. "It would be my pleasure. To do that, and to make love to you so slowly that your pleasure takes hours. To lose myself in you after you take my bite."

"Where would you?" I asked. "Alex told me his."

"I'll show you while I heal your cuts," he said, shifting up and back, treating me to a delicious view of his body. That was the only thing I missed about last night. It had been dark enough that I hadn't been able to drink him in.

Those tattooed thighs that straddled my hips. The abs that I still hadn't had a chance to lick. Arms that I could probably dream about and get off to just on their own.

"Cuts?"

His hands brushed over my ribs. "You're scratched up from the trees. And me. But I couldn't reach them when you had my knot."

"Need help?" Alex asked.

Erik paused, a gleam in his eye. "She does have a lot of cuts." He bent, licking just beneath my breast. A tiny flash of pain flickered where his tongue touched raw skin, and it soothed.

"That's a really convenient talent."

"I'm quite enjoying it right now." He licked the same spot again, even though there was no longer any scrape.

Alex appeared at the side of the bed, hair tousled and smile wicked. "He's right. There are a lot of little scratches. Some bigger ones too."

The next moment, his tongue ran along my ribs, and I squirmed, feeling that strange magic again. "Care to tell me why this is one of the things you guys can do?"

Marius rolled onto the bed on the opposite side, dragging his tongue along my collarbone and in the hollow of my throat. "Self preservation, mostly. It doesn't just work on flesh. It works on our stone form as well."

I giggled, and it turned into a moan when Alex found a spot on my thigh. "Whatever decided what magic gargoyles got really fucked you over when it chose for you to have to *lick* yourselves to heal."

"I'd say you're benefitting nicely," Erik murmured into my skin, tracing lines of heat across my lower stomach.

"Can't argue with that."

Marius took my hand and healed a scrape on the inside of my wrist. Alex lifted me long enough to reach my ass and heal everything there. I blushed when he groaned. "This is mine, *mon amour*."

Erik snorted a laugh. "Don't forget Marius said he'd fight us for the first chance at your ass."

My eyebrows rose into my hair, and I looked over at my blond mate. "Would you?"

"Yes."

"As long as I have a chance," Alex said. "I'm happy."

Erik's mouth returned to that spot below my breast, teasing it. "Here. I want to bite you here."

An uncontrollable shudder shook me. "Why?"

"That's where my instinct tells me," he said. "I don't know why. But that's the place." Sealing his mouth over the skin, he sucked deeply, sending pleasure down in a straight line to my clit. After the amount of orgasms he wrung out of me, I didn't anticipate being able to come for a couple of days.

My body clearly disagreed.

"What about you?" I asked Marius, arching my body as he looked me up and down. Heat was banked in his eyes, and I felt something spin between us. He was the only one that I hadn't fucked alone, and we both knew it.

Soon. That needed to happen soon.

"Here." Fingers brushed low on the outside of my hip. "This spot is mine."

"And you're sure we can't do this?"

Erik chuckled. "As soon as the show closes and you have three days to spare."

I knew I was pouting, but I didn't care. What they'd told me about it? I wanted that. I wanted to know what they felt and what made them tick. To know when they were aroused with simply a thought.

Pushing myself up on my elbows, my back hit the bed again. My arms shook like I'd just done a hundred push-ups. "Woah."

"You're still exhausted."

"I'm fine."

He rolled his eyes. "If you can't push yourself upright, you're tired, not fine." Spreading himself alongside me, he pulled me to his chest, tangling his legs with mine and making sure I was fully wrapped in his arms. Bondage with nothing but his body.

I was comforting and warm, but I also knew it was his way of making sure that I didn't try to get up again. Sneaky.

Alex still sat on the bed in front of me. It wasn't just heat in his eyes now, but a depth of emotion that I didn't fully understand. Couldn't fathom. "I'm sorry," I said. "About earlier."

The fact that he'd just had his tongue on my body

assured me that everything was fine, but I still wanted to make sure.

He stole a hand away from Erik. "We didn't consciously choose to hide it. I want you to know that. Our instincts got the better of us."

Marius came around the bed so he was in sight, arms crossed. "It's impossible to describe."

"What is?" My words came out a little strange sounding, and Erik kissed the side of my neck. Was I falling asleep again?

"The terror that hits when there's any possible danger to you," Marius's voice was measured and even. "The drive to protect you overrides everything. Every single thing. To the point where we don't even want you to have to think about danger."

I didn't like that they hadn't told me, but when put like that it was kind of sweet. "I still meant it, though. I want to know."

"This is new for us too," Alex said. "And it won't be the only time we don't know something or mess up. Just because we're mates and a perfect match doesn't make us perfect."

"Yeah." I closed my eyes, that exhaustion catching up with me suddenly. They felt heavy, like I couldn't even open them again. "You're going to leave me too soon."

Purring started behind me. And then in front of me as Alex slid in beside me there.

Erik turned my face up so he could kiss me. Even with my eyes closed I could feel the intensity leaking through the gentleness. "Baby girl, I promise we're never leaving."

"When you go to the roof." I knew they weren't actually leaving, but my heart dropped anyway when I thought about it.

Because when they were here, I wasn't lonely. That stark, awful loneliness that had been my life since the video came out. In the days I'd been here with them, I'd barely checked my phone.

Not one part of me missed it.

Something released in my chest. I hadn't really wanted to say it because it would seem ungrateful. A million people would kill to be in my position. But fuck, I hated being famous. I didn't want it.

Before I became 'the opera girl,' I'd been *happy*. Just like Meg said. I loved my quiet life and my job. Loved dancing. And yes, I loved singing. Was great at it. But all of this?

The production was going to be amazing and beautiful. But there was no true joy underneath it. Not the way I'd had when I was a dancer. I missed being able to go places without security or knowing that I was going to be photographed. I didn't want to worry that one tiny mistake would be blasted over the world.

I loved what I did, but it wasn't worth it.

Meeting my mates had been worth it. Which was why I didn't want them to leave. Not even to go up to the roof.

When I was more awake, I would have to deal with these thoughts. Because it wasn't like I could put being famous back in the bag. It happened. Mark hadn't intended for it to blow up the way it did—he'd been supporting his friend who wanted to sing more.

Looking backwards was always crystal clear.

There wasn't a solution that I could see. At least not while I was sleepy and surrounded by miles of delicious man. I cracked my eyes and saw Marius at the end of the bed. "Don't be left out," I mumbled.

A low laugh rolled across my skin and his mouth pressed a kiss to my ankle.

I never thought that my ankle would be a piece of my body that I could be turned on by, but here we were. "I'm not left out, sweetheart. I need to finish reading your book. It's giving me ideas."

"Oh my god."

"Should I read some out loud?"

My eyes flew open. "*No*."

He just smirked at me, retreating back to the

chair with a wink. The man was wicked, and he kept his eyes on me until he'd sat down and opened the book again. "The three of you are going to be the death of me."

"Hopefully the opposite," Alex said.

Sleep was pulling me down, but I resisted. I had the morning off. If I wanted to sleep, I could do it after they left. Instead, I held on, just relaxing and enjoying the feeling of being held. And for the first time in forever, not feeling lonely.

CHAPTER TWENTY-SEVEN

CHRISTINE

*T*he window nearly crashed open under the force of Marius pushing us through it together. We took the back way, or the scary way, as I now put it, so we didn't have to wait to get into my apartment.

The days had passed so quickly that they were a blur. Rehearsals were longer and longer. Going late into the evening in order to get the technical aspects perfect. Late enough that there hadn't been proper time with them since that night with Erik.

There'd been plenty of pleasure between us. But hasty moments, stolen between when I had to be on stage and when I had to sleep or not be able to function.

We were three days away from opening night. Tomorrow was the gala and the massive press boost that was hoped would already rocket the massive ticket sales. I was exhausted and horny.

The second I'd walked through the curtain into their home below the theatre, Marius had been with me, wrapping me up in his arms, and carrying me back out the door. "Where are we going?"

"Your place," he said, voice clipped. "So I can fuck that look of exhaustion off your face."

I laughed, but even that sounded tired. Burying my face in his neck, I groaned. "I don't know if you fucking me is going to make me less tired."

"No," he admitted. "But it will make you more relaxed. I could see how tense you are from across the room."

Of course he could. They were more in tune with my body than I was most days, being able to see and notice things that no human would be able to.

Which was how I was now, sprawled on the floor, laughing as we lost our balance in our desperation. Marius's wings were out now. The veined, reptilian shape of them was stark in comparison to Alex's angel wings. Marius, my dragon. His dragon tail, too, was already moving, curling up around my waist and lifting me upright.

"The fact that any of you can lift me with your tails is a surprise every time."

His tail, spikes pinching and tickling, lifted me off the floor and dropped me on the bed while he stripped his shirt off.

"Show-off."

His eyes were already dark, swirling into the blackness of the gargoyle. In one of the stolen moments that we'd had together, Marius had knotted me. *Deep.* The way it pressed against me rubbed my G-spot and it was like holding back a hundred orgasms not to move and beg him to fuck and make it bigger.

I'd barely made it back to rehearsal on time, and had been on the verge of distraction through the whole damn thing. Tonight, though, they'd given the cast the rest of the night off. It wasn't early, but it wasn't late enough that we couldn't do this.

Relief was thick in the air.

"Where are Alex and Erik?"

"I'm the only one you need to think about right now."

I rolled my eyes. "Marius."

"They're watching," he growled.

Every day that passed without Callum making

good on his threat was one that they became more tense, the protection instinct buried inside them ignited by nameless danger. The couple of nights that he'd stayed with Désirée, I'd stayed in their beds. I didn't want to be close to him any more than they wanted me to be.

I got my own shirt off and tossed my bra across the room. Marius's hands were in the waistband of my leggings, pulling them down and off before burying his head between my thighs.

All my mates loved tasting me. Had made it a point of pride to lick me into shuddering orgasms even when I didn't have the energy to fuck the way we all wanted to. Marius liked to go slow. Liked to draw it out until I was shaking like I'd run a marathon before he let me come.

If I came before he was ready, he delighted in edging me until I begged him. It was his favorite thing. "Marius," I said. "I don't have that kind of time."

"Hmm, I think you have time for this." His tongue curled around my clit and I stifled a moan. Forcing myself to sit up, I dragged him out from between my legs and kissed him.

"Please," I gasped when we broke apart. "I haven't been properly fucked in more than three days. And that was barely enough. You guys have made an addict out of me, and I can't take long and slow today. Please."

He shoved the pants off his hips, yanked me to the edge of the bed and sank into me in one swift motion. We both groaned. "This is what you want."

"Yes." I meant to say something else, but I couldn't. "Yes."

He drove into me, the piercing in the head of his cock dragging over the perfect place inside me. "Not long and slow," he growled. "But if I keep going like this, it will be far too fast for the both of us."

My breath came in bounces, driven out of me with every thrust. "What do you suggest?"

Marius pulled out of me and flipped me onto my stomach. I bounced on the mattress, laughing, and froze. His hands were on my ass, spreading, and I suddenly couldn't breathe because his tongue was *there*. Oh *fuck* that felt good in a weird way. Not weird. New. Strange. My brain was short-circuiting with the unexpected sensation.

All I knew was that I was wet, and my mate's tongue was fucking my ass like it was the only thing he wanted in this lifetime.

"Marius." His name was a drawn out moan.

His only response was that of a starving man, pushing his mouth closer to me, consuming my ass seemingly without the need to breathe.

"Oh god." My hips sank down to the bed, yielding to the new and the strange.

"I told you I would fight for the chance to take you here first."

I curled my hands into the comforter, savoring the sensation of his hands squeezing my ass. Massaging it. Stroking it. I felt his gaze on it like he was admiring a piece of art.

"I've never done that."

The sound of his zipper reached me, along with the low, sensual growl they managed to make that sent my mind into overload. Even without being bonded to them, the deepest part of me responded to that sound.

"Are you saying yes?" He asked, voice dropping into an inhuman register. "Because the thought of completely owning your ass—you won't have to worry about long and slow."

"Yes." I couldn't say that I hadn't thought about it. In moments when I drifted off into my thoughts and imagined more nights like our first, where they used me together.

I wanted all of them to fuck me. At the same time. There were three of them, and there were three ways to fuck me. A match made in heaven.

Marius stroked his palms down my back, landing at my hips. A soft kiss brushed over my tailbone.

"Let go completely," he whispered. "It's better that way."

The metal of his piercing was the first thing that I felt, pressed by the warmth of his cock. I gripped the blanket tighter, forcing the rest of me into a state of utter relaxation. It wasn't fear that caused the tension. It was the unknown. The alien feeling of a cock pressing into my ass.

I almost laughed. Of all the things that I'd done while here in Paris, anal sex was arguably the most normal. This was nothing.

Marius thrust forward, slipping past the tightest part of me, and I gasped. Buttons that had never been pressed before were coming to life. Nerves that had never been used simply because no one had endeavored to touch them.

"*Merde.*" He cursed, sinking all the way in. "Your ass is perfect."

It was a strange sensation. To be full and empty at the same time. My clit was swollen and sensitive, begging for attention. I was on the hazy edge of pleasure.

The amplified sensation of my mate was intensely apparent, tingling heat pulsing outward in waves from where I was impaled on his cock.

Those waves were enough. Marius didn't even

have to move, and eventually, those waves would carry me over the edge and into pleasure.

My mate lined himself up with me. Back pressed against mine, thighs bracing against the outside of my legs, hands holding my wrists. Mouth at my ear. I was entirely surrounded by him. Filled with him.

They made me feel so small in comparison. Towering over me when we stood together and overwhelming me with their bodies when they loved me. It was amazing not to have to think or worry about anything.

I'd never had that with anyone. Now it felt effortless. They settled into that empty space in my soul like a key in a lock.

"Did you think about this?" He asked, rolling his hips so he dipped out and in. A swirling sensation rippled through me. Little flickers of shivery pleasure. "After I told you?"

"Yes."

He rolled his hips again, slow and sensual, exactly the style he loved. "Tell me."

I bit my lip. They were trying to open me up. Pry every fantasy that I had out of me like a clam. Even after they told me that I couldn't hide from them, it wasn't always easy to say things like that out loud. "The three of you. All in me at once."

"More." Another slow stroke. Each time the ball

of his piercing pressed something deep in me and made me shudder. I already knew what kind of orgasm this would be. The kind that you saw coming in from a distance. That gathered depth and speed and a sudden trigger made the tsunami fall and dash you on rocks made of sparkling, diamond pleasure.

I took a breath and shook my head. It was hard to focus on talking when I felt like this. He was grinding me down into the bed, the barely there scratch of the blankets against my clit creating sparks that I saw behind my eyes.

All at once Marius moved, spreading my hands wide on the bed and transforming his own to stone. I was pinned beneath him, face pushed into the bed. He still moved. On his knees, fucking my ass with maddening steadiness.

"Tell me, Christine."

"I did." My voice was a desperate whine.

"Not enough." His teeth scraped my ear and moved to bite my neck. Hard. Not enough to break the skin, but enough to make me gasp and wriggle.

I wasn't sure the way they gave me pain would ever make sense. But I was soaking wet now. "I want to hear all the details of how you want to be fucked."

"Or you could just keep saying things like that." I

tried to move. To gain leverage so I could push back into his cock and take more. Urge him faster.

He wouldn't move an inch.

"I know you like dirty words, baby girl." Another thrust. "So tell me, and I'll make sure that you get all the ones you need." He pulled all the way back just to slam home again.

A sound that wasn't quite a scream slipped out, but we would get there. There wasn't one of my mates that didn't love to make me use my voice.

"Tell me, and I'll make sure that we fuck you like a whore," he murmured in my ear, speeding up. "Until you're sloppy with all of our cum and you can't speak because you've lost your voice from screaming our names. Or your throat is raw from taking our cocks over and over."

"Fuck." My voice broke into a cry.

"Tell me *now*."

"You just like this," I forced the words out. "Alex in my mouth. Erik fucking me. You switched places and didn't stop."

Marius pulled me up onto my knees, pushing cock deep as he did so. "Good girl." He turned my head to kiss me, dragging me back by the hair. Everything they did made me feel wanton and powerful, even when they pushed that dominance that made me shudder.

"You're going to feel just a taste of what that's like," he said. "So you can think about it. Let it make your mouth water and your cunt wet and so desperate for us to fuck you together that you'll *beg*."

His tail slid around me, the tip drifting up the inside of my leg. He did it often, and I'd wondered what it would be like, and then pushed it away.

The shape of it looked dangerous. A dragon's tail with the tip like an arrowhead. It wasn't sharp, but it looked it, and the spikes on the rest of it made his gargoyle form appear the most deadly.

He dragged the tip around my clit, teasing me. Flicking it the way he would with his tongue. Curling under it, and circling it, finding that spot that made my hips jerk in response.

Marius held me still, thrusting upward into my ass again as he teased. This was no phantom orgasm now. Pleasure was building under my skin and spreading, that mating amplifier so much stronger in their monster form. The second his tail touched me it was like dragging lines of blissful heat under my skin.

"Don't come," he said. "Not yet."

I whimpered. His denial wasn't a surprise, but I was already halfway there.

With aching slowness, the tip of his tail slid lower, tracing a path to my entrance. And it paused. "Hands." He took them before I had a chance to give them to him and pulled them behind his back. Made me clasp them just below his wings.

"Don't move them."

His body was broad—powerful—the effort to clasp my hands behind him plastered me against his chest. Made my back and hips arch. Placed my head on his shoulder.

Which was exactly what he wanted when he thrust his tail into me.

I was momentarily blind from the fullness. The inexplicable feeling of *rightness* at being so stuffed with him. My mouth watered, craving that third element, knowing that right now that I couldn't have it.

He was right.

I was going to beg.

Deeper and deeper still, pushing his tail into me, the slick friction of stone at once familiar and new. It curved, seeking my G-spot like a missile and finding it just as accurately.

Pleasure spun back and forth inside me, feeling both holes filled. Marius was still as the statue he embodied. The only movement came from that clever, sinuous tail, fucking me once and again. Deeper, until I couldn't take more.

My orgasm was hovering on the edge, and he knew it.

"Don't you dare come."

"I can't stop it."

His growl tore through me. "You will."

And then he fucked. Tail and cock together, pulling back and spearing deep. Empty and then full. Together. Again and faster. He wasn't holding back anymore.

The world went white.

My only focus was on holding back that tide, which felt like me pushing one hand against a tornado and expecting it to stop. I was pleading with him. Outside my brain, my voice was loud.

I was holding on by a thread. My hands were where Marius placed them not because I wanted to keep them there but because holding onto him was the only thing keeping me from flinging myself over the cliff into nothing but light.

"That's right," he growled in my ear. His hand was still in my hair, another way of binding me to him. "Hold it back. Because every part of you wants to obey your mate, even at the cost of your own pleasure."

The rhythm changed. Instead of together, they were opposite. Tail and cock and tail again. All I could do was hold on.

Speed built, Marius's breath ragged in my ear with his approaching orgasm. The sounds he made with every thrust made me wetter. Wilder. Until I was a drop lost in a wave that was about to break.

"Come."

The dam unleashed itself, the orgasm cutting sharp through me. Melting me. Covering me in rich sensation. I lost my grip, falling to the bed, my body out of control. The pleasure took and took and took, working me on both cock and tail until I was spent and gasping, heaving on the blankets.

Marius was catching his breath too, leaning over me. It was only when my pulse calmed and I felt like I could move again that I realized he was still deep in my ass, and knotted.

"You are so fucking gorgeous when you come."

"I told you guys that you'd kill me with orgasms. That was close."

He laughed, lifting me up and settling us at the head of the bed. Sitting like this made everything feel tighter. Full of him.

"Spread your legs."

I was too limp and relaxed to do anything but follow his command.

"Wider."

I did.

"*Wider.*"

With a moan, I pushed my legs as far as I could in this position. He made sure my legs were over his, so he could control how wide they were. Just like the first night we were all together.

"Now that I'm knotted inside your perfect, delectable ass, we have time for long and slow."

"Your knot will get bigger," I said in a rasp. These next few days weren't ones that I could risk that, much as I loved being locked to their bodies.

Weaving his fingers with mine, Marius pulled my hand to his lips, kissing my palm. "If I fucked you with my cock, it would. But as you now know, that's not necessary."

His tail—still shining wetly from fucking me—caressed my leg. "Should we see how long and how slow we can go?"

"You're sadist and you forgot to tell me."

I was wet again the second he growled, tail easing in so slowly I almost couldn't tell that it was moving.

Almost.

"I'm going to fuck you with my tail, Christine. So fucking slowly that you're going to shake with it. I'm going to take you to the edge and stop. I'm going to torture you with your own pleasure and I am going to love *every second of it*."

I cursed loudly, telling him exactly what I thought of that. And the fact that I hated the idea and thought it was the hottest thing I'd ever heard at the same time.

"How long?" If I knew how long I could make it.

"As long as I choose. And you're going to be a good girl and let me."

Arousal dropped onto my skin like rain, my mind blanking out to nothing but the awareness of him.

"What are you going to do?"

"I'm going to be a good girl and let you fuck me, long and slow."

Marius's tail started to move, and he did.

CHAPTER TWENTY-EIGHT

CHRISTINE

"You're sure?" I asked Anne.

"Yes." She finished fastening the necklace for me. "The replica we have won't look the same in close proximity as it will on stage, and you'll have the most security. I'd rather we double up and protect you and the necklace at once rather than try to split it up just to put the necklace on at the studio."

It made sense. There wasn't a time today that I would be alone or without security. Which was good, because I had to leave the opera house, and my mates had to stay here. Not only was it light out, but where I was going was beyond their range.

I was walking the red carpet at the gala, singing live, and then hopefully coming back. Tomorrow was dress rehearsal. I wanted to get at least *some* rest.

And the necklace made me feel better. It was that strange, near-singing sensation that I felt whenever I wore it. I had the vague impression that it liked me. Weirder things had happened. I was mated with living stone. Why couldn't a diamond like me?

"You look perfect," Anne said.

"Thank you."

My apartment was a mess now, having been invaded by makeup and wardrobe. But I loved the dress that they'd put me in. Silvery and strapless, the dress clung to my body and then flowed out in a ruffled skirt that reminded me of falling petals. It was an effort not to twirl around in front of the mirror.

My hair was curled and blown out into big waves, and my make-up shimmered, designed to match the dress and the necklace. Under the lights on the red carpet and at the studio, I would shine like the diamond I wore.

And we needed to leave, but I needed something first. "Give me a minute. I'll meet you at the artist's door."

"Okay. Not too long," she said with a grin.

"No."

The door closed behind her, and I blew out a breath. She probably thought I had to use the restroom. That wasn't it. I reached forward next to the full-length mirror that they'd set up and touched the wall.

Hello?

Hello, beautiful. Alex said.

I smiled. *Can you see me? I thought it was just sound.*

Erik's voice. *We can't see you. But I would do a lot of things to be able to right now.*

But, Marius interrupted. *We will be watching your performance and waiting for you when you get back.*

Sighing, I pressed my palm more firmly to the wall. *I wish all of you could come with me.* Having the three of them by my side in tuxedos would make tonight infinitely better. The idea of a gala was exciting until you realized that the whole world was going to be watching you, and a decent portion of those would be hoping that I would do something mortifying like falling on my face or having this strapless dress slip down.

They had a television down in the bat cave. I barely even noticed, but then, I hadn't been down there to watch things on it. We had better things to do. That's how they were going to watch me on the show.

I'd started calling it the bat cave, much to their

amusement. It was the only thing that fit in my head. What else did you call what was essentially a luxury apartment below the floor of a fucking opera house? Batman would be proud.

The simultaneous, unheard but *felt* sound of purring came from all three of them. It felt like someone was drawing a hand down my back.

We wish that too, mon cherie.

I have to go.

Erik whispered. *Be careful.*

There was a blank space after it, like there should be more words. But I pulled my fingers away from the stone. It was time.

I grabbed the little bag with my phone, keys, and back-up lipstick before locking the door behind me. The matching suits that had gotten me to the door that first day were waiting at the artist's door, along with the limo driven by Raphael.

"Miss Daniels!" His eyes crinkled with a smile in the rear-view mirror. "You don't call, you don't write."

"I'm sorry," I laughed. "I've been busy. I hope you haven't been too bored?"

"Not at all, *Mademoiselle*. As long as you know you can still call on me."

"I do know that," I said. "Thank you."

Anne was typing away on her phone, barely

aware of the conversation. She was often on her phone, and that wasn't surprising, given the number of hats that she wore at any given moment. Her sleek black dress was the exact opposite of what I wore, but it was very French.

I cleared my throat. "Anne?" She looked up. "Just quickly walk me through what I can expect?"

She nodded once and finished her typing before slipping her phone into her own clutch. "A bit of a whirlwind. The red carpet—lots of pictures. A couple of interviews, but we'll need to move quickly. No signatures, and I'll make sure they don't hold you up with too many questions."

"Okay."

"The gala itself. You won't be there very long. Only introductions to the highest donors and a photo with the cast and those same people. The rest of the cast will take care of them after that, and we'll be going out the back to get you to the studio. Because the show is popular, they've asked you to do some signatures and selfies after, and we agreed. But there's extra security."

"Then I get to sleep?"

She smiled and reached across the seat to touch my shoulder. "And then you get to sleep."

It was a testament to Anne herself and the power of this show in this city that we were now driving to where the gala was being held. From what I gathered —and what Meg had told me was making its way through the rumor mill—was that this party for the donors and important people in Paris had been moved half a dozen times. They originally wanted it to just be at the opera, but that was inconvenient so close to the opening. The Louvre wasn't available. Neither was the Ritz.

Which was why we were now making our way to the *Place du Trocadéro*, where the red carpet rolled across smooth marble and the Eiffel Tower loomed in the background.

I hummed under my breath, going over the aria. My voice was plenty warm. It always was right now, with all the rehearsals and my regular, screaming orgasms.

The lights were brighter than the afternoon sun. I saw them even through the tinted windows of the limo. Camera flashes and blinding overhead flood-lights to make sure they could get good images of us despite being silhouetted by open sky. No one wanted to block the view of the Eiffel Tower with a backdrop.

"Ready?" Anne asked as we pulled up to the end of the carpet.

"Absolutely not."

She laughed like she thought I was kidding. I

wasn't. My new realizations about fame and about being here made me dread stepping outside into the view of all the cameras. I just had to make it through all of this—the entire run of the show—and I could make some decisions.

Hopefully ones that involved my mates, though we'd been circling around talking about what happened when the show closed.

Anne left the car first, stepping aside before I could exit so the pictures would be perfect.

The sheer wave of sound when I stepped out of the cat was enough to knock me backwards. So many people. So many cameras. It was like staring straight into fireworks, the amount of flashes.

I waved to the crowd, following Anne's lead up the steps and passed the first stable of photographers. I posed. I smiled. I pretended that I was anywhere but here. And that right this second there weren't hundreds of thousands of people judging my hair and my dress.

Instead, I imagined that I wasn't alone. If I stood here with my mates, three huge, gorgeous men at my back like armor. What would it be like if I were open about it? There would be pictures of the three of them in various poses. Holding my hand, kissing my cheek, and if we dared to go a little further, them actually kissing me.

The thought brought the first real smile to my face, and the flashbulbs went off like shattering stars.

Anne touched my shoulder, and I moved with her, letting the fiction sustain me. There wasn't another way to do it. I could hear nothing but the brute force of a thousand shouted questions.

I used to wish that I could go to the Met Gala, and now, it was possible that I could get an invitation.

If this was the experience, I would pass.

"We're going to skip the interviews," Anne said, touching my shoulder.

"Why?"

"Don't worry about it." Her lips were pressed together in an expression that I knew meant she was unhappy, but this wasn't the place to ask.

Ahead of me on the carpet, Désirée was getting ready to enter the architectural museum where the gala was being held. "She said something?"

"We'll talk about it later," Anne said.

That was my cue. I smiled and waved for the last bank of cameras, and we finished the walk into the museum. As soon as we were through the doors I turned, voice low. "We don't need to talk about it now, but I *do* need to know what she said in case I'm asked."

Anne looked at me, and I could tell she was

considering whether to give in. She sighed, unlocking her phone and flipping to a new screen. Bold, thick letters made the headline stark.

Christine Daniels doesn't care if half the cast of Joan D'Arc *hates her. She's doing it her way.*

"Fuck."

"Quickly," she pulled me to the side. "What happened?"

"Désirée confronted me in the costume shop. She called me an ungrateful bitch." I outlined the rest of the conversation, including the part where I told her to keep being a bitch to me and turn half the cast against me, because it was a reflection on her.

Anne sighed.

"I'm sorry."

"I'm not upset with you, Christine. What you said was correct. Of course, I wish that you hadn't said it at all, but I can work with that. We'll take care of it."

I wanted to ask her more, but there were more people entering behind us now. Our time was up. I shifted into party mode as Anne brought me to the investors and other prominent people at the gala. This wasn't merely for the opening of the show. It was a celebration of the restored historical icon that was the opera house.

Meg waved from across the room. She was standing with Tori, who smiled and waved as well.

Between rehearsals, fittings, and everything else, we'd barely had time to see each other. Right now was no exception, as someone intercepted me.

"It is incredibly wonderful to meet you," a tall, handsome man said.

It took a full three seconds for me to realize that it was the president of France. "I'm honored to be here." No matter how I felt about the situation and the way it might turn out, this was an honor. And I would do everything that I needed to the best of my ability.

"I'm looking forward to your performance. I'll be there opening night."

"That's…incredible, thank you."

"Speaking of performances," Anne said. "Christine needs to leave soon for her next one."

"Of course."

"Yes," a new voice said . Monsieur Chagny clapped the president on the shoulder. "We mustn't hold up our star. Especially when she wears that necklace so beautifully."

"Thank you." Raoul was a shameless flirt. I was used to it now, knowing that he meant nothing by it more than playful banter. "And thank you for letting it out for the evening."

I took a picture with the president before gathering with the rest of the cast. Of course I was next to Désirée. The smugness was practically radiating off her. "Nice work," I told her.

"I only told the truth."

Hiding my sigh behind a smile, I said nothing. The last thing I needed to do was give her more ammunition.

Cameras flashed, and the picture ended. Taylor made some kind of comment that had the people around him laughing. And it gave Désirée her moment. "I'm just getting started."

"Are you threatening me?"

"What if I am?"

"Then that's good information." I checked the time on my phone. "I have to go. Enjoy the rest of the party."

Catching Anne's eye, we made our way out the back entrance and down to the street where the car was waiting. They'd done a good job making sure that everything was secured.

Anne slammed the door harder than was really necessary as she slid in. "You should be prepared," I told her.

"Why?"

"Because Désirée just told me that she's only getting started. I don't know what she's planning, but I don't think the one headline is going to be enough for her."

She cursed, French spilling out under her breath. "Fine. I'll figure it out. Just try to avoid her as much as possible, please."

I snorted. "Not a problem."

"Just focus on your performance for now. You'll be great."

I hummed again and started a vocal warm-up. This performance was one of the few things that I wasn't worried about right now. Because they would be watching. The sun was slipping down behind the buildings and casting long shadows. They would be free soon.

And with my mates truly watching me for the first time, I wanted to remember what it was like to *sing*.

CHAPTER TWENTY-NINE

ALEXANDRE

*T*he large television that slid out from the wall was dusty. We hadn't used it in a while. The refurbishment of the opera house had affected our power down here, and after Christine, the last thing I wanted to do was watch TV when there was an opportunity to have my head between those perfect thighs.

Now on the screen was a man that hosted one of the late-night shows. This was a special edition of the program—live—featuring Christine singing and interviews about the rebuilding, and the choice of *Joan D'Arc* as the opera itself.

"I don't like that we haven't seen Callum," Marius

cracked open a bottle of beer. Of the three of us, he drank the least. It showed what kind of state his mind was in.

I, for one, agreed with him. He'd come to see the other singer a few times, and we'd kept Christine away from him as soon as we heard him enter the building. But he'd been suspiciously silent in all other regards. Especially surrounding his threat against Christine. "He's waiting. Until the spotlight is less bright."

"Or until it's brighter," Erik said.

"How would that benefit him?"

He shrugged. "It doesn't. But he wants so badly to beat us and prove that he's more and better. To take her when everyone is watching and get away with it seems like something that he would do."

He had a point there, and I hated that he did.

Just the thought of him getting anywhere near her had energy snaking under my skin and my skin rippling to stone and back. I stood, pacing across the space and back again. She was out in the world, too far for us to get to her. The helplessness it shot through me was un-fucking-believable, and I hated it.

Panic was just under that, and the knowledge that the time we had to figure this out was coming to a close, and I had *nothing*. No fucking clue how to get away from this building. I'd searched. Looked for anything I could on gargoyles—the data one could find in modern times was unbelievable—and there was still nothing.

Of course, other gargoyles around the world weren't putting up blogs or accounts of their experiences, either. We weren't as rare as people probably wanted to believe, but in the world of monsters, we were still few and far between.

A growl ripped out of me. My monster wouldn't feel settled until she was back here and safe. I wanted to go to the edge of our boundary and wait for her to come back. Maybe after she sang.

From the screen, the host stepped up to the front. His English was nearly perfect, having so much practice with the celebrity guests he welcomed. "I'm excited about our next guest," he said. "She's the star of the revival of *Joan D'Arc*, singing the song that made her famous. Please welcome, Christine Daniels."

The applause from the audience faded, and the camera zoomed in on the stage, where pink lights glowed to life, illuminating Christine's face. We hadn't been able to see her before she left, and if I had a beating heart, it would have stopped at the sight of her.

The dress she wore exposed her shoulders and

flowed down and away. She was a gorgeous mess of rustling, ruffling silk. Like cherry blossoms caught in the wind. Her eyes closed, and the first notes of *Il Dolce Suono* began to play.

During the rehearsals, we listened to her. But it wasn't the same as watching her perform. When her eyes opened she looked straight into the camera. Straight at us. Her voice was clear and pure. Absolutely fucking beautiful.

All three of us were pinned to the earth—incapable of moving. The notes climbed to the first high, and it was like the world itself stilled. The emotion visible on her face tore at my heart.

We'd been so caught up in her and the fact that she was our mate that even after hearing her rehearse, this had become secondary. Awe. That's what was sinking through me. Sheer awe at her beauty.

I needed to tell her—wanted to make her sing while we came together so we could both be wrapped up in her voice. Our plan for opening night was to surprise her. Living here had its advantages. Including knowing the ways into the box office and being able to adjust the reservations.

The three of us now had a box to ourselves where we could watch her perform. Safe to say that I would be hard the entire time, waiting and counting down the moments when I could have her underneath me again while at the same time soaking in the exquisite creation that was her voice.

Christine's voice soared and hung in the air as the music faded, suddenly replaced by applause. The audience of the show was on their feet for her. Hell, if I hadn't already been standing, I would have.

On the screen, she took a bow. Cheeks pink and eyes shining. She loved that. Not the applause that she was experiencing now, but the singing itself. That was what she loved and why she'd gone viral in the first place. You could *feel* the emotion she poured into every note.

Another bow, and the host gestured. There was a door outside the studio into the evening light, where a whole crowd of people waited for her. Security lurked everywhere. Three men stood near her, with more lining the barrier that people pressed against, trying to get Christine's attention for a picture.

"That was incredible," Erik whispered.

"It was." No other words to describe it.

We didn't deserve her.

There was no known reason for mates. A happenstance of energy and resonance. But having a mate was far more than that. There was an inevitability to it—a deep knowing that it wasn't just chance.

Whatever forces ruled this world had woven the four of us together, and I would spend the rest of Christine's life making sure she understood how lucky we were to have her.

The host spoke over the footage of Christine signing autographs. These people had been waiting all day to meet her. She was smiling, but I saw the tension in her shoulders as she swiped her sharpie over images of the show's poster, pictures of her, and other *Joan D'Arc* related things.

I liked the bodyguards that were watching her. Hovering. Moving her along quickly and never taking their eyes off the crowd or off her. I was watching the crowd too, in case Callum made an appearance.

A young girl reached out, holding a phone. She was wearing armor just like Joan of Arc, and it was the first real smile I'd seen Christine give. She turned her back to the crowd, holding up her phone and posing.

It happened fast. One hand darted out and grabbed Christine's arm. Another person wanting a picture. And another. Suddenly, hands were all over her and she was being pulled back into the crowd. They would pull her over the fence.

All three of us roared loud enough for the building to hear, and I didn't care. We shifted. My wings flared and the claws on my feet dug into the floor, cracking it.

Mere seconds passed, the bodyguards around Christine leaping forward and dragging her away from the crowd. No more signatures and no more pictures. They walked here away from the people and toward the limo waiting for her at the end of the carpet.

She was shaken and shaking. Pale.

The crowd shouted after her, but she didn't turn back. Good. She needed to get the hell out of there or I was going to break myself getting her back. She needed to be here. Now. Never leave my sight again.

On the screen, the limo pulled away. *Let's meet her upstairs.*

All three of us in stone form heard and felt the others, and we were all in agreement. Our mate would be protected. At any cost. In those seconds, she could have died, and she didn't understand how precious or fragile she was.

The camera panned back toward the crowd. Most of the people there were showing concern and remorse as the host commentated over the footage of what had happened. They replayed it in slow motion. Christine was grabbed, pulled, and lifted off her feet.

My whole world turned black and red. Primal

rage from the bottom of the world burned in my gut. I would tear the city apart brick by brick if it meant keeping her alive. No one was safe from this fire that singed the depths of my soul.

Because on the screen, in the crowd, just beyond where Christine had been, was Witt.

CHAPTER THIRTY

CHRISTINE

"*A*re you all right, *Mademoiselle?*" Raphael asked. Security had instructed him to drive. Anne hadn't made it to the car—they just wanted me out of there as soon as possible.

"I think so."

Was I? My heart was still racing. One second I was taking a picture and the next I was yanked backwards and up, bent and lifted toward the crowd.

I didn't think it was malicious—too many people excited about pictures and overreacting. But it was scary.

Talk about swinging between extremes. Performing that song had been...it felt incredible.

Something magic about singing that song in public for the first time and owning it. Breathing it in and letting myself go.

That feeling was what I loved. If a career was only moments like that, it would be perfect. But it wasn't.

It was Désirée trying to sabotage me and people trying to grab me and screaming fans trying to get my attention. And it would always be like that.

I pressed my hand to my chest. My pulse was felt everywhere—fingers, toes, and I heard it in my ears. The adrenaline hadn't left me yet.

"Are we returning to the opera?"

I nodded before I managed to find my voice again. "Yes. Please."

Thankfully, that was the last public outing I needed to navigate for more than a week. Maybe by then my heart would be calm again.

The artist's entrance was a welcome sight, along with the security guards. Once I was inside, I could drop one level of my guard. And when I got to my mates I could drop another.

"Thank you, Raphael."

"Any time, Miss Daniels."

Someone had called the guards. The speed with which they got me into the building stole my breath. And I didn't stop moving once I was inside. No one else was here. The whole cast would still be at the gala. I needed to be somewhere safe, and the only place I wanted was their arms.

The familiar staircase and hallway drew the adrenaline out of me. Suddenly I was tired like I was the one made of stone and I wasn't strong enough to support my body. I unlocked the door and slipped inside, turning to lean my head on the door.

Déjà vu struck before I could stop it, the scream coming out of my throat as I was yanked backwards and held against stone, a knife at my throat. It ran against my skin under my necklace. "One movement and these pearls would scatter all over the floor."

Erik's voice broke through the panic, and I shoved his arm away, spinning on him. "What is *wrong* with you?"

He was in his gargoyle form. All of them were— Alex in the shadowy corner near the windows and Marius in my kitchen. "Why the hell would you do that?"

"To show you how quickly you could have been dead. Do you know who was in that crowd?"

"I'm not dead. And I was looking forward to coming back here and being comforted after a terrifying experience. Not held at knifepoint by my mate."

He had the sense to look embarrassed.

"It's too dangerous," Marius said. "Witt was in the crowd. One more second and you could have been gone. Or dead."

"But I'm not," I snapped, reaching up to take the heavy necklace off. The box was sitting on the bar. "I'm here."

The knife was gone when Erik stepped toward me, but I backed away a step. "Don't. Don't touch me right now."

"A knife is no different from claws."

I glared at him. "That's a stupid response, and don't pretend that it's not. You know there's a difference, starting with the things that I agree to *before* you use your claws."

Alex was lingering in the corner, the space he occupied clouded with dark, thundering energy. Like a true predator waiting to pounce. "What is going on?"

"He would have killed you," Alex said. "And we would have had to watch. Able to do nothing."

My breath hitched. "I'm okay."

The emotion running under my skin needed to get out, and it was building. I wasn't going to be able to hold it in for long.

"You almost weren't." That was Marius.

I rounded on him, everything that I was feeling bypassing the ramp-up and diving headlong into anger. "Can the three of you get your heads out of your asses long enough to realize that I'm okay, you're okay, and that your instincts don't equal something happening to you?" There was an uncomfortable silence, and it was so much worse than the first time. "Not one of you has asked how I am."

My voice broke on the words, and I hated it. It didn't matter that I already said that I was fine. I wanted to sink into comfort, and this was anything but comfortable.

Marius took one step forward, and then another. I saw the effort it took to pull back his stone form into something softer. By the time he reached me, his arms and chest were flesh, and that was enough.

He barely opened his arms, and I stepped into them.

"Christine." My name was agony on his tongue. Arms pulled me so tight that I couldn't breathe, and for the first time, I started to relax.

"You need to move downstairs," Erik said. "With us."

"Why?"

The growl laced through his words. "So we can protect you."

Alex finally took a step out of the corner. "One of us should be with you at all times. We can't take chances."

I turned toward him, taking in the seriousness on both their faces. "How's that going to work during the day? You're already with me as much as you can be."

"Your security should be with you then."

"Safe to say after that incident I think they'll up the security anyway. And definitely for the concert." They'd set up a charity concert featuring songs for the show. Not at the opera, but under the Eiffel Tower itself. We weren't the only people singing. Bands from all across the world were coming to help raise money for a selection of charities.

I'd chosen one that helped underprivileged kids gain access to the arts.

"You can't go to that."

I didn't even register which one of them said it. "Excuse me?"

It was Alex. "You can't leave the opera house until this is over. It's too dangerous."

Marius released me, and I stepped away from him. "Alex, this is my job. That concert is important, and I am the star of the show. I don't have the luxury of just saying that I can't go, no matter who is coming after me. I'll tell Anne that there's a concern, and they'll double—hell, she'll probably triple the security."

"You're not going." He didn't budge an inch. Both

his face and body were hard. Unyielding in more ways than just stone.

"Yes, I am."

I was stepping backward out of instinct before my conscious mind even registered the deadly sound. "You're not. I'll tie you down if I have to. It's the only way."

"Alex—" I stopped and looked at my other mates. Their faces were identical. My stomach hollowed out. "You agree?"

"You need to be safe," Marius said.

"Yeah," my voice snapped like a whip. "I fucking get that. I'm the one that was just yanked off my feet into a crowd of people that apparently contained a murderer. But I am your mate and not your prisoner."

"Being our mate—"

I cut Erik off. "I swear to fuck if you say that being your mate means that you have to protect me I am going to throw something at you."

"Doesn't change the fact," Alex said.

"Apparently it doesn't change the fact that you all are being assholes right now, either."

None of them said anything.

"I love being your mate, but that doesn't mean you get to order me and I have to obey."

A feral grin crossed Alex's face. "You like being told what to do."

"That's not the same thing, and you know it."

Erik drew up to his full height. "I'm not going to let you throw yourself into danger for no fucking reason."

My anger rose again, matching his. "When did I say that I was going to do that? How ever will I throw myself into danger if you're with me every fucking second? I couldn't throw myself into danger if I *tried*."

"The concert—"

"The concert is over a week away, and given the people who will be performing, it will probably be one of the most secure events on the *planet*. This isn't about the concert."

"No it's *not*." The word broke out of Marius and echoed off the walls. "We get one lifetime with you. Do you get that? That's all we get and we're trying to make sure that you stay alive to *have* that life. Stop trying to make us the bad guys and let us fucking *help you*, Christine."

Ice drenched my spine. "So you're trying to protect me? Your goal is to lock me in a building. Never going outside. Never being able to be alone. Always looking over my shoulder. Always being fucking afraid of what's coming around the corner.

Are you trying to protect me or my body? Because there's a fucking difference.

"Right now, I'm standing in the middle of my mates and I feel anything but safe. The only thing I wanted when I came back here was for you to hold me, and I can't even look at you, knowing that all you want is to lock me up."

It wasn't that simple. I knew that. We all knew that. But it was still the truth of how I felt. And they weren't doing anything to change it.

"Get out," I said. "Do what you have to do. Watch the windows from outside, stand on the roof and watch for Callum. Whatever you need to in order to satisfy those fucking instincts, but I want to be alone. And *don't* fucking listen to me."

"Christine." Alex's voice sounded human now. And broken.

"Get out," I said again.

They went; near silent in their exit. But I felt when they were gone, the sudden emptiness of the apartment obvious. That's when the tears came.

I sank onto the bed. My chest ached because this wasn't what I wanted. Any of it. I didn't want to be sad or scared or fighting them. If I called them they would come back, but that wouldn't fix it. They needed to see that.

No matter how deep the hole in my heart was at the moment, I had to face it alone.

This wasn't the first time I'd cried alone. Plenty of times in my New York apartment—when I saw how vicious people online could be. More when I realized that I could be putting my friends in harm's way just by continuing to do what I loved.

But things were different now. I thought now that I had my mates, I wouldn't have to do things like this alone. Not that I imagined we'd get through life without fighting. But the stark contrast of loneliness right this second was...jarring.

And so I cried, curling in on myself and letting it all pour out.

My phone chimed.

Somehow I'd held onto my clutch through all of that. Anne had texted.

Are you all right?

No. Absolutely not. I felt broken and sad and I wasn't sure how to fix it.

I'm fine. Back at the opera.

. . .

Good. That won't happen again—I'll make sure of it. Arriving shortly. I need to secure the necklace.

There was something comforting about the fact that Anne was all business. She wasn't coddling me, nor did I expect it of her. The necklace was worth more than I was. It needed to be protected.

There was another text too, from Meg.

OMG! I saw what happened. I'm coming back ASAP. With ice cream.

That got a hiccuped laugh out of me, but it didn't do much to fix the hurt.

I let myself cry a few minutes longer. The initial burst of emotion was fading. If I thought about it for more than a second I welled up, but I didn't want Anne to see that. Being grabbed like that...it was essentially nothing. She didn't know that a dark creature was hunting me because he was jealous. Which is what it boiled down to.

My phone chimed again.

. . .

Here. Heading up.

I kicked off my shoes and made sure that my make-up wasn't completely running down my face. And when the knock came, I looked through the peep-hole into the hallway. I wasn't stupid—I knew the danger was real. The fight wasn't about that.

Anne stood in front of the door, and I opened it. Her smile was tight. "I apologize. That never should have happened."

"That wasn't your fault, Anne. You couldn't have predicted that."

She laughed once as she entered, beelining for the necklace on the table. I touched my neck. I missed the feel of it, strangely, even though it was heavy. "It's my job to predict things. We'll make sure you're not put in that position again."

"I do appreciate that."

She looked me up and down, and I saw her mark my eyes. I knew they were red. "You sure you're all right?"

I took a deep breath. "I'm as well as I can be right now."

"I suppose that's all I can ask." She patted the top

of the jewelry box. "You'll see this again on closing night."

"Can't wait."

"Sleep well, and I'll see you at dress tomorrow."

I walked her to the door and watched her leave. She was always so purposeful. Whenever she was walking, there was a motivation behind it. Just looking at her move, I felt lazy in comparison. Her phone lifted to her ear. "I have it. Returning to the car now."

Closing the door, I sagged against it. This dress needed to come off now. If I wasn't going to cuddle with my gargoyles, then I was going to sleep.

I didn't even make it across the room before the knock came again. I looked around. Had Anne left something?

"Did you forget something?" I opened the door.

My mind saw three things at once. Anne was nowhere. The door to Désirée's apartment was open. And Callum stood in front of me.

He moved with the speed of a monster, covering my nose and mouth with a cloth before I had a chance to scream.

CHAPTER THIRTY-ONE

CHRISTINE

I wasn't in the opera.

Callum shoved that cloth over my face, and I knew that if I inhaled, it was over. Thankfully, I still had breath in my lungs, and it was my job as a singer to be able to hold it.

I fought him—kicked him and tried to scream. But he had the same abilities as my mates. *More* than my mates because he wasn't bound.

His hands had turned to stone. There was no way to push him off, and no way he was leaving me conscious. So I went limp. I had to breathe eventually, and I got enough of the drug to be woozy. Limp without having to try.

Enough that I couldn't fight. But not enough to knock me out completely, which was the goal.

I wasn't in the opera, and that was fucking *bad*. But where the hell was I? It was almost completely dark around me, and I was being carried. Not slowly. They were moving fast, to try to get me as far away from the opera house and my mates as possible.

To get me outside the radius where they could reach me. Dread, slick like oil, ran through me. I had to get away from them before then. Surprise was the only advantage that I had—I had to make it count.

My breath shook in my lungs. These were monsters. Ones that wanted to kill me. It wasn't a game, and the element of surprise wasn't much.

It was all I could do to keep myself steady. Because I could die, and the last thing I would have said to them was *get out*. That hole in my chest came back, and I blinked in the darkness. I didn't have time for the tears that pressed behind my eyes.

But my chest ached. I sent them away. Told them not to listen to me. They wouldn't know where I was, and if they didn't know where I was…

They wouldn't know where to find me.

Focus, Christine.

I turned my senses to what was around me, trying to figure it out. Obviously we were in the tunnels. But the dark, along with the weakness of my human eyes, didn't help.

Multiple sets of footsteps.

Low, French words that I couldn't fully understand.

The air was damp, the scent familiar. Why was it familiar?

I'm taking a piece of clothing every time I catch you. And when you have none left, I'm taking you.

That was the scent. When Erik pushed me up against that first tree. That particular scent of water was burned in my memory. Were we close?

I opened my eyes, and very intentionally didn't move. My whole body remained limp. Even my eyes. I kept them mostly closed in case they were watching. But the tunnel was getting lighter. The watery, blue air was floating in. They were cutting through the forest to get me out.

How did they know about it? Was it a coincidence? It didn't matter.

They reached the door, and the French they spoke was curses and surprise. So they didn't know. That was good. They weren't familiar with the place as it stood now. I was. One extra sliver of an advantage.

Down the steps and into the woods. They moved slowly—cautiously. Good. The same thick fog shifted through the trees. Even more than on the night that Erik and I had spent here. It wouldn't matter. They would scent me and follow.

I needed to be close enough to the other side to have half a shot of making it above ground.

So I watched. I listened to the deadened, fog-laden silence. Even my captors were quiet in the eerie expanse. Every second that passed, the effects of that drug loosened. If I hadn't held my breath I would still be asleep—that was for fucking sure.

There. I spied a shift in the fog from my awkward, upside down view. We were close to the other side. The wall was there. And they'd been moving to the stairs. What I needed was *stone* and not *grass*.

Slowly, I inhaled. Long and steady until my lungs were full to bursting.

And I screamed.

Callum startled, dropping me, and I was ready. I sprang to my feet and ran. My life depended on every ounce of speed that I could force out of my body. This wasn't a dream and it wasn't a game. The reality of it was sharp.

The roaring snarls behind me in the fog rumbled beneath my feet. They were so fucking fast. The stairs were right there, and they were right on my heels. I just needed the stone. I reached the stairs. Slick with damp, and I slipped, sprawling onto the sharp edges of them, absorbing the pain.

I screamed again. This time it was their names. I was touching stone. I was their mate. My only hope was that they would hear me. That my desperation would carry the sound farther than it should be able to go.

The hem of my dress stuck under my foot, tripping me again, but I forced myself upward. Up the stairs. But they were there. Stone hands yanked me back, pain sparkling behind my eyes when I landed too hard. "You little bitch."

He pulled me to my feet, hand banded around my arm and forced me up the stairs. "I suppose this is for the best. If they hear you, I'll take you over the line and kill you while they watch. If they don't..." he laughed darkly. "I guess you sending them away like that did even more damage than I hoped."

"You don't have to do this," I begged. "Please."

"I do." He said, dragging me up the stairs when I resisted. The two others were behind me, following. Even if I managed to slip out of his grip—which was impossible without breaking my arm—they would catch me in seconds. "I promised them that they'd watch you die, but the thought of them not coming for you? And watching your heart break before you go? That's something I'll savor."

"You're insane," I breathed. "This is insane. Why do you want to kill me?" His very touch on my skin felt alien. Like the gargoyle resonance that he had was directly opposed to mine.

"Because I can."

We were almost to the top of the stairs, and I needed to keep him talking. The longer he talked, the better my chances. "That's not a reason."

He snarled, every hair on my body standing on end. "The hell it's not. There's a reason I rule here. I have the power. You are a threat to that. I would say it isn't personal, but it is. Your three mates have been a thorn in my side for more than two hundred years. And your death will finally put them in the ground."

We were in the tunnels again, the light from the woods fading behind us. This part I didn't know. Where were we going? Erik said that the river was as far as they could go. If I passed that boundary, I was going to die.

The difference between the threat of death and the certainty of it was striking. Everything drew into sharp clarity. Every mistake. Every choice you wished that you'd made differently. Your favorite moments.

A lot of those last ones were from the past couple of weeks.

My bare feet slipped on the stone, and Callum yanked me upright.

HELP. I shouted the word silently into the stone. *HELP ME.*

Another set of stairs loomed in the darkness. The sound of traffic, and the sound of water. We were at the river. "No." I didn't mean to say it out loud.

"Yes." He pulled. The stone digging into my arm would bruise—not that it mattered if I was dead.

Oh god. Oh *fuck*. I was going to die, and there was nothing I could to stop it.

The last rays of light were dying in the sky as we came above ground. Darkness gathered in corners and in shadows. *Pont Royal* was right there. So fucking close. All he had to do was get me over that line. But now we were above ground. *Scream, Christine!*

I opened my mouth to do that, and a hand clapped over it from behind and transformed to stone. The scream that came out anyway was muffled. "I don't think so." The new voice said, and the third grabbed my other arm.

HELP ME. I was shouting to the void through the stone, tears stinging my eyes. All I had right now was regret. That I hadn't let them stay and let us work it out. That I hadn't told them outright that I loved them, even though I did.

It hadn't seemed right. I'd wanted the timing to be perfect and romantic. But there was no perfection in letting someone love you. It was messy and complicated, and sometimes it hurt. But it should never have to wait.

Please.

They lifted my feet from the ground. I was no longer touching any stone but theirs. "No one can hear you now, Christine. But don't worry. If you're good, I'll make this quick."

The roaring didn't make sense. It wasn't an animal sound, or a human one. It sounded like—

Water slammed into us from the side. All four of us thrown towards the wall that guarded the river. Pain bloomed behind my eyes, and I fell to the ground in a puddle as the wave receded and a great hand sank beneath the surface of the water.

I didn't question it—I was free. There was shouting from people who'd seen the wave. Honking cars. I sprinted toward the steps that led to *Pont Royal*. Close to home. More distance from the boundary.

They were right behind me. The water had only slowed them a few seconds, but it was a chance.

Cars were stopped on the road, slid and out of place because of the water that had overflowed the banks of the *Seine*. It gave me a free crossing. But they were right there.

My legs and lungs burned. I fled for the building that was across the street. Ancient and palatial, there was no chance that it would help. But buildings meant people, and it was in the right direction. That was all that mattered.

They caught me on the sidewalk. Arms came around me from behind, nearly knocking me to the ground. "You thought you could get away twice tonight? I was looking forward to taking you from that crowd. Guess this will have to do."

Witt. Witt held me, and Callum was limping across the road, holding one of his human shoulders. One arm hung uselessly at his side, and his face was the picture of rage.

Witt laughed. "Guess you didn't want it to be quick."

A dark shape dropped from the sky, slamming into the sidewalk so hard that it shattered, cracks radiating outward like a spiderweb. Two more followed like missiles.

Witt's head snapped backward, the cracking in his neck final. He fell away from me just in time for me to turn and see him crumble. His body turned into stone and then into gravel, collapsing down like rain.

Further down the sidewalk, the third friend met a similar fate, Marius's hands still on either side of his head. Where it was separate from his body.

All three of my mates were here.

They were here. And they stepped toward Callum. That was all it took for him to run. Back to the bridge and over the boundary where they couldn't touch him. His glare promised death when he looked back.

Alex was in front of me, and I couldn't process it. He was here. They were here. "You're here."

The rawness in his eyes nearly broke me. He placed one hand on my cheek, gently tilting my gaze to his. "Did you think we wouldn't come for you?"

I did break then, all that fear racing to the surface and coming out. Ragged sobs tore out of my chest. I couldn't stop them. Alex crushed me to his chest, arms so tight my bones creaked. "I'm sorry," I managed the words into his shirt. "I'm so sorry."

"Shh," the sound was gentle. "You're safe."

He lifted me off the ground, and I melted into him. This time being carried was comfort. We crossed the street, retracing the steps they'd used to try to take me.

Once again the hand rose out of the river. "She saved me," I whispered.

"We'll thank her," Alex whispered.

They only kept human speed until we descended into the tunnels. And then they *ran*. We were at the opera house in minutes, taking the back way through my window before anyone had a chance to notice.

"Oh my god!" Meg ran to me, mascara running down her face. "You're okay."

"I'm okay." The words sounded blank.

Alex reluctantly set me on the bed. I felt the way his hands lingered as he set me down, and I didn't want him to let go.

"I came back and your door was open." She pulled me into a hug. "You were gone, and I just…I knew."

"She called us," Erik said quietly. "She's the reason—" His voice cracked, and he cleared his throat. "She's the reason that we weren't too late. We heard you scream."

I held her back, squeezing my friend. There was a chance that I wouldn't have seen her again. I whispered. "Thank you."

"Are you okay, though? Really?"

"No," I said. "But I'm alive."

Marius stepped closer. "Would you like us to give you some time?"

There was pain in his voice, and the same pain echoed everywhere in my body. "No. Please don't."

Meg looked at me. It was clear on her face that she wanted to stay and hear everything. To make sure that I was whole. So when she stood, I took her hand. "Tomorrow morning. Breakfast. You can tell me."

"Are you sure? You don't have to go."

She squeezed my hand. "Yeah. I…think you need some time."

I stood, my legs shaking, and walked with her to the door. She wrapped me in a hug. "I was so scared."

"Me too."

"They love you. You know that, right? I've never seen anything like it."

It took a couple tries for me to speak. "We fought. Before it happened."

"That doesn't matter now." She pulled back and smiled, but it was forced. "I'll be back with breakfast."

"I love you."

"Back at you." Meg winked before closing the door.

Silence hung thick in the air, all three of them standing perfectly still, looking at me. "Please touch me," I said. "I need you to touch me."

They all moved at once. Alex pulled me into his arms again, slamming his mouth down on mine. It was *right*.

Marius tugged me away from him, wrapping me up in a hug that I never wanted to break away from. All warmth and strength.

Finally, Erik pulled me to him and lifted me into his arms. He sat on the edge of the bed with me, kissing my forehead gently. "Let it go, baby girl."

It was the permission I needed.

So I held onto him and cried.

CHAPTER THIRTY-TWO

MARIUS

*A*s long as I lived, I would never forget the sound of Christine crying. Wracking sobs that shook her shoulders—her entire body—that took a very long time to fade.

I didn't want to think about how close we'd come to losing her. Again. First on the roof, and tonight. The instinct to protect her still moved within me. But it was held at bay by the site of my mate weeping, and the satisfaction of tearing Sebastian's head off his shoulders.

There was a part of me that thought I should feel sorry for killing him.

I didn't.

"He was here," she finally said, hiccuping through the words. Her fingers were curled so tightly into Erik's shirt that her knuckles were white. "Anne came to get the necklace, and I thought she forgot something. Désirée's door was open. He must have been in there."

The fact that we didn't know—

With mighty effort, I pushed the wild rage back down. Callum knew our weaknesses just as we knew his. We could hear through the stone, but we couldn't see. He would have made no sound entering —or such little sound that the scraping and scuffing faded into the background noise.

He must have come in when we were in the basement, lost in the haze of instinct and rage. When we were so preoccupied with what happened outside of our boundaries, we weren't paying attention to what was within them.

"Do you think Désirée is a part of it?"

Christine leaned her head on Erik's shoulder. "I don't think so, but I don't know. She made me look bad in the press today, and she told me she was just getting started. But I don't think she wants me dead."

I agreed. The woman was a snake, but she wasn't a murderer.

Alex leaned forward where he sat in the arm chair and dropped his face into his hands. "You told us not to listen, and...I couldn't help it. Then we heard you cry, and we didn't want to betray your privacy after you asked us not to. So we stopped. I'm so sorry, Christine."

"I shouldn't have sent you away."

Following the impulse, I knelt in front of her, taking her hand. "You were right. We couldn't see through the haze. It was like a film dropped over my eyes, and all I could see was you getting pulled backward and Witt's face in that crowd." Now I would have to live with the image of the bastard tackling her from behind before Erik snapped his neck. "We're supposed to protect every part of you, and we didn't."

Erik gently placed his hand over her heart. "You're not a prisoner. Never a prisoner."

She looked at me. Her eyes were red from crying, what was left of her make-up streaked on her face. She was still the most beautiful creature that I'd ever seen.

"I didn't want that to be the last thing I said to you." Her face crumpled again, but she pulled it back. "I never told you that I love you. And I do."

Light exploded in my chest, hearing those words. I knew—of course we knew. We could feel it even when she'd sent us away. But hearing it was like having the aurora borealis poured directly into my soul. Glorious, awe-inspiring, and like nothing else in the whole fucking universe.

I kissed the back of her hand because it was the closest skin that I could reach. Alex was on his feet and with us in a flash, leaning down to kiss her bare shoulder. Erik's face was buried in her neck. "I love you," I said. "I hope that you knew that without me having to say it. I loved you from the first moment, and I'm never going to fucking stop."

Alex whispered the words into skin. Erik wrote them on her lips. If anything had happened, and she hadn't thought that we loved her...

It was unthinkable. Soul-shattering and life-altering.

Christine swallowed. "I know that you said we can't. Because we don't have time for the frenzy. But...please. I don't want to feel like that again. I want to know where you are and for you to feel where I am." She straightened, finally releasing her death grip on Erik's shirt. "I want to know what you're feeling so we don't have to say it. We can fit the frenzy in between rehearsals and shows. I don't care. But after feeling that, I can't wait. Please."

I lifted her hand in mine, turning it to kiss the center of her palm. "You don't have to convince me, mate. But I think the three of us agree that we have something to fix first."

"What?"

It hurt to say it. "We broke your trust. You said that you didn't feel safe with us."

Christine went still. She opened her mouth to protest and stopped. "I shouldn't have said that."

Erik shook his head. "You should always say things that are true. Even if they're not comfortable." He smiled a little. "Even if we have to fight about it."

"We don't want you to have any doubt," Alex said, pulling her to her feet. "It's not something that you can take back."

"I want it." And she cut him off before he could say anything else. "I wanted it from the beginning. I'm not going to change my mind."

"I know," he murmured. He slipped his hand behind her neck, touching where he'd chosen to mark her when the time came. "Will you do something for me?"

We didn't deserve the way her body eased under his kiss. Not after we almost let her die.

"Let us love you," he said, the words still pressed against her lips. "Get rid of any thoughts of that asshole. That's as long as I'll be able to wait to make you *mine*."

I couldn't agree more.

She glanced at the two of us, and I smiled. There was no party of me that didn't want her.

Her teeth pulled over her bottom lip, showing the nerves that were still there, regardless. "I need to wash them off. I'll be right back."

"Want company?" Erik winked.

Christine shook her head. "I want to leave them in there, and come back to you."

It was hard to watch her disappear even just into the bathroom. I let my feet transform to stone in order to root myself into the ground. The protective instinct was pacing back and forth in my mind, wanting to make sure that the bathroom was empty and that she was okay.

The water turned on, and I heard the soft shuffle of fabric as she let her dress fall to the ground.

"He's still alive," Alex said. "This isn't over."

The mess on the bridge I wasn't worried about. There were monsters in the city that took care of public perception, because things like this happened. It would be a freak accident of some kind. An incredible specific earthquake that caused a wave out of the Seine, or something like that. The humans were happy to accept it and move on rather than delve into the possibility something strange existed in their world.

"I need to find the biggest diamond in existence for Penelope."

"Fuck," Erik said. "Yeah."

Alex crossed his arms, wings growing out of his back and flaring. "What do we do when he comes back? Because he will."

"That was a declaration of war, whether he wants it to be or not," I said. "Can't you feel it?"

There was a difference in the air now. When I reached out and touched the stone of the wall, I could hear further. If I concentrated, I could listen to any place stone touched within our boundary. Our power—a part of the earth itself—reacted when threatened. And he'd threatened the deepest part of us. If he so much as made a sound within our hearing, we would know.

"Of course," Alex said. "But there's nothing stopping him from trying again in the same way. Complete silence."

"Tonight isn't about that," Erik said. "He knows that he has no chance if he struck tonight. Alone. Tonight is about bonding with our mate—fuck everything else. Tomorrow, we make sure she's safe." Even Callum wasn't stupid enough to fuck with feral mates.

I nodded. The last thing I was going to do was let my instincts get in the way of anything else. Would I fuck up? Yes. But this was a stark and brutal reminder that Christine's life was fragile, and protecting all of her—soul, body, and mind—was more important than the monster that rested inside me.

The monster grudgingly admitted that, though he was snarling with anger that Christine was out of sight.

The water shut off, and our mate came out of the bathroom in nothing but a towel. Water clung to her skin, dripping from her hair into the towel, and that fresh, floral scent of her filled the room like incense.

I stripped my shirt over my head and tossed it aside, crossing to her in three steps. Not touching her would be like ripping off my own hands. She shuddered when I touched her, releasing a shaky breath. "If you're not ready," I whispered. "There's nothing wrong with that."

Her eyes snapped open with new fire. "I'm ready."

"Bonding with us when we can't leave the opera," Alex said. "You have to think about what that means."

"Stop trying to talk me out of it, Alexandre."

His purr filled the space at the sound of his name in a flawless French accent, and I looked at him. "Get her on the bed."

"I'm standing right here," but she was smiling.

"Yes you are. And soon you're going to be lying where Alex can hold you still." Her heart sped up, and I stepped closer. Our bodies were separated by a mere inch, and she had to tilt her head all the way back to see me. "We fucked up. You're not a prisoner, and that conversation should have been a discussion between all of us. But I think we both know that in the bedroom? We own you. And you love that."

The richer, thicker scent of her arousal reached me. She really did love that.

Christine's eyes danced. "Technically this isn't only a bedroom."

Alex came to stand behind her. "I have no qualms about carrying you down to a room that is exclusively a bedroom. But you'll be doing it in the towel."

She shivered, leaning back into him. "Here is fine."

"Then drop the towel."

I saw the curve of her smile before she ducked her head. "No."

One of his arms banded around her waist, and the other grabbed a fist full of wet hair, tilting her face back. "Want to try that again?"

My mate's chest rose and fell, breath coming fast as she came back to us. Met us on familiar ground where we could drive her to new heights.

I could see down into the hollow of the towel where I stood, thoroughly enjoying the tempting glimpses of her skin. "Let's agree to it." Her eyes were already glazed with pleasure, but she looked at me.

"To what?"

"Exactly what I said. Everything outside of this is equal. But when it comes to this?" I pressed a knuckle beneath her chin and tilted her head further into Alex's hold. "You're ours, little mate. Owned. Bound. To pleasure and fuck. To knot." I leaned down and pressed a kiss to the corner of her lips. "You want something, you tell us. But let's not pretend that the reason that I'm drowning in the scent of your cunt is because you *don't* want that."

Her face flickered. Emotions that I couldn't yet feel playing underneath them. Erik joined us, closing her in just like the night we'd finally gotten her to say she was our mate. I let my tail unfurl and trail up her leg, getting the tiny inhale that I wanted.

"Yes," she finally gasped. "In the bedroom, yes."

Erik slid his hand up her body and across her chest to her throat. We knew she loved it there, and I knew he was reminding her of what they'd shared in those woods beneath the ground. "You need to say it."

Christine's body arched, something between a moan and a whimper escaping her lips. A perfect blush painted her cheeks. My mate. *Mine*. The declaration was as solid and fervent as the day her scent had floated to me on the wind.

The words were shaky, but not from true fear. Now that we'd seen the difference, we would never never make that mistake. "In the bedroom," she swallowed. "I want you to own me."

The air around us eased. Relief and what we needed coming back to us. Our monsters needed to take, and our mate needed to be taken. In this moment, nothing else fucking mattered.

"Then take the towel off," Alex growled. "Or I'll take it off for you."

She dropped it, the fabric dropping to the floor and revealing dewy, wet skin. Nipples that were peaked and rosy. And bruises. I growled at the sight of them—they weren't something we could heal with our tongues, and the thought of who put them there was enough for me to go outside and shout for Callum to come and face us.

"Get her on the bed," I told Alex again. This time, he did. Just like I'd pleasured her the other day. He settled her between his legs, leaned against his body so he had full control.

Owned.

Erik and I watched him touch her. Dragging his fingers up her ribs and allowing his hands to shift into claws. She arched into the sensation. Watching those pink lines appear on her skin where he touched…

I was so fucking hard I was going to come before we even started. But I had an idea. "Do you trust me, Christine?"

Her eyes were glassy when she looked at me. Already so aroused I could see it. Scent it. My little mate wanted to be fucked.

Alex dragged his claws across her breasts and throat. "Yes."

"Good." I transformed my hand and dragged it down her stomach all the way to her delicious cunt. "You're going to come all over my claws. After that, I'm going to make you mine."

CHAPTER THIRTY-THREE

CHRISTINE

*P*ure, deep arousal flowed under my skin. I was drunk on it. My mind was too exhausted to allow anything else. And they were right. When we were alone and in whatever bed or room we were sharing, I wanted to surrender.

If I could accept the fact that I want to be chased and taken—that I would willingly share my life with monsters—then I could accept the fact that I wanted to be owned by my mates.

Alex dragged his claws up my skin, whispering filthy words in my ear. "The way you drip for my claws makes my cock harder than when it's stone."

I didn't have to ask how he knew that I was dripping—I was.

Marius climbed on the bed. "Do you trust me, Christine?"

Alex chose that moment to rake those exquisite claws over my breasts and my throat, dragging attention to what I'd told them I'd wanted. "Yes." The word was barely voluntary.

"Good." He held his hand up, and I watched it shift, fingers elongating into claws that he ran along my skin. Riding the edge of pain that I'd come to crave straight down my body. "You're going to come all over my claws. After that, I'm going to make you mine."

I gasped. "Your claws?"

Alex laughed. "You do love them."

They'd fucked me with their fingers. Cocks made of stone. But never with their claws. Marius's in particular were long and sharp—the claws of a dragon.

Erik stood at the side of the bed, watching. Casually, he dropped his pants to the floor, stripped his shirt away. So I could see everything. His piercings and the muscular thighs covered in stormy tattoos.

Eyes flashed to mine, and he stroked himself, thumb working over the silver studs in his skin.

"Keep looking at me like that, baby girl, and you're going to be gagging on my cock."

It was a threat that only made me wetter, and every single one of them knew it.

"Have to make sure she's ready," Marius said, bending his head and dragging a long, slow lick up the center of me. "Fuck."

He teased me with his claws like Alex had done that first night, toying with their sharpness to amplify the pleasure. When he turned his hand, I tensed. He was going to put his claws inside me.

"Are you scared?" Alex asked.

I swallowed. "Yes."

"Enough that you have to stop?"

My voice was shaky. "N-no."

His, in comparison, was silky smooth. "This is about trust." Lips on my neck to distract me. "About us *owning* your pleasure, and you knowing that we will never harm you. Even when you're getting fucked with claws that could rip you apart."

My body clenched and dampened. I was slick with it. My breath raced in and out like I'd been running.

"So spread your legs for your mate," Alex whispered. "Present him with your soaking cunt."

Holy god. I did. Wider than they already were.

Marius's breath cooled the wetness between my thighs, and I moaned.

Alex's purr melted me. I relaxed into him, every thought emptying out of my head. He wrapped his arms around me, and I felt them harden, keeping me still. "Good girl."

I squirmed with those words. Nothing felt like the glow of his praise in my chest.

"Look at me," Marius said. His green eyes were alight with mischief, and he slid a claw into me.

"Oh my god." It felt good. Strange. Hard and sharp—not like they were when they were stone. My brain shouted *danger* at the razor point touching inside me. My body wanted more.

"Stay very still," Erik said.

Another claw slipped in beside the first, the deadly tips of them scraping over my G-spot. My hips bucked, and Marius growled. "Seems like someone needs to listen."

Erik stepped forward, releasing his cock and placing his hands on my hip bones, pushing me down into the bed with unrelenting force. Stone arms weighed me down and wrapped around my waist. They never needed any other restraints than themselves—they were living restraints.

"Mmm, perfect." Marius ran his tongue over my clit, and I was unable to move even if I wanted to.

He fucked me with his claws.

Slow and steady, making sure every time he moved in and out they teased the spot that made it feel like I was staring into the sun. Deeper too, drawing sharp constellations inside me. His tongue worked me in circles, drawing up pleasure from where it was buried.

Quivering, shaking sensation moved through me. It was just out of reach. The orgasm and oblivion that I wanted, but it was dancing around the edges.

Lifting his mouth, Marius looked up at me and grinned. "Trust me."

The claw of his thumb curled up and over, dragging across my clit. Inside, twin points of pleasure and pain pressed into me, and I cracked open. The orgasm raced out like a burst of flame, singing along my nerves and consuming my voice so everything was silent. I arched and pressed against their hands, trapped exactly where they wanted me. The very fact that I couldn't move made it better. Stronger.

"Christine."

Marius looked at me. Erik had released me, and now my mate's mouth hovered above that place on my hip that he'd claimed. Exactly where he wanted to bite. He was waiting for one final confirmation.

"Yes. All of you, yes."

A chased kiss against my skin. I closed my eyes,

and cold pain ripped through me as Marius's stone fangs bit into my hip. I screamed, the sound muffled my Alex's hand. It was the worst pain that I'd ever felt. Bone-breaking, soul-shattering pain.

And just as quickly as I thought I was going to die from that pain, it warmed and soothed and became heat. Ecstasy. It wasn't an orgasm, it was a hundred orgasms rippling outward from that spot into all-consuming need.

"I love you," Alex whispered, and sank his teeth into the place where my neck met my shoulder.

That true pain melted into the pleasure and lifted it. Heightened it. Both at once made the pleasure sweeter and the pain worse and I couldn't say which was winning. Only that I would never forget what it felt like to burn without fire.

"One more, baby." Erik's tongue soothed the skin beneath my breast before ice sheared into my body. He bit the tender skin beneath it, and I was gone. That new pain unlocked something—a shift that was only beneath the skin. Harmony and resonance that it was impossible to describe.

It felt like a perfect twelve-part harmony. Suspended chords that resolved into lovely, lingering echoes.

They weren't holding me anymore. My body arched off the bed, lifted by the crescendo of what was rising like a geyser and collapsing just as fast. I was being rewritten like new music. They were right —it could never be undone, and I didn't want it to be.

I came to rest, gasping, grasping at the blanket beneath me. Everything felt strange. Like my soul was too big to fit into my body. Wait—that wasn't my soul. It was theirs. I could *feel* them.

Alex's dominant passion that wanted to see me beneath him, undone. Erik and flickery, fiery need that felt like he was about to start running and chasing me any second. Marius's deep and steady want to take his time and wring pleasure from me just because he could. They were all inside me.

And love. I felt that most of all. Love that ran to the core of the world and deeper. The love they had for me was the thing that rooted them to the earth. It was the only thing that mattered. Couldn't be lost, or their world would end.

For the first time, I truly understood.

"I feel you."

The emotions shifted to delight, and then wicked anticipation. They could drive me to madness like this, I realized. As soon as their thoughts turned, I was ravenous. The need to fuck and be fucked and *not stop* came over me.

It had me climbing back into Alex's lap. This was

what they meant when they talked about the frenzy. I needed them inside me more than I needed to breathe. I'd happily suffocate if it meant one more second of their cocks inside me. "Take your clothes off," I begged him.

No matter who owned who, it didn't matter.

Erik was behind me, mouth on my spine. "*Mine.*"

The sound was guttural. Feral.

Truth.

I wasn't tired anymore. The only thing that mattered was them and me. Every last bit of control snapped, we were everywhere.

Flesh and stone caressed my skin. Mouths and teeth and tongues. Hands and claws. Tails and wings. Everything that wasn't them ceased to be.

They took me to the floor—the bed wasn't big enough, and we were a tangle of instincts and pleasure. I savored the feeling of their souls inside me, along with their cocks. Delighted in the taste of them on my tongue.

Before them, I thought there were limits on pleasure. There weren't. They played with me. Conspired to drive me higher now that they could feel exactly what made me come. I was theirs. Made to sink into their control and their pleasure and reflect it back. To be wrecked on their shores.

Destroyed by the feel of them and put back together with nothing but the sound of a purr.

It was clear why this could last for days.

We had until dawn.

I slipped down into the rhythm of hands and the song of sighs, and I let my mates prove how thoroughly they loved and owned me.

CHAPTER THIRTY-FOUR

CHRISTINE

*W*e didn't want to stop.

When dawn came, I was both exhausted and exhilarated. Covered in *them*. There was no part of me that hadn't been licked and sucked. Pleasured. The scent of sex hung thick in the air, and still I wanted more of it. But they had to go.

Marius sat up. "We have to stop."

"No." I dropped my mouth onto his cock, sucking the head between my lips. The woodsy scent of his skin and the deeper scent of his cum filled my nose. I was addicted.

He groaned. "Baby, you're going to kill me."

It was impossible to laugh when I was shoving him down my throat. The sound was more a moan.

Alex yanked me up off him in one movement, and dropped me on the bed. I squeaked at the unexpected movement, laughing. His hand came down on my ass, the sharp crack of sound echoing through the room.

All it did was make me wet all over again.

"He said you needed to stop."

"I don't want to." The words drew out in a whine.

He spanked me again. Harder.

And again.

I wiggled my ass into his hands, silently asking for more. His tone was a warning. "Christine…"

Pouting, I let myself go limp and still, a sign of submission. His hand drifted up my spine until it rested on the back of my neck. "Good girl," he purred. "You know what good girls get?"

His hand slammed down on my skin, over and over again, until I could feel the skin going red and I was moaning and begging into the blanket where he held me. One more spank on either side, and he dipped his fingers between my legs.

"Good girls get reminded of what happens when they're naughty."

I was so turned on, I wasn't sure if it was a punishment or a reward. If he kept going, there was a chance I would come from his hand on my ass alone.

He pulled me back off the bed and into his arms. "Guess we'll see what kind of girl you are tonight."

I melted into his kiss, and then Erik's, and finally Marius as they pressed themselves into me. Trying to make it last. "It's going to be torture," I said.

"Yes," Erik said. "It is."

They couldn't delay anymore, letting their touch linger as long as possible as they slipped out the windows and onto the roof. Now, even though they were gone, I carried them with me. Echoes of the longing that they felt like they were buried in the center of my chest. Similar yet distinct.

It was early, but Meg would be here soon, and I needed to shower them off me.

By some miracle, I wasn't tired, the frenzy having injected me with seemingly endless energy. But I was still human, and now that I wasn't getting my guts rearranged by the monsters I was hopelessly in love with, my body ached.

In the shower, I leaned against the wall on purpose.

We hurt you? Marius asked. His concern echoed in my chest.

No. But I'm also not used to twelve-hour sex marathons. I'll be fine.

Erik's laugh echoed in my head. *You* are *fine.*

I rolled my eyes and let them feel it.

On a more serious note, Alex said. *You should tell Anne that you have a stalker. To heighten security further while not getting into the details.*

The thought made me cringe. Not being protected, but the idea of admitting that I had a stalker. With the way Désirée and the cast already felt about me, I didn't want them to think that I was being a diva.

A near silent growl came through the stone, and in the new place where I felt them, all three of them became stern. Loving, but unyielding.

Better a diva than dead, baby.

Okay.

The water didn't feel as warm now. I shut it off, stepping out, and wrapping a new towel around myself. The one from last night was...very dirty.

I opened it in front of the full-length mirror in the apartment. In the frenzy, I hadn't looked where they'd bitten. But those points had been touched and licked and pleasured, and even now when I brushed my fingers over the bite on my hip, I shivered.

You couldn't see them unless you were looking, the shapes of their jaws marked in pale, silvery scars. I loved the way they looked on my skin. They felt right.

They didn't have to hear me speak to feel what I was feeling now, and their amusement quickly turned to possessive arousal from knowing that I loved their marks on me. In turn, my own arousal crashed over me like a wave. "You guys can't do that," I whispered. "If I'm in the middle of rehearsal and suddenly horny it will be a disaster."

I felt absolutely no remorse from any of them.

Clothes felt strange now, when all I wanted to do was be naked and fucking. But I pulled them on, anyway. Meg and I were close, but we weren't that close.

By the time she knocked on the door, the coffee was brewing, and I'd managed to settle myself. The knock on the door still sent my heart racing. They soothed me from the inside out, and I made sure to look through the peephole. It was Meg, and she was alone.

"Okay," she said, brushing inside. She was carrying a large paper bag. "I didn't know what you wanted, so I got the whole fucking bakery. Literally, I think I bought one of everything. Tori mocked me, and it was one hundred percent worth it."

"You didn't have to do that."

"I did." She dropped the bag on the counter and yanked me into a hug. "Yes I did. And fuck you look so much better."

I snorted. "The kind of sex I had last night will do that to you."

"I knew it." She smirked. "They better have taken good care of you."

"They did." I lifted my shirt and tugged down the band of my leggings to expose Marius's bite.

Her eyes widened. "What the fuck is that?"

I grabbed us both mugs and explained what happened and what we'd done. What that meant.

"So…are you going to stay in Paris?"

They were listening, of course, so I had to be careful. They could feel me anyway. "I don't know. I haven't thought about it that far. All I know is that I can't live without them."

"If you stay here, I'm coming to visit."

I laughed and dug into a *pain au chocolat*. "That won't be a problem."

Meg's face sobered. "I was terrified last night. It was like that night at ABT all over again."

"I'm sorry. The guys want me to tell Anne that I have a stalker."

She stood up. "You should do that. And you should do that right fucking now. Let's go."

"Meg."

"Christine."

My best friend was a force of nature when she wanted to be, and her glare was a good way to get me to do things. I was going to do it anyway, but I hadn't meant right this second.

Inside my chest, they were laughing.

"Anne's here this early?"

Meg laughed, digging through my cupboards for two travel mugs. "She's set herself up in the back of the house. Has like three laptops around her and I swear I think she might be a hacker. She never stops. Tori and I saw her on the way to the bakery."

"Okay. I don't want to interrupt her."

"I swear to God, Christine, if I was able to call your mates right now and get them down here, they'd agree with me."

They very, very much agreed with her. "You don't have to call them. They'll agree."

"Great. Let's go." She handed me my coffee, looped her arm through mine, and practically bulldozed her way out of the apartment. There was no reason to be as nervous as I was. I just didn't want any more attention than I was already receiving. Doing my job aside, if I could disappear with no one noticing back into my low-key life—this time with mates in tow—I would do it.

Meg's description of Anne was absolutely accurate. The woman was dressed in the most casual clothes I'd ever seen, with jeans and a long-sleeved t-shirt. There were glasses on the tip of her nose that

I'd never seen before. She looked like she'd been awake as long as I had, with none of the benefits.

"Anne?" Meg called.

She looked up over her glasses and glanced between the two of us. "Yes?"

Meg looked at me expectantly, and I took a breath. "I need to talk to you about a security problem."

She nodded. "I promise you, that won't happen again."

"It's actually unrelated to the incident at the studio. I…have a stalker. After you picked up the necklace, he came to my apartment. He'd been hiding in Désirée's. I know that because her door was open."

Anne stared at me for long seconds. For the first time since I'd met her, she looked flustered and pale. "Were you harmed?"

"He tried. I got lucky and managed to get away from him." I considered what to say next, and I felt the urge for caution from my mates, as well as support. "I've been seeing someone while I've been here. And they helped me."

The warm glow of their approval lit me up from the inside.

Anne was already dialing her cell phone. "Get down to the house. I need to speak with you." She hung up and dialed again. "It's Giry. Tell Monsieur Chagny there's been a security breach at the theatre and that we will need additional bodies. As well as private personnel for the principals' apartments."

"I—"

She held up a hand. "He can come here to discuss it, but I won't be speaking about the breach over the phone." The call ended with a quick swipe of her finger. "That's taken care of."

I stared at her for a second. "Thank you."

"The safety of everyone in this show is not something we take lightly. No one should have been able to get that close to you, and I'm very sorry that happened."

A scoff came from behind me. "If you called me down here to scold me about the article at this time of the morning, Anne, it could have waited."

Anne didn't react to Désirée's voice, still focusing on me. "Would you describe what happened last night as an attack?"

"If she won't, I will," Meg said. "It was."

"Very well." She turned to Désirée then, who was glaring daggers at me. "Last night when Christine returned to the opera, she was attacked by a man who was hiding in your apartment. Yesterday, you told her that you had more of this behavior planned. Did you have anything to do with this?"

Désirée blanched. I'd never seen anyone go white so quickly. She turned to me. "You assumed it was me? How *dare you*."

"She didn't assume anything," Anne said. "Christine never mentioned you, other than to say that your door was open, indicating that's where the attacker came from. *I* am the one who's asking. Did you have anything to do with this?"

She was still pale, and now she looked nervous. "No. I swear. I might hate your guts, but I'm not going to have someone attacked."

My mates were wary at her tone, but they didn't see the way she reacted. As far as I knew, it was impossible to pale at will. I believed her. They did too.

Anne stared at her for what felt like an eternity before she nodded. "We're adding security up there. A guard at the end of the hallway at all times."

That would be inconvenient for my mates, but they would make it work because they were happy about the extra guards.

Meg was hiding a smile like she knew I was thinking about the implications of a bodyguard on my sex life. And of course, I was. "I appreciate it, Anne."

"Of course. Please try to relax before dress rehearsal. If you need anything, let me know."

"I will."

We didn't make it all the way back to the apartment before I heard her. "Hey."

Meg was here, so there was a witness. Whatever she had planned, she wouldn't do it with someone else here. I turned to face Désirée.

"That's really low."

"Anne didn't lie. I didn't bring you into it." I shook my head. "I never suggested that you were involved. For all I knew he came in through your window."

She looked at the ground and down at me. "I don't like you." she said. "It's not a secret. But I wage war in the press. I don't hate you enough to kill you, or have you attacked."

"I know," I said.

"Doesn't mean I'm going to back off you either."

I chuckled. "I know that too."

"Good." She shoved passed me and into her apartment, slamming the door.

Meg followed me into my apartment and we closed the door before we collapsed into giggles. "God she's a piece of work. You really believe her?"

"Yeah. I do. Callum was using her from the beginning to get to me."

She took a long swig of coffee and sat dramatically on my couch. "Well, your mates are busy being rocks."

The emotional response was both amused and annoyed. "They hate that."

"I know, but it's good for me. We get to hang out instead of you having sex that I'm jealous of. Did they ever find a gargoyle for me?"

The reaction startled me. "Based on the laughter in my chest, maybe."

"I'm going to need a firm answer on that."

"Noted." I sat beside her and leaned my head on her shoulder. "Thanks for having my back."

She knocked her mug against mine. "I always have your back. Even if you might live in France with your fucking monster mates."

I laughed, but I couldn't help but think about that. We had a couple of weeks to figure it out, but they knew as well as I did that a lot could happen in two weeks.

And it wasn't very much time at all.

CHAPTER THIRTY-FIVE

CHRISTINE

J felt him a second before the hand clamped over my mouth from behind, and I gasped into the fingers. My mate, come to see me in the middle of the performance.

After opening night, when they surprised me by watching the whole show looking like supermodels on the red carpet, and coming to my dressing room to show me how proud they were.

Or when I'd come back from the concert that we'd fought over and their protective instincts hadn't let us speak at all before they were pushing me up against the wall and taking me. I loved every second.

They'd gotten into the habit of surprising me backstage. Making me moan between scenes when the frenzy that hadn't stopped took over. The number of times I'd *almost* missed a cue was growing. I hadn't yet, and after tonight there was only one show left. I wasn't going to break the streak now.

"Quiet," Alexandre said, voice nothing more than breath. "Don't make a sound, or you'll miss your entrance."

I smiled, not moving. We were in the wings in a shadowy corner. No one could see us. For now. "What are you doing?"

"Thinking about how embarrassing it would be for you if it was discovered that you missed your entrance because you were gagging on my cock."

"Alex—"

"I said quiet."

I fell into silence, heat blooming where his hands curled around my body. The command he wielded never got old. The time would not come when my body didn't respond to that power. It was a part of my DNA now. In my chest, I felt the sharpness of his arousal, and the sense of steel that was present when he expected me to obey.

And oh, did I want to obey.

This was the end of the opera. The thin costume that I wore to be burned as Joan of Arc hid nothing from him in the same way that it did nothing to protect me from the heat of his hands.

"Joan D'Arc," he whispered. "The famous virgin. Imagine finding her fucked. Ruined. Covered in nothing but sweat and what was left of her lover's orgasms. Sticky."

Fucking hell. My voice rasped. "They would have burned her much faster."

Alex pulled me back against his body, the line of him hard, straining in his pants. "When you're done burning," he said, voice velvet in my ear. "I'll be behind the forest set, waiting. I expect you there when you come off stage, on your knees, and I want your pretty make-up smeared on my stomach by the time I'm done with you."

The implication of that sank through me. "Curtain call," I breathed.

"If you're lucky, I'll give you a chance to clean up before you have to go out there."

I didn't have a costume change after the burning. Just an addition of some accessories. "What happens if I don't show up?"

"Do you want to find out?"

Kind of. I liked his punishments, and he knew it. "What will it be?"

"Nope. Not telling." I felt the curve of his wicked smile against my ear. "You'll just have to risk it."

I moaned just before the click of my microphone came on. The tiny mic embedded in my hair was a constant danger.

My cue in the music was coming. One long, slow kiss pressed just beneath my jaw, and he was gone. Like a ghost, and I was flushed, trying to wrap my head around the words that I needed to sing.

There was my cue. I stepped forward out of the shadows, up between the cast members meant to lead Joan to her death. In a strange way, Alex's command gave me more to work with. There was now desperation swimming in my veins. The same desperation that I imagined Joan would have even though she'd resigned herself to her death.

It went perfectly. One of those moments of synergy where the cast was all on the same page. The emotion was palpable in the air. We had the audience without a doubt.

The best show we'd performed so far.

Just in time for the run to end.

I was relieved. Everyone wanted the run to be extended but me. People were clamoring to put up shows, and now that there was interest, the city and the opera thought it would be best if *Joan* had one successful run. Fine by me. I was ready.

My voice soared through the theatre, and I went limp as the smoke and false flames went up around me. Joan had died. The set pulled off, and I practically leapt off the piece. Through the shadows, I made my way behind the set pieces where Alex waited.

I brushed my fingers over the mic gently. It was off. Thank fuck.

Alex's hand fisted in my loose hair. "Knees, mate."

I went. His cock was already hard—already waiting to be shoved into my throat. And it was. This wasn't a long and slow seduction. I had done that, spending time exploring every inch of their bodies.

This was hot and hungry and raw. Need spiraled up from the floor, misting in front of my eyes. Alex pushed in deep, stealing my breath. I could take him the deepest of all of them. All the way down my throat so my nose pressed to his skin just like he wanted.

And he fucked my throat. Holding me still, taking what he wanted. He pressed deep, holding my face against his body. "What I wouldn't give to knot in your mouth," he growled. "Keep you just like this, milking my cock."

A moan escaped me. The minute I got out of costume, I needed to be fucked. It wasn't enough. Never enough. Whoever told them days for the frenzy had lied. It had barely lessened. It would take *years*.

Alex fucked deeper, still holding my face to his skin. He pulled me back, air rushing in. I hauled in a breath, bracing my hands on his thighs.

"One breath is all you get," he warned. "Make it count."

I did, filling my lungs seconds before he slammed back in. He was rigid in my throat, grinding into my mouth with every thrust. His arousal fed my arousal, the pleasure coming through our mating bond nearly enough to make me come.

His breath went short, fingers tightening in my hair. One last time he drove all the way in, bracing my face with his hands and keeping my lips locked around the base of his cock.

He came, heat flowing into my throat. Filling my mouth. My eyes fluttered closed. Not even Meg understood when I tried to explain how much I loved this. The smell and the taste of them. The sensation of being helplessly used while at the same time loved and cherished.

His cock jerked, spilling more cum into me. "Swallow it. Go out there in front of that sold-out crowd knowing that you taste like me. That minutes ago you had a cock so far down your throat that their favorite soprano couldn't sing if she wanted to."

I swallowed.

On stage, the final crescendo of the show was happening. They would need me soon. He lifted me to my feet, using his thumb to clean up the mess of my lipstick. He didn't have to say the words 'good girl'—I felt them resonating in my chest.

Winking, I left him there, and went to take my bow, his cum still on my tongue. The crew hand saw me slip into place from a different direction and gave me a look, but nothing more.

This was always the best part. More than performing, which was amazing in itself. The curtain call was the drug that kept performers coming back over and over again. Nothing felt like the wash of energy from the crowd surging to their feet when you appeared.

Tonight was no exception.

The curtain fell, and Meg jumped on my back, squealing. "Good fucking job! That was fantastic, girl."

"Thank you!"

She laughed as I carried her towards the wings. "What's the rush? Somewhere you have to be?" She was teasing me.

"You know it."

"Go get 'em. Breakfast tomorrow?"

I nodded. "Last time."

Breakfast had become a solidified tradition now. Morning was for Meg, and the night was for my mates.

Tori appeared and smacked Meg's shoulder. "Hurry up, the last one at the bar buys the drinks."

"I'm coming!" She jumped off my back toe shoes loud on the stage as she followed Tori. After a show, it was all glorious chaos.

I changed quickly, grateful that my complicated costumes came at the beginning of the show and not the end. Because it took me less than ten minutes to clean up and slip down the back stairs to the bat cave. With all the extra—very needed—security, I spent a lot more time downstairs. But it also made it hard for Callum to reach me. There'd been no sign of him.

All three of them waited for me. Staring at me.

The feeling in my chest hit a second later. They were all serious and subdued. I paused. "Given the way that Alex just fucked my throat, this isn't the reception that I was expecting."

He smirked. "And you took it so well."

"Then why this?" I touched my chest.

"Because we need to talk," Erik said.

I sat in the armchair alone. Touching them led to kissing them. Which led to other things. "Okay."

"The end of the show is tomorrow," Marius said.

"I'm aware." I pulled my knees up to my chest and smiled. "It'll be nice to have some rest."

"And..." Alex sighed. "We've been looking. Whenever we can. For a way out of our predicament. We don't have one."

A knot formed in my stomach. We'd come up against the discussion before and hadn't been able to bear talking about it. We were out of time now. "It's okay." It wasn't. What else could I say? I was planning to stay with them in Paris for a while, anyway. "There has to be a way. We'll find it."

"It might take time."

"So?"

Erik looked at me. "We don't expect you to stay here, locked in a basement, while we try to find a way to free ourselves."

I froze, terror and dread pinning me to the chair. "You want me to leave?"

"No." All three of them said at once.

Marius shook his head. "Of course not. But you're Christine Daniels. They'll want you for shows. And most of those won't be here."

"What if I didn't want to be?" I sighed. "Maybe I could just be a one-hit-wonder celebrity. Someone they'll think about in twenty years when they think about that one opera girl."

Erik's gaze fixed on my face. "Is that what you want?"

I wasn't sure what I wanted. What I knew was that I was tired, and I wanted to eat and sleep and fuck for a week without thinking about anything else, and then I could figure it out.

"Do you have any ideas?"

"We do," Alex nodded. "There's a lot of modern technology that exists now that didn't when we were made. Maybe a temporary shift in energy that would get us across the boundary."

"It would be easier if you could just get struck by lightning again," I muttered.

We all burst into laughter, as if that were actually easy. And wouldn't turn them into smoking gravel.

"I'm not leaving you," I said. "I don't care how long it takes. We'll figure it out. And if we don't, then I still want to be with you. I didn't bond with you just to leave because I don't like your apartment. Which isn't true. This place is amazing."

Alex hid his smile for a second before leaping out of his seat and kneeling in front of me. "We don't deserve you."

"Yes you do."

He pressed a kiss low on my stomach. "We have a surprise for you tomorrow."

"What is it?"

Marius laughed. "If we told you, it wouldn't be a surprise, would it?"

I flopped back in the chair. "Fine. Keep your secrets and be glad that this connection doesn't let me read your minds."

"I don't know about that," Erik said. "What am I thinking right now?"

The emotional image slammed into me. Him pinning me to the bed and fucking. It was almost crystal clear. "Don't make promises you can't keep," I teased.

That was all it took to have them pouncing to carry me to bed.

CHAPTER THIRTY-SIX

CHRISTINE

I was out of breath when I came off stage. Adrenaline fueled me. Screw yesterday. That was the best show we'd ever done. One hell of a finale.

The necklace hummed against my skin. Anne had been backstage after my scene with one of the bodyguards to put it on. A way of acknowledging the history of the show without long speeches.

"Christine, they're doing encores."

I took a swig of water and jogged back to the stage for another curtain call. The audience was still on their feet. There were flowers on the stage from the close rows, and Anne was there with a giant bouquet of roses for me. The other principals were given flowers as well.

This was a moment that I'd never forget. The curtain came down four times, and they stayed standing. Tears flooded my eyes, and a quick glance around told me that most of the cast felt the same.

Even Désirée looked like she was about to cry.

Finally, the curtain dropped, and it didn't rise again. I hugged Anne. "Thank you. For everything."

"Thank you, Christine. You were the perfect Joan."

I pulled back from the hug before I overwhelmed her with emotion. She wasn't the touchy-feely type. Even her eyes sparkled as she walked swiftly away, ever on to the next task.

All around me, people were hugging and celebrating. The entire cast was planning on painting Paris red tonight. Not me. I had a surprise waiting.

None of my mates had given me a hint. Not even when I begged them this morning before they took me sneakily back to my apartment and then went to the roof.

But they teased me all day. Sly touches through our connection here and there. Flashes of heated breath and endless orgasms. Which was a given now, but they said a surprise, and they were serious.

In my dressing room, there were more flowers. A gorgeous bouquet of white roses with a single card.

Meet us on the roof.

I smiled. The roof was where it all started. I hadn't been up there since. No time, and even though I knew they would catch me, once you fell off a roof, you were a little hesitant about being on top of them.

Throwing on clothes, I left all the roses in my dressing room. I would come back for them later. I had mates to meet. They were in my chest, delighted. Holding back what they were truly feeling until they could show me what they had planned.

Sound grew louder as I approached the roof. It was raining. Scratch that—it was a full on thunderstorm. The boom shook through me. They couldn't be on the roof during a thunderstorm, it was too dangerous. What were they thinking?

The rain poured down. It was dark, the city glittering like a reflection in a lake. "Hello?"

I shouldn't be here. My gut screamed it. This wasn't right.

"You're not the only one who has friends," the voice said. My stomach dropped, and I turned for the door. It was locked from the inside. I smacked my fist against it, refusing to look at Callum behind me. "Turns out the *Sacre Coeur* weather spirits were more than happy to stir up a thunderstorm for me. They even know where to center things like lightning."

They knew. Rage and panic were singing in my chest. Close this time, and on their way. My mates would be here in minutes, and in danger the second they stepped on this roof.

Lightning flashed, thunder crashing loud enough to hurt my ears. I was already soaked through, and the hum on my chest like the force of that lightning was close.

But it wasn't me. It was—

I turned to him. "You lost. Why won't you just give up?"

I could barely see him in the dark, in his stone form, dark against the roof. "Of all the people in the world, I thought you'd understand. I know who you are—I've researched you. You came from nothing and now you have everything in the world.

"That power will change your life now that you have it. In a few years, you'll understand that you never want to give it back."

He took a step toward me, and I took a step back.

They were racing upwards now. They just reached ground level. "I *do* want to give it back," I shouted. "I want my quiet, boring life again, and I would do anything for that. This was amazing, and beautiful, but the only good thing it's given me is them. The rest of it has only given me people like you. People who want to use me for their own gain. Forgive me if I pray to God that I am *never* like you."

"Then you're foolish," he snarled, advancing toward me. "Power is the only thing worth something." The next flash of lighting showed me his gargoyle form, and I gasped. This was the first time I'd seen it, and it was horror.

Skeletal limbs and carved rotting flesh. His face was a snarling demon, legs with stone flames encasing them. Half of his body was designed to be rotten and dead, a gargoyle in the truest sense— meant to scare away the real demons.

Again with the lightning, a sense of flowing power. Strange resonance that I couldn't quite place.

"What happens if you lose your power?" I swiped the rain from my eyes and ducked around a statue and around the corner, trying to stay away from the edge. "What's the worst thing that happens besides not being the one that everyone bows to?"

"Monsters are already given scraps in this world.

Going back means going back to nothing. It was easy to let your mates rot in this place when they were an example of what happened to people who got in my way. Now they have you. And a shiny, golden new home. I have to fix that."

He lunged, and I leapt back, not fast enough. He landed on me, driving me down onto the stone as I heard the door burst open. They were there, staring at Callum as he yanked me to my feet, hands around my throat. Even at monster speed, he could snap my neck in a second.

"Lightning," I shouted. "You have to go back inside."

Marius growled. "Like hell."

Alex's wings flared, voice rumbling like the thunder above us. "Take your hands off my mate."

"Doesn't this seem familiar?" Callum mused. "Like two hundred years never really passed. I suppose the bitch is new."

Growls shredded the air, and lightning lit up the sky. My skin buzzed and Callum jerked like he'd been shocked. Terror lived in my chest. It was theirs. They knew that one breath could change this for all of us.

I pushed love back at them. No matter what happened, they were mine. I loved my monsters.

Now it wasn't just my skin that was prickling. My hair stood on end. Like static. "That's my cue," Callum said. "Time to make your choice, kings."

Callum picked me up and threw me across the roof. I screamed, the sound pulled from me. It was too dark to see, and I only had time to force myself limp before I crashed into a corner, skin tearing, head cracking on the rough surface.

Energy was restless under my skin, and it didn't feel like mine. Lightning was crackling in the air, illuminating a strobe show. Callum leapt from the roof, and I understood the choice he was giving them. Save me, and die. Or follow him to kill him, save their own lives, and let me die.

They were my mates, and to them, it wasn't a choice.

Above our heads, the clouds circled ominously, lightning swimming just beyond their edges. Static clung to the air. It was going to strike here.

"Don't," I begged. "I can't watch you die."

They jumped for me anyway, cracking the stone next to me as they landed. They would take the strike to try to save me. "Please."

"I love you," Erik whispered in my ear. "I love you."

Alex said it, and then Marius.

"Stop it," I hissed. The rain mixed with my tears. "Don't say goodbye."

It was too late. The light cleaved the sky in two, and it headed straight for us. That singing, buzzing hum rang in my head. And time froze for the blink of an eye.

I was still wearing the necklace. The one thing to survive the fire inside. The one that seemed to hum every time I touched it. The one that was vibrating on my chest, shaking and crackling, desperately begging me to hear it.

When we met, I said it. *I just thought if you could like...ground it to something else. Channel it like a lightning rod.*

Marius said it too. *Finding something that matched our energy* exactly *would be impossible.*

And it would be impossible. Unless it had been created when they were created.

Calm wrapped around me like a blanket. This was a chance. If it didn't work, then we were dead anyway. My mates held me from every side, and I raised my hand to the storm.

Pure power slammed into me. I was the lightning, every cell screaming. I was lit from within like a thousand fireflies lived inside me. The electricity crackled over all four of us, searching, and it found a way out. Through that stone. A little lightning rod.

Just like them, I was changed. My energy shifted. Their energy shifted. We shifted together, always perfectly aligned.

All I felt was relief.

And my heart stopped beating.

CHAPTER THIRTY-SEVEN

ERIK

*W*e were alive.

The lightning tore through my body and it felt exactly like I remembered so viscerally that I had it tattooed on my body. Pain so clean and pure that it cut you in two. I closed my eyes and accepted that it was the end.

Dying to save my mate was no hardship.

But the pain receded, like it was pulled back. Reversed. Changing us, shifting us, releasing us.

Christine collapsed in the center of us.

"What the fuck just happened?" Alex dropped next to Christine. "Christine?" His fingers touched her neck, and he swore. "She doesn't have a pulse. *Christine*. Hold on *mon petit etoile*."

He moved his hands to her chest when I saw it, shock overcoming the raw pain of seeing her there. Broken. Dead.

"Alex." I grabbed his hand, keeping him from starting the movements to start her heart.

He looked at me, and I was staring at our beautiful, precious mate. "She's breathing."

Christine's chest rose and fell steadily.

I dropped to my knees, scooping an arm beneath her shoulders and lifting. Her lips under mine were still warm. Her breath soft and floral. She was just as soft as ever, and couldn't accept the possibility of anything other than a miracle. If I did, it would break me.

"Come on, baby girl. Open your eyes for me."

She sighed out a breath. "Erik."

"Christine? Come on, baby. We're here. You're here."

Those gorgeous eyes opened, blinking against the rain. She was alive, but her heart wasn't beating. "Inside," Marius said. "Quickly."

I got my other hand under her knees, lifting her. Alex nearly snapped the door off its hinges getting it open. We were soaked, the thunder and lightning still going on outside.

Confusion was strong through our bond. "Erik, you can put me down. I'm fine."

"You were just struck by lightning, Christine. You don't have a fucking pulse. I don't think you're fine."

She blinked. Then she smiled. So wide that it lit up the whole goddamn world. "It worked!" Squirming so much that I had to set her down, Christine reached for her neck, quickly unhooking the necklace. *The* necklace, I realized. No more.

The stone that laid in her palm was no longer that gorgeous pale pink. It was blackened and cracked. Dead. "It survived the fire. The night the building was *struck by lightning*." Then she looked at Marius. "Something that exactly matches your current energy."

He stared at the stone. "Holy shit."

What she was actually saying sank in. "We're free?"

"Only one way to find out," she said.

Alex growled. "We have a different problem."

I scented it a second later. Smoke. It curled up from below us, already spreading. "The fucker set the place on fire."

Acute panic filled my chest. "We have to get people out."

Marius had his hand to the stone. "They're doing it. Everyone is evacuating. They can't stop it

—to many places, but I don't hear anyone in danger."

"Except us," Alex nodded to the stairs, where the orange light was glowing.

I pulled Christine into my arms again. "Let's go."

We burst out of the door and ran straight for the edge. We weren't going to be struck again. That would be death, or another life sentence. And this time we wouldn't have a diamond.

I leapt into open air.

Christine screamed as we dropped. My legs shifted to stone, absorbing the impact perfectly. Shouting came from the front of the opera house, people pouring out of every exit. Flames were already licking at the windows. Callum had done his job thoroughly.

The rain slicked my skin. This night was all too similar to the one that trapped us here. I couldn't resent that night now, because it led me to the woman cradled in my arms.

"Laurent," I said. We could test our range and make sure Christine was okay at the same time.

We started to run. Christine tucked her face into my neck against the rain, and we ran. As fast as I could. The streets blurred, and I didn't slow until we reached the boundary.

The pull didn't drag on my limbs. There was

nothing threatening to crumble me into dust. We stepped over the line that had bound us for two hundred years, and I took a breath.

Exhilaration and adrenaline and speed. I ran again, speeding through the streets that I still knew like the back of my hand. "You're free?" Christine curled a hand around my neck.

"We're free, baby."

Joy spread through my chest—Christine thinking through all the possibilities that just opened to us.

Marius knocked on Laurent's door, and I didn't blame the shock on his face when he opened the door. We were the last people he expected to be here. "It's a long story," Alex said, pushing through the door.

"Yeah, I would think so."

We switched to French for speed. "She was struck by lightning, and we need a place to be safe while we go hunting."

Laurent nodded soberly. "You'll kill him?"

"He tried to kill her. Twice."

The doctor snorted. "You won't hear any argument from me."

I placed my mate on the couch and lifted her gaze to mine. "Stay with Laurent. I trust him with my life, and your life."

"Where are you going?"

Smiling, I kissed her quickly. "Hunting."

She grabbed my hand. "Be careful."

"We will."

Outside, I crouched, my hand placed to the ground. My power rushed through my veins like it hadn't in forever. I was no longer limited, my awareness singing through the ground like fire. Searching. Seeking Callum like a missile.

"Found him," Marius called. "North."

"Let's go."

Fuck, it felt good to be unleashed. I didn't care if people saw. The streets flew by, blurring. He didn't get far enough, because he didn't even know to run. Sloppy. In his hate, he'd gotten complacent.

The bar was one for monsters. Silence fell when we stepped inside. And as one, all the gargoyles in the room stood. Except for one.

Callum stiffened, form rippling into stone before he turned. He had to sense the return of our power. "You just won't fucking die, will you?"

"He tried to kill our mate. Twice." Marius scanned the room. "Does anyone stand with him?"

Silence so thick you could hear the sound of the rain outside. No one moved.

"Good."

He didn't stand a chance. We moved the way we used to, perfectly in sync, the gargoyles that the very earth recognized as kings. In one breath we had his arms. In a second Alex twisted his head so far the stone of his neck broke. Marius and I ripped his arms off for good measure, even as his body was crumbling.

The asshole didn't even have the time to scream.

Silence still reigned as I brushed the dust of Callum off my hands. Finally, an older gargoyle in the corner snorted. "It's about time."

It broke the spell, people going back to their conversations and drinks as if a dismembering was commonplace. I hoped that whatever remained of Callum's soul witnessed the way the world moved on without him.

"Drinks?" The bartender asked.

I waved. "Another time."

We had a mate that was waiting for us now. And she was *safe*. My monster hadn't felt this calm in centuries. If it was possible, we ran faster on the way back.

Christine leapt to her feet, jumping into my arms the second we passed through the door. "I felt it," she said. "You got him."

"We got him." I kissed her, deepening it until I wasn't sure where we separated. The need to spread her out on the floor and worship her rose. My cock ached.

A throat cleared. "I have a spare room," Laurent said.

"Sorry." I wasn't remotely sorry, and neither was Christine. Alex pulled her in for his own kiss.

I looked at the doctor. "She's all right?"

"More than."

In my chest, a feeling I didn't understand. A combined terror and excitement. "What is it?"

Christine flushed pink, the way she looked when she was about to come. My favorite fucking color. "Laurent thinks that I'm immortal now. Human, but immortal. Because my energy shifted with yours."

All three of us looked at the doctor, and he shrugged. "I don't have an explanation, but she's alive, and you're right. Her heart is still."

"I guess we'll see in a few years."

Alex kissed her, the joy from her leaking through to all of us. Forever. We could have forever with her. I couldn't begin to wrap my head around it.

"The opera house is burning," Marius said. "If you don't mind, that room for the night would be appreciated."

"Of course." He bowed.

I held out a hand. "Laurent. Please don't."

"But—"

"Our world doesn't need more kings."

Smiling, he inclined his head. "That reason alone

is why people will want to bow to you. I'll get it ready."

We were alone then.

"We need to go back," Christine said. "They're going to be looking for me. What if they don't think that I'm alive?" The three of us went still, and she felt the shift. "What?"

Alex lifted her chin. "What if they don't think that you're alive?" He said gently.

Marius stepped in, wrapping her up. "If you want to go back, we will. I don't give a shit if you're famous, Christine, as long as you're mine." He paused. "But Alex is right. If you want a way out, this is one."

"What about Meg?"

I smiled, noticing her first response wasn't to protest that she didn't want to.

Alex chuckled. "I believe your friend is more than capable of keeping a secret."

The rumble of emotions in my chest told me that she was thinking, and quickly. If she was immortal, sooner or later she would have to disappear. The fire was a convenience. Especially since the opera thought she had a stalker.

Finally, she smiled. "I never thought I'd be relieved to be dead."

"Are you sure?" I asked.

She nodded. "I'm sure. I love to sing. I love to dance. I love to perform. But I can live without it. I hate being famous. I'd rather travel the world with you. Sing in places where only you can hear me."

Marius kissed her hair. "I love you."

She closed her eyes, basking in the kiss. His words. "I love you too." Only peace radiated through our connection. "Tomorrow, I want my monsters to take me away."

I grabbed her hand and pulled her behind me in the direction Laurent had gone. "We will, baby girl. We will."

EPILOGUE

CHRISTINE

"Christine Daniels, the viral opera singer who stunned the world with her voice, has been declared dead after the fire that destroyed Paris's newly renovated opera house. Reports that she had a violent stalker aiming to harm her were backed up by signs of arson. Hope that she's alive remains among her fans, as no human remains have been reported in the wreckage. However, that hope grows thin as the third week since the deadly fire passes.

"The opera house, which burned in a similar fire during the same opera two hundred years ago, will be turned into a museum in its current state and not refurbished a third time."

Meg's voice came through the speakerphone. "The reports are getting less dramatic, at least. That's good."

"It is." I took a sip of coffee and leaned back on the couch. The news anchor moved on to a different story entirely. I flipped the TV off.

I called Meg the night of the fire, and she was already crying, thinking I'd died. She was absolutely furious. Rightfully. But she'd come around to the idea of faking my death faster than I expected, and helped the stories along.

My funeral was televised. People wept, and even Désirée managed to find some mostly kind things to say in the press. I felt bad for deceiving everyone. Enough that I almost came back. But I didn't.

Every time I realized that I didn't have to look over my shoulder, I was relieved. For now, I was still careful. My face was plastered all over the media. But sooner than later, they'd forget all about me, and I'd just be another girl walking on the street. With three men in my shadows.

I had nightmares now. Callum appeared wreathed in lightning, ready to kill me and my mates. They were always there when I woke, soothing me back into sleep with warmth and kisses.

"How's Greece?"

I snorted. "Fabulous. I think we'll stay here for a while. Being on the beach with nothing to do? Excellent life choice. You should try it."

"I would, but I don't have infinite wealth at my fingertips."

"You know we'll pay to fly you out."

Being mates with three monsters who could find gems in the ground at will made money easy.

"In a couple of months, yes. If I suddenly disappear, people will ask questions."

She wasn't wrong.

In my chest, I felt a pull. My mates were returning from the beach. They'd decided to take up surfing while we were here—not that Grecian beaches were known for their surfing. They were walking up the beach towards me, bodies shining in the setting sun, dripping.

"Christine?"

"Huh?"

She snickered. "Get distracted?"

"Maybe."

I could practically hear the eye roll. "Go get some dick and call me later."

"Will do."

"Love you!" She hung up just as they entered the back door.

Alex shook the hair out of his eyes. "Meg?"

"She says hello. In a manner of speaking."

A purr radiated from Marius, along with a stroking across our connection. Arousal and need that fed mine.

The frenzy had faded.

Barely.

All it took was one look from one of my mates and I was climbing their body like a tree trying to get closer.

It wasn't just Marius that was teasing me now. It was all three of them. "What are you guys doing?"

Marius pulled me to my feet and tossed my phone aside. In one move, he ducked and folded me over his shoulder like a caveman. "Marius." My voice was a squeak. He carried me up the stairs to the absolutely giant bed that we'd rented this place for, and dropped me on the pure white comforter.

"You once told me a fantasy. All three of us taking you at once. It occurred to me that we never fulfilled that little fantasy."

I flushed. That was the day he fucked me with his tail and pulled the images from me. Suddenly my mouth was dry, and other places were very, very wet. "No, we haven't."

"No time like the present," Alex said, stripping off his shorts.

"That's it?" I raised an eyebrow. "Where's the foreplay? Where's the romance?"

He stalked toward the bed, crawling over me until I was forced to lean back underneath him. "You don't like foreplay," he murmured against my skin.

"That's not true."

"No?" His teeth scraped over his mark, and my whole body arched. "You like being told what's going to happen, and then taking everything we give you. That's your foreplay. By the time I'm done talking you'll be wet enough that Marius's cock will slip right out of you."

I was already that wet, but I bit my lip, waiting for him to keep going. Because he was right—their filthy mouths ruined me.

He lowered his lips, brushing the shell of my ear with his breath. "You're going to take all three of us, just like you wanted. All your dirty holes filled with cock down to the root. We're *all* going to knot you, so you're trapped, helpless, and writhing. And if you're very good, we'll do it again."

"Fucking hell," I muttered, and he laughed softly.

"I'm going to enjoy this."

Erik was naked now, too. "I think we're all going to enjoy it."

Alex lifted off me long enough to strip my pants

off. "I can smell how wet you are, Christine. You'd think we never fuck you."

He smirked, but it was true. They barely *stopped* fucking me, and it wasn't enough.

Marius grabbed me as he slid onto the bed, rolling me over him and driving up into me in one movement. *"Fuck."* My hands landed on his chest. Right over those pierced nipples that matched the silver ball that was currently teasing me.

"Such a dirty mouth," Alex said. "I need to do something about that." He yanked me closer, pulling my shirt off in the process, and guided my mouth to his cock. Which left Erik with my ass.

I gasped. He was huge. I didn't think he would fit there. Pulling back, my head met Alex's hand. "I don't think so."

A moan left me as he drove deeper, matching Marius's thrust upwards. Erik's hands drifted over my ass. "Trust us baby. We've got you."

Oh, fuck. His tongue was there, wetting me. Teasing me. It would be nothing compared to his cock. Soon enough, that thickness pressed against me, and I whimpered. He was so, so thick. The head of him slipped in, and I moaned, the sound muffled by Alex.

They were all in me, and they wouldn't stop. Not until they got exactly what they wanted. My hands shook, braced on Marius. He grabbed my wrists, taking away my leverage. It made me lean harder on him, let Alex slip further down my throat. And in my ass, Erik pushed. The first studs on his cock entered me, and my mind went blank.

I could take them—my body was made to take them—but it still shocked me when I could and did.

The slow movement of his hips was at odds with Marius. Even when I'd been filled with his tail I'd never been *this* full. All three of them in me. Erik was inching further, and I couldn't breathe. I couldn't move. I couldn't suck Alex's cock. All I could do was feel.

The second set of studs pushed inside me. I came, pleasure soaking through my body and brain. Faster and deeper than the waves at high tide.

Alex released me to breathe, my voice raw and groaning. "Oh fuck. Oh *fuck.*" It kept going and didn't stop, curling under me and through me.

"Take me, baby." Erik used the pleasure to plunge deeper. One stroke, and then two, and he was all the way in. I stilled, my body trembling with the fullness.

"Fuck, Christine. Such a good girl." Alex sounded in awe, and those words that unlocked the honey-sweet glow of his approval eased my body. Relaxed me. So this felt good. Felt fucking perfect. I could take a full breath.

He reached for me again. "Fuck her onto my cock," he told Erik, slipping between my lips. "Make her take me all the way."

That was exactly what they did.

Erik moved, pulling back far enough to slam back into me and drive me onto Alex. Marius moved too, opposite and then together. The world was nothing but this.

It was everything that I wanted when Marius made me speak the words. New pleasure rolled over me, and it wasn't going to stop. Through our connection their pleasure was my pleasure, and mine was theirs. It was like having four orgasms at once. Mind-melting and gorgeous.

Alex stretched, placing his hands behind his head, showing me just how hard Erik was fucking me to drive me all the way down his length. Into my throat. Until I was almost as far as he liked me to be. Lips pressed to the skin of his stomach.

Marius rolled his hips, the ball of his piercing hitting the spot so deep inside me that I saw the whole fucking universe behind my eyes. I was going to die from this pleasure, and I was immortal. It was too much too much too much.

Something shifted, and they moved in unison.

Alex wove fingers into my hair and fucked. Erik grabbed my hips, thrusting to the hilt, and Marius matched. They were hardening. Getting closer. And I was lost in the swirl of golden glitter that was the never ending orgasm.

Marius came, cock turning to stone and swelling larger, locking himself to my body. The knot stretched me, and it made Erik's cock feel that much thicker. Delicious heat inside that made my whole body contract.

I squeezed both of them, and that was the trigger. Erik roared, driving home, releasing his pleasure, and letting himself shift. It was torture and it was pleasure. Somewhere, I screamed, throat still stuffed.

Rough, hard stone stretched me, his knot growing and pressing against Marius's. If I moved, I would come again simply from being stuffed full. Everything hung on that precipice.

Alex pulled me closer, grunting as he fucked my throat. His pleasure unspooled in my chest one second before I tasted him. "Swallow. Do it now."

I obeyed, going limp and feeling him slip deep. His cock hardened. Thickened. The knot at the base of his shaft filling my mouth. I could barely breathe, and I couldn't remember the last time that I'd been this content.

Marius rubbed slow circles on my wrists, soothing. Moved one hand to my clit and made those same circles. He would draw out that pleasure as long as I could, and I could do nothing. I couldn't move. Utterly helpless, just like they wanted.

Every time I did, bolts of lightning moved through me. Delicious and precious.

"Look at our mate," Erik spanked me. "Stuffed full of us."

I floated in a silvery haze. I knew they spoke, but I didn't hear it. I was happy and satisfied, lingering in this mist like the underground forest that Erik made for me.

Alex's knot released me first, and my jaw ached. He leaned down and kissed my forehead. Kissed my lips. "You have no idea how much I love you, little star." He laughed. "And not because you just kept my cock in your mouth for an hour."

"An hour?" I felt dizzy and drunk. High on the very essence of them.

Marius confirmed it. "An hour." His knot loosened. "You were floating."

"I'm still floating."

Erik was finally able to release me, and I sagged down to the bed, unable to do much more than that. He laid behind me, cuddling me to his chest. I loved the warmth. Briefly, they lifted my head to rest on Alex's stomach. Marius was in front of me.

The big bed was fucking worth it.

"It's a good thing that I'm immortal." My voice scratched. Raw from screaming and fucking. "Because I think that might have killed me otherwise. In a good way."

Marius smirked. "We can't kill you. You're already dead, remember?"

"Smart ass."

I closed my eyes. Sleep was coming, and I still craved them. Their touch. My monsters. "I love you."

Hands tightened where they touched me, the response clear through our connection. No matter what, I knew that when I woke, they would be here with me.

I curled up, tangled in tenderness, limbs, and love, happy knowing that we now had forever.

Me and my monsters.

The End.

Meg's story, *All the Devils Are Here*, is now available!

Hello my beautiful readers! I hope you enjoyed THE POINT OF NO RETURN, my first ever monster book! This book challenged me in unexpected ways, but I got lost in the story, and I truly love Christine and her harem. I hope you do too!

But I do have one request—if you like this book, would you consider leaving me a review? I love hearing from readers about what they loved, and even what they didn't. Reviews like yours help others find books!

There are more words coming to you very soon, and I hope to see you there.

Devyn Sinclair

KEEP IN TOUCH!

Devyn's Newsletter:

Be the first to hear updates about my new releases, sexy exclusive content, and the occasional dessert recipe!

https://www.subscribepage.com/devynsinclair

Devyn's Facebook Group:

Come hang out with us! We talk about books —*especially* the sexy ones—share memes and hot inspiration photos and more!

https://www.facebook.com/groups/devynsinclair/

ABOUT THE AUTHOR

Devyn Sinclair writes steamy Reverse Harem romances for your wildest fantasies. Every sexy story is packed with the right amount of steam, hot men, and delicious happy endings.

She lives in the wilds of Montana in a small red house with a crazy orange cat. When Devyn's not writing, she spends time outside in big sky country, continues her quest to find the best lemon pastry there is, drinks too much tea, and buys too many books. (Of course!)

To connect with Devyn:

ALSO BY DEVYN SINCLAIR

<u>The Carnal Court</u>

Fevered

Euphoria

Shameless

Breathless

<u>War of Heavenly Fire</u>

Queen of Darkness

Queen of Torment

Queen of Annihilation

<u>Shifter's Curse</u>

Moon Enchanted

Moon Entrapped

Moon Exalted

<u>The Royal Celestials</u>

The Virgin Queen

Made in the USA
Las Vegas, NV
16 March 2024

87273602R10288